GLOW GIRL

JENNIFER LUCIC

UNDERGROUND
HOUSE

Glow Girl

ISBN: 978-1-7368383-0-3 (paperback)
ISBN: 978-1-7368383-1-0 (hardcover)
ISBN: 978-1-7368383-2-7 (eBook)

Library of Congress Control Number:
2021905375

Author: Jennifer Lucic www.jenniferlucic.com
Cover Design: Sarah E. Miller www.sarahvision.com

For my husband, thank you for believing in me.

For my daughters, always chase your dreams.

Contents

ONE

Lilly
_____

"We really shit the bed this time," Lilly said. Her entire life reduced to sitting shotgun as the flashing blue and red lights crept up behind them. There was no sign of reassurance on Adam's face as his shoulders tensed and he gripped tighter on the steering wheel. *He's got this. It's all under control.* But it wasn't.

"Fuck! Lilly, here, take this. Hide it in your bra. I hid everything else. It's cool, we're cool, be cool. Fuck!"

He definitely doesn't have this. She took the baggie out of his hand and followed the order. Her head sunk into the palms of her hands. The lights were right behind them now. A glance in the rearview revealed the faces of two police officers, lit by the flashing light bar and focused like predators on the hunt. *Two cops, no big deal,* Lilly told herself, finding her own reassurance when she couldn't elsewhere. *Shit, there's two cop cars, four cops, fuck.*

They had to pull over, there was no other option. Adam directed the car off the freeway and into the unlit parking lot of a fast-food restaurant.

· · ·

THE FIRST TIME Lilly smoked pot was four years earlier. It was the beginning of the new millennium. Y2K had passed and she and her high school best friend, Beth, wanted to celebrate the non-ending of the world with the occasion. There were reservations on either side. Lilly was concerned because it caused the munchies, and, being fat already, she wanted nothing to do with that. Fat, in a derogatory sense, isn't fair to say. She was a beautiful girl, hidden behind rosy padded cheeks with a small mouth compared to the width of her face. But it was her hips that betrayed her. They made themselves so wide that she risked a panic attack every time she had to walk down a row of desks in a classroom.

Beth heard smoking the plant caused psychosis and one hit could land them in a mental hospital. This idea, compliments of an old PSA her health teacher had shared with the students.

"Oh my God, Beth, really?" Lilly laughed at Beth's seriousness as they walked through the hall after fifth period. But not having any experience herself, she had no room to refute the claim.

"You don't know! Did you see the film *Reefer Madness*? Mr. Barry showed it to us in health class. These people literally went crazy!"

"I don't think that's gonna happen. I mean, come on, everyone else is doing it. We're like the only losers who aren't."

Beth shrugged her shoulders and clenched her textbooks tight to her chest.

BETH'S older brother knew where to find it. His name was John, and he was a tall lanky dude with grimy blonde hair who wore expired glow stick bracelets and a chain of colored plastic beads around his neck, the center pendant of which was an infant's pacifier. Lilly always thought this was strange, but he was a strange guy. The details worked out when he told the girls he was going to introduce them to his pot-dealing friend, Shade. They would meet Shade at the local coffee shop after school on Friday.

The day came, and when the last bell rang, Lilly hopped and skipped her way through campus and into the parking lot. As the girls came into each other's view, they squealed and hurried to Lilly's car to begin the journey to meet John and this Shade character.

John was outside the coffee shop smoking a cigarette next to a man-ish-type-maybe? Only having been alive for a short seventeen years, Lilly had never seen a person like him. *This must be Shade.* Besides his high-gloss purple leggings, the five different pairs of colored neon G-string underwear, and the black mesh midriff top, his face was striking. His eyebrows didn't exist, except for the shadow of what used to be there above crystal blue eyes covered in glittery purple eyeshadow and a jet-black Cat Eye lining the lid. *Why does anyone need that many pairs of underwear?* Shade had strings of colored beads around his wrists and neck, just like the ones John wore.

The girls froze, mouths agape, as they both soaked in the sight that stood before them.

John called them over for the introduction. Shade had a flamboyant greeting ready for them.

"Hi! I'm Shade! Oh gosh, you girls are so cute!" He flapped his hand at the wrist and giggled at the girls, who stood with tense shoulders and faces pointed down towards the concrete.

"Uh.. hi, John's my brother," Beth said in a quiet voice. Lilly stood behind her, a hard gulp in her throat.

After a few minutes of easy talk and one more

cigarette, the transaction continued. Both the girls smoked, but they didn't smoke for real. It was in vogue at the high school to steal mom's cigarettes and sneak off campus during lunch to "fake smoke", that is, to puff on the butt until smoke filled the mouth but never inhale. As each other's only friends, Lilly and Beth tried this to connect with the larger group of girls that gathered off campus. It didn't work, yet still they persisted. Standing just feet away from the smoking girls, puffing their own stolen cigarettes, Lilly waited for the day one girl might bring them into their circle or compliment their blouse. Maybe that would lead to an invitation to a party or a date with a sexy senior boy.

Lilly relaxed into the metal outdoor patio furniture in front of the coffee shop.

"Okay sweetie, it's gonna be $20. You got that?" Shade asked.

"Uh, Lilly?" Beth answered Shade but gestured at Lilly to make the transfer of funds.

"Oh, yeah, here." Lilly fumbled with her cigarette and dropped it on the ground as she reached for her wallet, stuck in her too tight jeans. Embarrassed, she didn't know whether to pick up her cigarette or continue going for the wallet. She grappled with her decision internally. Her limbs and facial expressions followed her thoughts and advertised her struggle. The rest of them let her go through the process, silently watching without expression. A final shake of her head made her stand up to stomp out her floor cigarette and finish pulling the wallet out of her pocket. Lilly retrieved the $20 bill and sat down again before passing it to Shade underneath the mesh top metal table. He half-smiled at her.

A fuzzy purple elephant backpack sat underneath the table. Shade pulled it up from the ground and rummaged around inside it for a moment, drawing out a fist that hid something inside. He reached out to Lilly, a face that said, "Be cool, kid." This was the moment. It was happening. Lilly looked around and behind her with darting eyes, being so obvious, while John and Shade both laughed a little and shook their heads. Accepting the object hidden in Shade's palm, her first observation was its size. "Dude, I could fit this in my pocket and no one would even know. It's tiny!" These were the first actual words Lilly spoke through the whole encounter.

"Yup! Tiny, like a seasoning packet of Top Ramen!" John said as the two men laughed.

"Oh! Could you imagine? Sprinkle some of that on your noodles!" Shade said as he laughed with John.

Beth glanced at Lilly. Her face said, *I don't get it.* Were they supposed to be laughing too?

"Cool, alright, you ready, Beth?" Lilly said. Now eager to make their escape, the girls said their goodbyes and thanked Shade for the hook-up.

Lilly drove fast and far away from the scene. Neither of them could do this anywhere near their subsequent homes, where the threat of parental intrusion loomed like a grey cloud over their plans. Lilly's mother lived for any excuse to yell at her, their relationship strained from a drawn-out divorce that left her mother bitter and overwhelmed. Lilly sensed her mother's shame about her daughter, who had responded to the divorce by gaining weight and thus making herself unlovable.

Ending up at the movie theater, Lilly parked and turned to Beth.

"You got the pen cap?" Beth asked, reciting instructions she had received earlier from her brother.

Lilly pulled a plastic ballpoint pen out of her center

console and removed the blue plastic cap. Beth opened the tiny baggie of weed.

"Okay, so I think we just rip a little piece off and shove it in the hole. Right?" Beth asked, holding the pen cap in one hand and a small piece of marijuana flower in the other. Her head cocked to the side like a puppy trying to understand its owners command and her face scrunched up with confusion. Lilly didn't answer, rather made an *I'm confused too* sound and shrugged her shoulders. Beth loaded the green flower into the open end of the pen cap. Holding the tail, she brought it up to her lips. She held a lighter to the flower and flicked on the flame.

"Awwh, fuck! Ouch!" she shrieked, dropping the filled pen cap and lighter at the same time. "Burned my fucking finger and my mouth. This thing isn't long enough, it's not gonna work."

"Here, let me try." Lilly picked up the paraphernalia and made her attempt. This time she bent the tail back, so it wasn't in direct line with the flame. She held it to her lips, trying to leave as much space between her mouth and the emanating heat as possible. Her thumb flicked the lighter, igniting fire. She brought it close to the flower and sucked in a deep breath of air through the tiny cap. The green flower turned bright orange and a stream of smoke filled her lungs. Heated plastic burned her lips, but she didn't stop. She inhaled until she couldn't anymore, and the orange embers turned ash grey. Her exhale caused a cascade of uncontrollable coughing. Spit flew out of her mouth and onto the steering wheel. She couldn't breathe. But as soon as she recovered, her coughing replaced itself with a wave of laughter, followed up by more coughing as she handed the now ash-filled pen cap back to Beth.

"Dude," she said. "Go." She nodded to Beth, telling her this was something she wanted to try again.

Beth reloaded the pen cap and took her turn. Soon the two of them were in a fit of laughter that collided with harsh coughing and gasping for air. A few hits back and forth and the pen cap melted down to a pliable gum. Lilly took it as a sign that they should head towards the theater to watch the movie. "Okay, I think we should be high now, right?" Lilly said, inciting more laughter. Beth nodded in agreement.

Outside the car, Lilly watched the length of the parking lot stretch out before her eyes, each step forward, a step backwards, the door no closer until she was right up on it and walking through.

Once inside, the smell of freshly popped popcorn enticed her. She needed snacks. The line at the concession was only two parties long but moved so slowly, Lilly rehashed an entire inner monologue of an argument she'd had with her mother before they even reached the cashier. By then, she had forgotten what they were doing there.

"Wait, what's going on here?" Lilly asked as she approached the cashier.

"Uh… you're standing in line for concessions, you're at the movie theater," he answered.

"Oh, cool. Yeah, let me get a large popcorn and two ICEES." She stared at the cashier, and then turned to Beth as she, again, forgot she was ordering. "Dude, it's like taking me so long to say words, I forget the beginning of my sentence before I get to the end. Does that make sense? Wait, what did I just ask you?"

"Huh?" said Beth.

"What flavor ICEE would you like?" the cashier asked.

"Huh? Oh, uh… red," replied Lilly, forgetting she was in mid-conversation with Beth. Either a moment or an eternity later, the cashier returned and presented two large ICEES and a large popcorn. They both turned towards each other and gasped with wide eyes and grateful smiles. "Whoa? Did we just win a raffle or something?" Lilly's mouth and eyes were wide open, punctuating her surprise.

"When did we get raffle tickets?" Beth asked. "Wait… where are we again?"

"That'll be $16.07, please."

"Oh," said Lilly. Her mouth and eyes reverted to half-closed as she pulled out her wallet.

Inside the theater, time slowed even more. Lilly felt herself sinking inside her chair, as if it were swallowing her up. Sweat beaded her brow and her breathing became heavy as a throbbing heartbeat pulsated into her brain. Easy fix, Lilly requested that they change seats, the next pair being far less sinky and just sinky enough to relax into without feeling like she was being eaten alive. The previews began, but they weren't like previews at all. They might as well have been full-length movies because each one lasted hours. *How many movies were they watching? Was it over yet?* Lilly thought, all before the movie had even begun.

At some point, Lilly became bored with movies and focused her attention on the frosty, red ICEE in the cup holder next to her. She stared at the tasty beverage and watched as beads of condensation performed a sexy slide down the cup's exterior. Her mouth and throat were dry and chalky, and she took a long and glorious sip. The bright red flavor exploded in her mouth, so sweet and icy-cold, she couldn't remember a time an ICEE had ever tasted so delicious. In fact, she couldn't remember if she had ever experienced *anything* so wonderful as this. As soon as it left her mouth, thirst pulled her to take another sip. The next moment, she barreled over in pain.

"Brain freeze!" Lilly yelled out as if she were alerting the theater of a fire. The entire theater turned towards her. She slunk down into her seat, still wincing from the pain, and now red with embarrassment. Beth burst into laughter, lightening the mood and provoking Lilly to join her. When various "shhhhs" by other audience members hadn't proven strong enough to quiet the girls, an usher entered and whispered that they needed to leave. The two girls giggled all the way out of the double doors.

Lilly and Beth never tried smoking pot again after that. It was fun, but more of a bucket list check-off than a new hobby—as if teenage girls needed bucket lists. The experience had been enough for them and the two went back to their normal routine of talking about new diets they were trying and dreaming up the ideal versions of boyfriends they might like. Lilly considered her brief encounter with the underworld of recreational drugs behind her.

IF MARIJUANA DID anything for her, it was to spark a flame of rebellion inside her. Still in disharmony under her mother's roof, running away became a staple. The last time, Lilly had gone to stay with Beth and threatened that she would not return to school. She told her mother that she didn't need to graduate high school, and that she would live with Beth. Her best option for employment was the early shift at the nearby bagel shop. She would get the job, and emancipate herself from her mother. It wouldn't be legal, of course. She didn't have the resources for such a thing.

Lilly's mother had become tired of this habitual phase. "You know what, fine! Stay with Beth because you're not coming back to my home," she said, or shouted rather.

Lilly stood with her shoulders back and head up in front of her mother and father, who had both come over to Beth's after work to convince Lilly to come back home.

"But guess what, I'm taking the car, you're on your own!" her mother threatened.

Lilly had purchased the '91 Buick Regal from her mother's ex-boyfriend, a car mechanic who sold it to her for $500. "But it's mine! I paid for it with my allowance!"

"Too bad, it's under my name, and I'm the adult!" Lilly's mom screamed the words at her.

"You take her, you're her father, do something for her for once!" Now addressing Lilly's father, who had been standing there in silence with arms crossed against his chest while his daughter and ex-wife screamed at each other. "You know what, I'm done. I can't do this. I don't need this. Goodbye." Lilly's mother threw her hands above her and shook her head, not addressing anyone.

Once Lilly's mother left with her car, her options diminished. Only her father remained to offer guidance, and Lilly knew he stayed only out of obligation. He proposed Lilly move in with him and his wife, a woman Lilly despised because she was only six years older than her and no more of an adult than herself. Still, with no alternatives, Lilly accepted the offer and moved in with her father and stepmother, a woman Lilly referred to as the child-bride.

The two girls fought over insignificant things, like when the child-bride would order Lilly to put her laundry away, to which Lilly would refuse. This would cause the two of them to pursue an argument that had no ending until voices and emotions were so loud and overflowing that their faces turned red and their throats went hoarse from the screaming. An urgency to reinstate peace in his home overtook Lilly's father, causing him to convert his garage into a studio apartment for Lilly to live in, separating the girls and giving them both space to breathe. Being sequestered in the dark garage proved a reality Lilly could no longer ignore—that her mother didn't want her, and her father could hardly put up with her.

Although Lilly had the companionship of her best friend Beth, she ached for something more. A boyfriend, a warm body to hold her tight through the chilly nights in her cold garage studio apartment. With no willing participants to choose from, she settled for after-school hangouts with Beth that involved skimming the pages of *Elle* magazine and salivating over the male models.

"Oh! Look at him, Lilly! He's got so much muscle!" Beth pointed at the oiled chest of a sultry-looking man laid out on a sun-drenched beach.

"Oh, my God, he's a god! I wish!"

"Wish?"

"Yeah, I mean, come on. A guy like that would never go for a girl like me." Lilly's face held a polite smile, but inside her chest felt heavy. Her shoulders slumped forward as her body responded to the sensation.

"Oh, please, Lilly! You're amazing! You could have any guy you want," Beth said with bright encouragement.

"Ehhh… Girls like me don't get guys. Look how tiny her waist is, that's like the size of my big toe!" Lilly flipped the pages and pointed out various women.

"Your big toe? Oh, my God, stop it, Lilly." Beth laughed.

"I'm serious! These women are goddesses… I'm not good enough, and I never will be." Loud messages left over from her stay with her mother, and silent visuals she received every day all around her echoed in her own self-talk. "If I ever find a boyfriend, I'll worship the ground he walks on, 'cause no way a man's ever gonna love me like they could love her," she said referring to the tall and lean, beautiful women that graced each page.

. . .

TO COPE WITH HER REALITY, Lilly imagined what finding love, against all odds, would feel like. What would life be like with a boyfriend? First, she had to imagine the boy. She attached her thoughts to the various heart-throbbing celebrities she admired. There were a few, but first-and-foremost was a precarious white rapper who introduced himself to the world as Slim Shady. Once she had the image of the man, she imagined a world where she and he were together, patching the gaping hole that loneliness had struck through her heart. Lilly was like a little girl who was playing pretend, imagining herself as a homemaker with a make-believe husband and her baby dolls as children, with her Easy-Bake Oven and Fisher-Price kitchen set. But she was too old for toys now. Instead, she played these games in her mind, cuddled up under the covers, in the darkness of her garage studio. She imagined a world where these fairy tales belonged to her and she to them.

Over time, these fantasies took up more and more of Lilly's time. She excused herself from the family early, long before the sun had set, only so she could go to bed, close her eyes, and press play on the reel in her mind that made up the imaginary life of hers. She played this game with herself until she fell asleep, and it became her dreams, and she woke to pre-production planning for that evening's episode. Obsession worked for her. At least enough to keep her appearing level-headed on the outside, while on the inside she was falling down a rabbit hole too deep to catch the sunlight.

TWO

Adam

_____

The summer of 2000 was Lilly's first semester at Santa Monica College. The outdoor campus halls harbored the sounds of seagulls overhead and the palm trees made themselves a part of the landscape.

It was here that Lilly first met Adam. The class was English 101, in a large lecture hall with stadium seats. She found a seat towards the back of the room that wasn't too far from the door. It was the only row not filled with people and the easiest for her to get in and out of. Always at the forefront of her mind was her size and how she might save herself the embarrassment involved when it came into contact with places and objects meant for smaller bodies. She arrived a few minutes early, another strategy, ensuring she didn't have to face the possibility of bumping into people already settled if she were to come in late.

A few minutes after 2:00pm, start time, in walked a boy. He was tall with a gait that made him glide across the ground. Bleach-tipped dreadlocks fell down behind his ears, framing a handsome face and milky chocolate skin.

The way he presented, like he had nowhere to be even though he was already late, conveyed an aura of confidence that attracted her. He looked around the room for a seat when his eyes settled on an empty chair next to her. From right where he stood, he smiled and waved, as if to announce himself as a friend before they even met. Lilly's face flushed and her lips stretched to meet her ears.

"Hi, I'm Adam!" he whispered.

Lilly was too embarrassed to say anything, as the professor had already started talking. She smiled and waved and moved her bookbag so he could sit. *My God, is he handsome*, she thought. His figure, now up close, allowed her to appreciate the perfect chisel in *all* of his features. The cool factor enhanced in his soft blue eyes and burly forearms. Her mind stayed distracted by him. She wasn't paying attention to the professor as he talked about the required textbook or the syllabi or exam dates. Instead, the subtle yet masculine scent of his cologne consumed her. His effortless style, a fresh white T-shirt and baggy, dark blue jeans entranced her. Class ended and Lilly gathered her things in slow motion, giving him an opportunity to leave first, and hoped for a goodbye on his way. Which he did, as he closed his folder and capped his pen. She flushed again and couldn't wait to leave class to call her old friend Beth and tell her all about him.

Beth and Lilly remained friends through high school and now attended the same community college together. The summer before college began, Lilly had made more friends when she got a job behind Beth working at a local sandwich shop. Beth had helped her get the job when she put in a few kind words about her to the owner who was looking for new employees. The owner requested a phone call with Lilly and hired her on the spot upon hearing her bubbly, outgoing voice. At The Sub Shop, Lilly and Beth befriended several other girls their age, and they became a girl group. They called themselves The Sub Shop Hoes and they spent their free time begging their families to leave them behind on weekend getaways so they could throw parties at the expense of their parents' prized vase collections and lavish knick-knacks.

When she got home, Lilly grabbed the long, curly cord of her wall-mounted kitchen phone and called Beth. The rest of The Sub Shop Hoes were three-wayed in. The conversation focused on the new boy Lilly had met. Each of the girls listened to Lilly talk and asked questions about him as they all gushed over the thought of what kind of future they might have together.

Classes for that week came to pass, and that Friday evening, the girls got together at Beth's place to celebrate the first week survived in college. Beth's parents were out of town and the girls planned a huge party, inviting all of their new college friends. Before the party guests arrived, Beth pulled Lilly aside to tell her about a surprise in store for her.

"Come here, come here!" She motioned to Lilly, who was in the kitchen pre-gaming with the other girls. Lilly threw back her shot of bottom shelf vodka, winced, and made her way over to Beth in the living room. "Okay, I have a surprise for you. You know how you told me about that guy, Adam? Well, I think it's the same Adam that I have in my Health class on Wednesdays, and, well, I invited him!"

"Oh my God! Are you serious? He's so cute! Oh my God, am I wearing the right outfit? Oh my God, oh my God, okay…" Her mouth dried and her throat tightened. Her arms and legs shivered and her chest tightened in kind with her throat. "Hey guys!" she shouted back to the huddle of girls in the kitchen. "She invited Adam! That dude I told you about, remember? Hey, wait, pour me another one of those." The initial excitement waned. She shook out her body and let her eyes focus again on the bottles of alcohol waiting for her.

The guests arrived, and Lilly kept an eye out for Adam. The packed house held what must have been at least sixty college freshmen. By this late in the night, most of the girls had already broken off from the party and coupled up with their dates in the various empty rooms of Beth's 6-bedroom house. Lilly and Beth were the only ones left, Lilly awaiting the guest of honor and Beth hanging on to Lilly to witness her reaction when he first walked in, or to be her drinking buddy if he never did. But he did. He walked right through the front door and found Beth and Lilly. As he did in English class, he waved and flashed a bright smile right before making his way over. Lilly grinned hard as she hit her best friend on the arm several times in excitement.

"Hey, Beth, right? Thanks for the invite, and uh, you're in my English class, right?"

Lilly couldn't respond, she wanted to, but lost her words for a minute too long. Beth sliced through what had now become awkward.

"Yes, I'm Beth, this is Lilly. Hi, Adam, thanks for coming. There's a keg out back and shots in the kitchen. Help yourself."

"Alright, cool, see you guys out there?"

"Yup, we're coming!" Beth said after waiting long enough for Lilly to respond first, which she did not. "Oh, my God, Lilly! Don't just stand there! Talk to him! I brought him here for you, now go!"

"Oh, my God, like I know. I'm so lame. Come, do a shot with me and then I'll go talk to him?"

"No! Go ask him to do a shot with you, you're already

drunk, it'll be easy." Beth shoved Lilly over in his direction. Now free to do what she had been waiting to do and what the other girls were already doing, Beth grabbed the closest boy she could find and threw her tongue down his throat. Her proposal was met without objection.

Lilly met Adam by the shot table. Already with a group of people to talk to. He seemed in control of the conversation, and people were listening closely to what he was saying. Women gathered close and stood in provocative poses, but his attention stayed tied to the table of assorted alcohol in front of him.

"Hey! Got you a drink!" Adam offered a warm welcome to Lilly as she approached the table. He poured her a shot. "Lilly! Lilly! Lilly!" He shouted her name with a loud confidence, encouraging the rest of the crowd to join in. Within minutes, the entire party was shouting her name as she took it down. Clapping, whistling, cheering followed. She was the most important person in the room, all eyes on her, including Adam's. He turned the party into something Lilly never imagined a party could be, and standing next to him, she was at the center of all of it. She felt a sense of power, one he invoked simply by walking into the room, and she ate it up.

Lilly followed Adam around, but she wasn't the only one as many other girls and boys did that night too. It was like they all wanted something from him, even if that was only to soak in his presence. They competed for his attention, and he was receptive to each of them. Lilly studied his face, watched his expressions. A girl approached him and attempted to fall into him. He caught her, the gentleman he was, smiled to her face and with a gentle hand pushed her off in a direction away from him. As soon as the girl was out of sight, he rolled his eyes and chuckled to himself. Like he knew the girl had done it on purpose and was desperate. What was it about him that made people fall over themselves to get to him? Lilly couldn't identify it, but she felt it, and she imagined everyone else at the party did too.

At one point, Adam asked Lilly if she smoked and would she join him outside for a cigarette. Lilly teased him about how gross cigarettes were and how she couldn't. Not that she didn't want a cigarette, more so because she didn't want to risk him discovering her fake-puff-style of smoking she had held onto since high school. The two bantered back and forth until Lilly gave up her argument for Adam's viewpoint that cigarettes were not gross, they were in fact a good thing and even provided their user with unknown superpowers.

"Alright, alright, no cigarettes for you. How 'bout you be Ice-Cube and I'll be Chris Tucker. You wanna get high? Come on, take a puff?" Adam asked Lilly as he pulled out a thick, rolled joint from his pocket. She laughed out loud at the *Friday* reference, every college kid's favorite movie, and couldn't believe how nice he was being to her. Not flirty at all, but friendly and considerate, like they were old friends.

"Pfft, watch out, man, I drink." Lilly replied to keep the banter going, carrying on with the *Friday* reference to quote Ice-Cube. She was expecting him to respond with Chris Tucker's line, that she would laugh at, continuing their moment a little longer. But someone else chimed in with an offer to take him up on the smoke out session, breaking the scene and ending the fantasy.

"Oh dude, I'll burn one with you, bro," said a random kid Lilly had never seen. Lilly took in a tiny gasp of air as her eyes widened and mouth dropped open. Shocked by this person's audacity, she looked over at the guy who had interrupted their fun with an almost snarl. How dare he.

"Cool, man, I'm Adam, let's go."

Adam and the thief walked away, leaving Lilly behind. She wasn't sure what to do next, but concluded that she should go back in for a fresh wine cooler and to find Beth.

The next morning, the only ones left at the house were the girl crew. They all made it through their hangovers with a bagel and tall glass of water. Lilly regaled the girls with her experiences of Adam, told them how he was *so funny* and *so smart* and *so cool*. She couldn't wait for school next week to meet him again, this time as a friend she wouldn't have to be shy around. It was only Saturday, English class wasn't until Tuesday, she'd have to make it through the next three days first.

Tuesday came, and she arrived at the lecture hall early again so she could sit in the same seat where it would be easy for Adam to find and to recognize her if he came in late. She would position her book bag in a way that no one would sit next to her as long as other open seats were available. As before, class began and Adam sauntered in the door, scanned the room for an open chair, and found it right next to her. His smile and wave a little more familiar as he walked over to greet her.

"Hey! My girl, Lilly! Cool party last weekend."

"Shhhh!" A voice from behind them.

Lilly giggled, and Adam made a silly face in acknowledgement. Adam sat down and took out his notepaper and began writing tiny letters in the paper's corner. He lifted his hand and shoved the notebook over towards her, motioning at her to read. *Super fun party this weekend, you have cool friends.* Lilly used the opportunity to start a silent conversation. Passing notes was something she was great at. She had done it for years in high school and it made class time fun. The two passed notes back and forth and chuckled in silence. This was troublesome for Lilly as she paid zero attention to the content and instead only focused on Adam.

At the end of each class, Adam would say goodbye and Lilly wouldn't talk to him again until the following week. Despite the note passing, staying friendly and funny, never flirty, Lilly's cheeks still flushed, and her legs shook in his presence. Each Tuesday, as he appeared in the doorway, her heart thumped a little harder in her chest and her face warmed as he made his way towards her. She couldn't help but talk about him to her friends, and the girl group became frustrated at hearing about the same stupid boy over and over. Conversations with Lilly became presentations about one topic, Adam, with no room or time left for anything else.

After weeks of enduring Adam-talk, Beth brought up to Lilly that everyone was tired of hearing about him. That he was some boy that wasn't interested in her anyway, or something would have happened by now. The semester was more than halfway through and he had not shown up to another party nor invited her to any of his. Beth finally told Lilly that she needed to either make a move or move on because she and the rest of the girls were tired of hearing her pine over him all the time. This shocked Lilly, who didn't believe she was talking too much about him at all.

"What are you talking about, Beth? I don't even talk about him nearly as much as I think about him. You guys just don't know that."

"That's the problem, Lilly! You're thinking about him so much you don't even see the problem here! It's like you're totally, like, crazy! If you really think you don't talk about him that much, when's the last time you've let any of us talk about our stuff with you? Do you even know what's going on in any of our lives? Do you even know that Claire

had her heart broken last week by David? Did you know
Ashley found out Brian has been cheating on her? Or that
Desiree hooked up with Claire's boyfriend at that party last
weekend and is the reason she's heartbroken? The Sub
Shop Hoes are falling apart and all you can talk about is
Adam!"

"You know what, Beth, just shut up! I don't understand
why you're so jealous of me. Are you trying to get me mad
at him so you can have him for yourself? You guys have
health class together, but you never want to tell me what
you guys talk about, so, what? Are you trying to steal him?
What the hell, Beth?"

"Oh, my God! This is exactly what I'm talking about! I
just told you three things, important things, that are way
more relevant to us and our friends than Adam and you
didn't even hear me."

"I heard you Beth, you're the one not hearing me!"

"Oh, you heard me? What did I say about Ashley and
Claire then?"

"What? You said nothing about them. You just said
that none of you want to hear me talk about Adam."

"Oh my God, Lilly. Something is wrong with you! You
are so focused on the word Adam! You need to get a grip!
There's a major malfunction happening in your brain right
now. You might need professional help."

"See, there you go again with the jealousy. Find your
own man and stop trying to steal mine!"

"Okay. I can't even do this with you right now. You're
done. The girls and I don't want to talk to you anymore
until you figure your shit out or at least care about the rest
of ours." That was the last thing Beth said to Lilly before
walking away. A four-year friendship crashed into the rocks
over something imaginary. Lilly rolled her eyes at Beth as
she left. She didn't need to be around anyone who didn't

support her, and she didn't want to be friends with a man-stealer. It was only a matter of time, Adam would understand that Lilly was perfect for him. He would ask her on a date before the end of the semester, she was sure of it.

The next day Lilly settled her feelings and headed to The Sub Shop to work a shift with Claire and Ashley. Beth had the day off. She would talk things out with Claire and Ashley and if she got them to understand her side of things, Beth would too, and everything would be okay again. Lilly walked in for her shift and approached them both in the back of the shop, Ashley was slicing tomatoes and Claire was prepping turkey meat.

"Oh my God, so you guys will not believe what Beth said to me yesterday! She's totally freaking out for no reason! She's like so jealous of me and Adam and she wants to steal him, I swear."

"Uh, Lilly…" Ashley replied. "I don't think Beth wants to steal Adam. You can't steal something that doesn't exist."

"Wait, so are you saying you agree with her?"

"I'm just saying that we all agree that maybe you seem, I don't know, a little obsessed with him. Like why do you spend so much time talking about him? There's stuff going on in our girl group and you're just checked out!" Ashley's words became more tense as the conversation escalated.

"Well, maybe there wouldn't be anything going on in the group if someone hadn't hooked up with my man last weekend, that bitch!" Claire said, pointing all of her aggression towards the pile of turkey meat in front of her.

"I know, it's okay, babe, we're gonna get through this," Ashley said to Claire in her ear, snuggled up in a half hug.

"Oh my God, I can't believe this, you guys too? You know what, whatever, all you bitches are crazy, I'm not the crazy one, you guys are. You all want to gang up on me?

Fine! I don't need any of this shit. From now on, I'm just here to make sandwiches and you hoes can just leave me the hell out of it."

"Lilly, hold on…" Claire spoke in a soft tone to diffuse an already heated situation.

"No, no! Forget it. I don't need this! You guys aren't my real friends and I'm not focusing any more of my energy into this."

"Leave her alone, Claire." Ashley said. "She doesn't wanna be a Sub Shop Hoe anymore."

THREE

Obsession

L illy was alone again. Back in the dark garage she went, feeling like an unwanted troll under a bridge. But she was used to being alone. She had spent most of her childhood and adolescence alone; and had plenty of coping strategies to get her through. A half-smile brought itself forward when she thought about Tuesday, and every Tuesday in English class when she got to meet and sit with the boy she believed was her soul mate. She spent the week looking forward to Tuesdays.

With no other social interaction, it didn't take long for Lilly to recoil back into her thoughts. It had been a long time since she had fantasized about celebrity crushes, but this time was different. She didn't need fantasies anymore; she had a real boy to play the part now.

Lilly began spending more time in her bedroom. Her father didn't mention it—he assumed she was studying for exams. But her grades were slipping. Instead she was focusing all her energy on devising a plan for how she was going to convince Adam to fall in love with her.

Every Tuesday, Lilly came home from English class

with a skip in her step and a new story of their encounters to replay in her head. She re-read the notes they passed over and over, blushing and giggling as she did, becoming entranced by them as she ran her fingertips over the etchings on the paper, sensing the pen movements and living through the moments again. She took these little snippets each week and pulled energy from them, and soon came to rely on them as her primary source. Each Tuesday renewed her with a sense of purpose and fresh notes to consume. It was a high that kept her floating an inch off the ground for all of Tuesday, only to succumb to a slow decline as she memorized his scribbled words and ached for new ones. By Sunday and Monday, she was empty and dragging her feet, devoid of motivation to get out of bed, to step away from the reel in her head that held her imaginary life with Adam. Each Tuesday morning held a new opportunity.

There was a routine now. She would ask him questions to keep him writing to her, she would giggle and laugh at his jokes, compliment him when she could without appearing too desperate. Each passing week came with more information that she would put together to thicken her ploy of convincing him she was more than an English class acquaintance. She was actually the love of his life.

It was nearing the end of the semester and by now she had learned much about him. His favorite color was black. He was a smoker and drinker, and he had tried Ecstasy before, something she had never heard of and didn't intrigue her. Trivial facts like these she wasn't interested in, but memorized them nonetheless. She would have memorized his shoe size or arm length if he had given it to her, anything that pertained to him or who he was was important to her, much more so than Critical Theory or how to define Chomsky's Universal Grammar.

She learned that the reason she didn't recognize him from high school was because he had only moved into town that summer with his parents. His father owned a chain of hotels and they were wealthy in excess. He came to a community college, instead of a four-year, because it was close to a new hotel, owned by his father, who expected him to manage it in between classes.

He was the silver spoon type and his parents cared about his keeping his grades up and presenting with a front of success, a weakness he used to manipulate them into giving him whatever he wanted without having to work for it. Lilly could relate to this as she herself grew up in a place of privilege, not quite to the same degree, but she was keen to the concept of a parent that would rather buy a child's love than show it. Lilly's mother wasn't interested in her otherwise, but took her on shopping sprees in an attempt to convince her she was happier under her mother's roof than with her father. This worked in the beginning, until adolescence stole Lilly's passivity, and she became, according to her mother, unmanageable.

From the stories he told, Adam appeared to be a master manipulator who could get away with anything. He told Lilly about a time the cops pulled him over for driving intoxicated when he was only sixteen. Instead of being arrested, he convinced the officer to let him go with only a ticket for speeding, and, as luck would have it, the citation was later lost in the system. Another boozy evening out, Adam crashed his father's car into the main gate of their community complex of multi-million-dollar homes. He was able to convince his father it was an accident due to long hours of studying and the stress of upcoming finals, adding in a little gem that blamed his father for the accident because Adam didn't have his own car and instead had to rely on borrowing dad's. His father responded by purchasing him a brand-new Rav4 and sending him away for a long weekend on an all-expenses paid trip in the Caribbean to relax and clear his head.

In his circle of friends, Adam dominated all of them. Evidence of this she remembered from the party at Beth's house. He could show up alone and end up making friends with anyone and everyone. In all these stories, Lilly only became more intrigued by him. *He was so nice, so funny.* So what if he had a talent for manipulating his friends, his parents, and the police? He had powers of persuasion, but she was sure he only used his powers to do good.

As the weeks ran out, Lilly needed to create a situation in which Adam would perceive her as a part of his close circle of friends. She had so much information about him, but still nothing to hint at his interest in making her a more intimate friend. Until one class, Lilly took a risk and tried steering the conversation down a semi-flirtatious avenue. She mentioned a tattoo she had gotten in high school when she and her friends found a tattoo shop that would tattoo without ID in exchange for a flash at a pair of young tits. To make it a question, she followed it up by asking if Adam had any. No tattoos, his ultra-conservative parents would never pay for that, but he thought nipple piercings were hot.

Bingo! This was her shot, and she was going to take it. *So funny*, she wrote in the small corner of her notebook paper, *my friends and I are all going to get nipple piercings this weekend!* A bold lie—one, because she didn't have friends anymore, and two, the thought of piercing her nipples had never occurred to her and wouldn't have. But it became an opportunity to flirt with Adam, and that was her aim. *What! HAHA! Cool, promise you'll let me see next week?* Hell fucking yes! she said to herself when reading his reply, but responded with a cool and collected, *Ok, fine, weirdo.* A smiley face followed to imply her playfulness. Now she had a plan, and if it worked, she'd be flashing Adam by this time next week!

Having no one else to talk to, Lilly mentioned her nipple piercing plans to a girl in her Biology class. They weren't friends, but they had worked together on a group project and were friendly. She was the edgy type with tattoos and piercings of her own, dark black hair with bright red and purple streaks. Lilly thought the subject appropriate to bring up to her in particular. The girl asked if she could tag along with her to the tattoo shop where it would happen.

"You wanna come with me? Yeah! Hell yeah! That'd be cool!" Lilly replied, almost shocked at her luck. The plan was already working out better than she had expected. Now she had a "friend" to go with her, making it more authentic and not a half-assed attempt to win some boys' attention. Lilly could even bring along a disposable camera and have the girl take pictures of the whole thing happening. She would pose with this girl as proof that she had friends, and that this was a long since planned event. The pictures, she imagined, would arouse Adam and if he asked to keep one or two of them, that would be okay with her too.

The girls meet that Saturday, enough time for Lilly to get the piercings and have the photos developed before Tuesday's class. Lilly picked up her classmate and drove to a tattoo shop the girl was fond of, armed with a loose-fitting tank top and her disposable camera. Lilly bounced in her seat and let out an excited shriek as they pulled into the parking lot. It was a dingy little suite in a rundown strip-mall. The store front said TATTOO with blacked-out windows. A neon purple sign read TATTOO & PIERCING. *This must be the place*. Lilly took a hard gulp of air, then followed her new friend through the door.

A masculine-looking woman with long straight hair and a lip ring greeted them. "Hey, Sarah! You bring us another victim?" she said, opening with a serious joke.

"Hey! She wants the Peach Ring, both sides."

"Oh, okay, living dangerously, I see. Alright, I'll just need to see some ID and we'll get started."

"Wait, wait," Lilly chimed in, "what's a peach ring? Is that for the… uh…" the last word she whispered, "nipples?" Both women laughed at her innocence.

"A Peach Ring is both nipples pierced with hoops and a chain connecting them. You're gonna love it," the woman behind the counter responded.

"A chain? I can do that? Is that a thing?" Lilly questioned as her eyes lit up.

"It's a thing, and it's hot, I have it, see?" Sarah said as she pulled down her low-cut top to reveal two pierced nipples connected by a thin silver chain.

It was like jewelry for her cleavage, and Lilly wanted it. As the woman was setting up the piercing station, Lilly and Sarah took a couple pictures of the shop and took one or two "before" pictures. Lilly's heart raced in her chest as her mind whirled with the fantasy of how much Adam would love this. She couldn't wait to show him the pictures and the finished product in the flesh. This was going to make her visible to him. The pain she didn't think about, her mind left no room for anything else as she jumped head-first into the experience, only the word "Adam" running through her thoughts.

"Alright, missy, come and take a seat right here." The woman motioned to the bench in front of her and instructed Lilly to take off her shirt. "Okay, now sit up real straight for me, shoulders back, don't move… okay, I'm just gonna mark your little bits real quick so I know where to make the holes. We don't want any lopsided booby holes now, do we?" The woman chuckled to herself. Lilly followed the instructions and motioned to Sarah to take pictures. "Okay, deep breath in, we're gonna count down from three…" It was getting real now. Lilly let her eyes close and roll back into her skull as she relaxed into it. She breathed in deep, exhaled slow. The woman latched a clamp onto her nipple and brought a thick hallow needle up to meet the clamp. "Three… two…" The countdown faded off in the distance.

By the time she completed her exhale, she hadn't even heard the woman call out the number one when the needle pierced through the top layer of skin. She felt it push in and heard a crackling sound that came from inside her body. She was sure it wasn't audible to anyone else in the room—it was a sound she felt. Every millimeter of the needle pushing turned more intense than the last. She felt pressure inside the skin, through the nipple where nothing had ever touched before. The sensation was alien. She felt pain, but that wasn't as striking as the cold steel entering and then exiting her body, although still only skin deep. It exhilarated her. The woman looped the jewelry hoop into the hollow part of the needle, now sticking through the other side of the clamp, and pulled it back through, and she felt the steel again. This time the sensation was hot as the nipple had already swollen. Time to do the second one. Again, the clamp came up, the countdown began, another deep breath in, then out. The sensation came, then fell like a wave crashing over her.

"Oh, my God!" Lilly said as she let out another breath. "Wow! That was crazy."

"Those are always my favorite to do," the woman said with a smile as she cleaned around the wounds. "Now, I'm gonna give you the chain, but you'll want to wait until they're healed before you put it on. If you do it now, you'll pull on them and they'll reject and then you'll have split nipples and you don't want that, trust me."

"Okay, thanks." Lilly turned to Sarah. "Did you get lots of pictures? Here let's take some more." She stood up, a little woozy, and posed with Sarah for more pictures, topless and with a newfound confidence only the surge of adrenaline could invoke. Lilly paid the bill, and the two left the shop. She was so excited for Tuesday. Her nipples ached, but she didn't care. She was ready for the next phase of the plan, the reveal.

For the next three days, Lilly's nipples stung as they tried to heal themselves. Each time she entered an air-conditioned room, they would harden and send a shiver of ice down her spine. Getting ready for work, she pulled her ponytail through her uniform hat and an electric zing shot into her nipples outward through her breasts and again down her spine. The slightest touch brought on this sensation every time, and she wasn't sure if this would become annoying. She hoped it would lessen as they healed. Lilly cleaned and cared for them as she was told, but the pain and puffiness persisted. The healing would take at least two weeks, or so she was told. She didn't have two weeks; it was Tuesday again and time to follow through with her plan. As she got ready to head to class, she played over in her head the sound of the woman at the tattoo shop warning her against wearing the chain too soon, but rationalized that she had to wear the chain anyway because this might be her only chance to seduce Adam. The chain made it super sexy, and that was the whole point. She justified her choice to herself and clipped the chain to each hoop. The weight of the tiny chain pulled down on her and she found herself hunched over with a throbbing pain that pulsated through each breast and exited her armpits in a wave of heat. She was going to push through, at least for the next few hours. She straightened herself out, put on her bra and shirt, stuffed the pack of pictures she had developed at the 1-Hour Photo Stop in her backpack, and headed to class.

In class, as Adam walked in the door, that same electric sensation shot through her when his figure came into view. Lilly flushed and put her head down. *Great.* Now she had a physical sensation to match the mental stimuli that Adam brought upon her. Having no previous experience with this, she had no mechanism to mask it.

Adam sat down and pulled Lilly's notebook towards him. *So? How was your weekend?* he asked, going right into it, no beating around the bush or pretending to be polite.

Lilly smiled and pulled out the pack of photos, slid them over to him, and brought her pointer finger up to her mouth, making the universal symbol for him to be quite and discrete about it. Adam leafed through the photos, keeping them close to his body so no one else around could peak. He got to the images of Lilly and Sarah, both topless, showing off their jewelry. Lilly searched Adam's face for a reaction and lit up when the smile on his face stretched out across it. She blushed again as more electricity shot through her.

Wow! Who's your friend? He wrote.

Lilly's jaw dropped open and looked down at the photo. The image revealed how much bigger Sarah's breasts were than hers and how they had that stupid, sexy chain running across where Lilly's in comparison were puffy and red, so much smaller against her much larger belly, and chainless. *Fuck!* Now Adam was only interested in her big busted friend and she hadn't even considered the comparison.

Oh, that's Sarah, she's not my friend for real, she's kind of bitchy and I think she has herpes. Was that response desperate? Yes, but she didn't know what else to write to salvage the experience and push the focus back to her.

Haha, ok, yours look hot though. Nice. Adam must have sensed her frustration as he threw her a bone.

Lilly's head sunk down in defeat, her plan destroyed. She changed the subject to steer the conversation away from her friend's breasts and back to their normal routine of wasting time on other topics. Class ended and Adam said goodbye. He didn't ask to her to show him her actual boobs; he didn't invite her to a party or event where something like that might happen on its own. All he gave her was a goodbye and a see you next week. As he walked away, a lump grew in her throat, her body became heavy and weak, her breasts ached so much now that she couldn't walk without a hunch. *Why hadn't this worked?* She would regroup and come up with an alternative plan, a better one. Next week was the last class and final exam. It would be her last opportunity and she wouldn't mess it up again.

FOUR

The Smoking Section

I
t was Tuesday again. The last Tuesday that would
ever matter to her for the rest of her life. She had
spent the week devising plots to connect her and
Adam, something that would make her more to him than a
class acquaintance. She had quite a few creative ideas.
Maybe she could throw a party and invite him? No, that
wouldn't work. She no longer had the network of girlfriends to make such an event successful, her parents
weren't leaving town that weekend, and she had no clue
how to get beer without the help of her ex-girl group's
older siblings. Or she could convince a bouncer at the local
nightclub to give her VIP access? Lilly and Adam were
both underage, and getting VIP access to a bar would be
an exceptional way to gain some traction with him. He
would have to fall for that. But how would she even do
that? She didn't know any bouncers, only that it was a job
that existed. No, it wouldn't be worth it unless it was a
surefire shot to work. Second guessing herself was enough
to throw her off of the idea all together.

Lilly dreamed up different scenarios of asking him out

on a date; but never in a million years would that have
worked, she was fishing way out of her league here and if
it were ever going to work, it would be a long and slow
game of cat and mouse—one she had never played either.
It would have to work so slow that Adam, the smartest guy
in the room, wouldn't even realize he was playing until she
had caught him. If she did this right, it would take him by
surprise, and he would wake up one day realizing he was in
love and couldn't live another moment without her. Asking
him out on a date was not the way to do that. It would only
work if he thought he was the cat and she the mouse, when
in reality she'd been the cat since that first day in the
lecture hall.

Forsaking all other options, she could create an emergency, a situation in which she involved herself in an accident or got hurt. Giving Adam the opportunity to come to
the rescue, provoking a damsel in distress response, causing
him to carry her off to safety where she would praise him,
stroke his ego, and offer some romantic gesture as a thank
you. But if it backfired, it might end up in her becoming
wounded physically or dying of fatal embarrassment. She
concluded that neither was something she wanted to
happen in front of him. What if he was the one who got
hurt, and she saved him? He would have to want to date
her after that! Oh, but if she got caught, or if he ever
found out, that could be trouble. She never was smooth or
subtle when her actions involved consequences. That final
Tuesday morning, she settled on a plan. She would ask him
if she could buy him a beer to celebrate the end of the
semester. It wouldn't be a date, because it was beer, beer is
for friends. It would be as friends. That would work. It
wasn't embarrassing, and no one would get hurt. She
didn't know how she would get the beer, but that would be
another obstacle she would figure out later. Perfect.

That afternoon, the professor had prepared the room by blocking off every other chair with caution tape and signage that said, "DO NOT SIT HERE—FINAL EXAM PROTOCOL." *What the hell?* She couldn't even sit next to him! Would they talk at all? This was the worst thing that could happen! Forlorn and feeling like her plans were foiled yet again, she sat down and waited for his arrival, only this time she wasn't able to stretch out her bookbag to save him a seat. It wouldn't have mattered anyway, considering the distance between the open seats. As predicted, he was late and by the time he arrived, there were no open seats left anywhere near her. He still waved at, her from a distance, before walking to the front of the room to the only remaining empty seats. She smiled at his acknowledgement. Did that mean he liked her more than a class acquaintance? Her mind reeled with the symbolism of his actions. What could it mean? She searched the sea of heads in front of her for the back of his, but could barely make it out. Once the exam begun, her eyes left her paper every other moment only to land on a small piece of a random dreadlock, reassuring herself he was still there.

Adam, being the smartest person alive, finished the exam before anyone else and stood up to turn it in. He stepped towards the podium and tossed his completed Scantron sheet on the surface, took the couple steps back to his seat, gathered his things, and walked out. She had to think fast. He was leaving. What was she going to do? He was getting away! She stood up, walked down to the front of the class, and submitted her exam, face down so as not to reveal its incompleteness, and hurried to make it out the door before he had gotten too far ahead. When she emerged from the doorway, he was already several feet ahead of her—too far to catch up with a casual walk, yelling for his attention would have been too obvious.

There was no other choice but to follow him. Was it weird? Yes, but she had run out of options and time.

She followed him to a section of campus she had never been. He walked, and she trailed, in front of the theatre and past the box office to a shaded little corner on the side. It was a place that a person wouldn't wander to on their own. The area secluded itself from its surrounding and led to nowhere, and its name was "The Smoking Section" as referenced on various signs and local ashtrays. She found herself somewhere she had no business being. There were people there, none of whom she had ever met before, except for Adam, who now eyed her, a glare and a half-smile pointed towards her. He knew she didn't smoke; she knew he knew she didn't smoke. *Oh my God, what am I doing?* She hadn't thought this far ahead and couldn't think of anything to say that would justify her being there.

But Adam, being Adam, welcomed her with open arms and a warm greeting. "Lilly! Hey! Oh I'm happy you're here, I didn't have time to say hello in class." He spoke with exuberance.

"Oh, yeah, hi." She gave a sheepish response that high-lighted how nervous she was. All she hoped for now was that no one mentioned the flush of her face as she felt the blood rise to under the surface of her skin. She couldn't explain why she was there unless she was prepared to admit that she had followed him. He paused, as if to give her a chance to respond further, or explain herself, or stop being awkward, a moment that never came.

"Uh, okay, well, come meet my friends." He motioned for her to come near. He was surrounded by several people, all with cigarettes in hand. "So, this is Kyle, Ryan, and Neil." He pointed to everyone, each of them lifting a hand or nodding their head when they heard their name.

"Hi, I'm Lilly. Adam and I had English class together, I

just wanted to come say hi." A lazy answer, but it worked. The conversation continued and Lilly stood and listened. She laughed when appropriate, added commentary when she could. Soon she felt the heat dissipate from her face as her nerves relaxed and she found herself in normal conversation, with normal people that didn't seem bothered by her presence.

These friends of his were interesting. She would learn much more about them in the weeks and months to come but in this moment found that they were people who liked to smoke and talk about meaningless things, much the same topics she and Adam had discussed on notebook paper in class. Each of them had a unique style. The group looked like a mismatched bunch of kids plucked from their corresponding peer clusters and smashed together to make this one.

Lilly's first impressions of the guys focused on how unique they all appeared on the surface. Kyle was a flamboyant, glitter-faced, dirty hippie, gay boy. His long hair held up in a man-bun long before hipsters brought it to the collective consciousness of popular fashion magazines. He had dirt under his fingernails and caked in-between the colored but faded plastic beads of the bracelets around his wrists. *Those damn bracelets again.* Kyle wore Jenko fat pants with rainbow suspenders, wife beater tank-tops and a cartoon character backpack. It wasn't for holding books and notebooks though, as she learned Kyle didn't attend the college, he only showed up for the social interaction and free cigarettes.

Ryan could not have been a further cry from Kyle. Although both of them enjoyed the free cigarettes gifted by others that visited the hangout spot, that was the only thing the two had in common. Ryan wore a grey Fedora hat, a black jean kilt, and black jean vest adorned with metal hoops and chains and spikes with an occasional safety pin holding together two torn segments of a pocket. He had a chain connecting his wallet to his kilt and black on black Vans over black socks. His skin was deep black, and his dark eyes sat behind thick prescription glasses. Curly black hair poked out from the bottom of his Fedora, and crooked, nicotine-stained teeth rested in his smile.

Neil, besides Adam, was the most normal-looking of the bunch. Lilly would come to find out that Neil was a former serviceman and had served in the Army. Now retired, he was attending school on the GI Bill that educated him on good old Uncle Sam's dime. Neil wore raggedy band T-shirts and baggy blue jeans, and he still had his service haircut. He was the oldest of the crew at 28, while the rest were between 18-20. He had been out of the service for years but still spoke about it with fond memories as the years he spent there came to define the man he was after coming home.

These trivial facts she learned about the guys all while standing there and involving herself in their conversation. Neil brought up his time in the service about as often as he could, Ryan spoke about a hacky sack tournament he might attend that weekend, and Kyle listened while bobbing along to the silent music playing in his head.

Adam received a text. *A text message? Who even does that?* Adam pulled Kyle aside to tell him something Lilly couldn't quite make out over the sound of Ryan and Neil talking about final exams. Only a few seconds later, the two came back to the group. As they approached, Ryan and Neil stopped talking, almost in mid-sentence, expecting an announcement by Adam.

"Guys, let's go!" The words left his lips and the entire crew sprang into action, grabbing book bags and stomping out their cigarettes. Kyle, Ryan, and Neil all started heading off without saying goodbye, no pleasantries. They were on a mission too important to leave time for such things. But Adam was not like them. He paused, turned to Lilly and said, "Hey, so, we all have to go, we're going to my friend Shade's house and I would invite you, but…"

"Oh, I know Shade." Lilly cut him off before he could complete the non-invitation.

"Really?" He sounded surprised. "How do you know Shade?"

"He sold me drugs," she answered. Another shock. She was blunt and honest, revealing that she did know Shade because she told two intimate details about him, things that she could not have guessed by the name alone—that Shade was a guy and that he sold drugs.

"Oh! Ha! Okay, cool, well, do you wanna come? We're gonna smoke weed, though?"

"Uhhh…." She hesitated at first. Was she about to do this?

"Come on, you can be Bill, I'll be Ted, we can go on an excellent adventure together."

"Okay." She replied as her cheeks flushed and she melted at the sharpness of his wit. *He's so smart, so cute.* It would have been stupid to refuse the invitation—this was her in.

"Cool, let's go," he said, and they headed off with the rest of the group.

Once in the parking lot, Lilly turned to Adam, "I'm over here." She pointed toward her car.

"No, no, Neil's our driver, trust me, it's cool." Adam almost laughed at her suggestion she ride on her own.

Was this what it felt like to be part of Adam's crew? She could only hope.

They soon arrived at a late 80s model Astro Van, dark brown with a light brown and grey stripe across both sides.

Neil pulled back the sliding door to reveal a layer of wooden beads that draped down over the opening. Inside was a camel brown, shag-carpet floor, dark green curtains covering the windows, and darker brown leather seats. Scattered on the open floor were cushions, pillows, and blankets. An aqua blue and emerald green lava lamp sat attached to the center console, plugged in with an adapter to the cigarette lighter in the dash.

"Welcome to The Experience," Neil said to Lilly with a grin and relaxed chuckle. A pause before the reveal added drama. It was obvious he lived for the moment he got to introduce his van to new people. He even named it The Experience, a name so fitting for Lilly in that moment, symbolic of the very thing she had been searching for the entire semester as she pursued Adam. It was beginning. They all laughed a little and took a step aside, allowing Lilly to enter first.

Inside, every pullout ashtray was overflowing with cigarette butts and the tips of smoked down joints. There was a CD collection so massive it cluttered the front cup holders and back seat pockets, each one numbered and labeled. There must have been hours upon hours of studio sessions, live concerts, unreleased recordings, full-length albums, bonus tracks, all of it.

The group loaded into the back. Lilly took a seat while Ryan and Kyle opted for the cushy floor. The engine rumbled to a start, and they were off. Adam sat shotgun and he and Neil argued in lighthearted banter about what songs to put on for the audience in the backseat. Neil sang every lyric to every song as it played, hanging his cigarette out the window during the parts that required full vocal force. Lilly laughed along with the others when he belted his voice to reach the high notes in Tom Petty's "Free Fallin'."

"Dude! You don't know all these songs," Adam said.

"I do." His reply was confident and stoic.

"Okay, bet!" Kyle chimed in from the back, lounging on his side with his hand on one hip in a pose that reminded Lilly of old Hollywood glam, but dirtier. "CD number 14, song 8. Go!"

"Well, that'd be 'The Wall' by Pink Floyd, Disc 1, track 8 would be 'Empty Spaces'…" But he wasn't finished. He completed his statement in lyrics. "'What shall we use to fill the empty spaces…,'" he sang.

"Whoa!" the rest of them recited in unison.

"Okay, okay," Ryan said as he flipped through CD leaflets. "How 'bout this one? CD 27, track 12."

"Awh yes," Neil began. The rest of them stared at him with open mouths and silence. "CD's 20-102 are The Beatles collection, so 27 will have to be Revolver, their seventh studio album, track 12 is… 'I Want To Tell You.'"

"Oh my god, you're like Rain Man!" Lilly said, impressed.

"Well, I like to stay organized. It's the little things that are important in life."

"Okay, okay, dawg, stop showing off, we're here." Adam refocused the group as they arrived.

They had arrived at a rundown apartment complex. The five of them shuffled out of the van and walked up to a first-floor apartment. Loud music played inside. She couldn't place the genre. It was unlike anything she had ever heard before. If computers were musicians, this is the music they would write, repetitive and fast-paced, with sweeping melodies and big bass lines. They didn't bother knocking, but walked right in. No way any knock or doorbell would have cut through the noise.

It was the ultimate bachelor pad. Complete with a dirty kitchen full of empty beer bottles and a gravity bong made of empty and chopped up 2-liter soda bottles. The concept of which involved slicing the bottle in half and placing the top half into a reservoir of water, in this case, a dirty kitchen sink. The cap of the bottle was fashioned with a small hole in the top to hold a stemmed bowl of pot. The pot would be lit and the bottle lifted out of the water, the space inside would fill with thick, yellow smoke as it sucked air through the bowl and pulled with it the thick smoky byproduct of burning marijuana. Before the bottle came out of the water, the user would untwist the bottle cap and place their lips around the bottle mouth to inhale the milky smoke—and this was only the kitchen.

They moved into the living room with two tattered beanbag chairs, a single recliner that looked like a grandfather's hand-me-down, a box television sitting on top of a plastic milk crate, and a full DJ set up with a speaker system that stacked up to the ceiling. Behind the setup was a decorated banner that read "1 Earth, 1 Rave," in black-light reflective paint. Previous visitors marked the walls up with pens and pencils, the quotes and signatures of friends and memories. Spent glow sticks and those same beaded bracelets scattered themselves on the floor amongst random bits of cigarette rolling papers, receipts and the occasional stale pizza crust. Dirt and grime gathered in corners and crevasses, and the carpet outlined a clear walkway where others had passed.

"Hi everyone!" It was Shade who greeted them, only he looked nothing like the Shade she had met as a nervous high school kid buying pot for the first time. There was no black cloak, no platform shoes, no neon-colored G-strings, and no glittery purple eyeshadow. He had eyebrows, a plain brown T-shirt and khaki cargo pants, short hair and the same piercing blue eyes. It was those same striking blue eyes she remembered; this was Shade. His voice was lurid as his dress from back then, but without the wild costume to match.

"Shade! What up, dawg!" Adam exclaimed. They met in the center of the living room for a handshake and a hug. "Sick beats!"

"Oh thanks, this is my newest track, just testing it out on the decks." Shade directed his attention to Lilly. "Hi, I'm Shade," he said as he stretched out his arms for a hug.

"Oh, hi, you probably don't remember me, but we've met before."

"Really? When? Why don't I remember you? Impossible, I always remember faces."

"Um, you looked... uh... different back then. You didn't have eyebrows."

"Oh," Shade said, followed by a nervous laugh. "You knew Shade Destiny! Okay, I don't remember a lot from back then. Don't do drugs, kid." He paused and chuckled at himself. "Yeah, you're cool. Welcome!"

"Tight, tight! Cool, man, so you wanna Poke?" Adam chimed in, changing the subject back to the point at hand.

Did he say poke? What could that mean? Lilly turned to Adam, puzzled by the word and the question that made little sense to her.

"Oh, you don't know." Adam chuckled as he explained. "Poke is short for Poke Smot, which is code for Smoke Pot. See, when you switch the first two letters of Smoke, and the first letter of Pot, you get Poke Smot. That's how we say it, so you gotta say it like that now too."

"Uh, Poke Smot. We're gonna Poke Smot."

"That's right! Good job!" Adam laughed as he reassured her.

"Okay, but why the secret code?" Lilly almost whispered this, not wanting to feel dumb for asking what was probably an obvious question.

"Well, silly," said Shade, "it is illegal, so, can't be too careful!"

Lilly nodded in agreement. She had so many more questions about what she had observed in the apartment. What did the banner behind the DJ set up mean? Why was the music so repetitive? And all these beaded bracelets. What the heck was up with these things, and why were they everywhere? But she didn't want to reveal her naivety; maybe it was better to save those questions for another time.

"Let's do it," Adam said, arms held open as if he were offering the room a hug. With those words, the crew sat in a circle on the floor, almost like they already knew their assigned spots, legs crossed in front of them and only an arm's length away from the person on either side. Lilly waited for everyone to sit before she found an empty place to put herself, one that the rest of them had left for her, Shade on one side and Ryan on the other. While the space was already there, they both scooted out a little more to make sure she felt welcome.

"Sit, sit!" said Shade, as he patted the ground next to him. "This is what we call a pot circle, and this is how we smoke, or poke, actually. It makes it easy to talk and pass the pipe and it's comfy." Lilly's particular shade of green shone bright to all of them as they each took her under their wings to teach her the ways of their subculture. Lilly sat down and Shade passed her a pipe with a bowl of fresh, packed flower. "You want Greens?"

"What's that? Some type of drug?"

They laughed at her like big brothers laugh at a little sister learning how to ride a bike.

"Well, yes, but really Greens means to take the first hit off of a pipe. It's the cleanest and tastiest hit, kinda special." Those familiar to the culture knew that Greens belonged to whoever packed the bowl or supplied the pot, or was offered to guests in the same way someone might set out fancy seashell soaps in a bathroom when expecting company.

Lilly took the pipe in her hand and held it up to her lips. She lit the bowl and sucked on the opposite end, but the bowl wouldn't ignite. She had never smoked out of a proper pipe before and was sure she was doing it wrong. They all laughed again. A couple of them shook their head and rolled their eyes with smiles.

"Oh, my god this is gonna be the longest smoke out in recorded history!" Kyle shouted from the opposite side of the circle.

"Shut the fuck up, Kyle," Ryan hushed him.

"Joking, joking, sorry, jeeze!" Kyle raised his hands in a gesture of surrender and quieted down.

"Here, there's a little hole in the side, it's called a carb, short for carburetor, put your finger over it when you light and suck, then let your finger off to inhale the smoke," Ryan explained as he pointed out the various parts of the pipe and the mechanics of how smoking worked.

Lilly's heart thudded in her chest as she listened. Her inability to grasp these concepts made her feel childish. She wanted nothing more than to impress these people she was around, but her nerves took over as she squirmed and twitched with all eyes watching her. She followed the instructions offered by Ryan and tried again. The bowl lit and she inhaled a deep cloud of smoke. This one didn't even compare to the tiny wisp she had got the first time with the pen cap. She found herself sunk down into the ground. A wave of euphoria washed over her as the melody in the background swept her away.

The pipe continued around the circle; the group continued talking amongst themselves despite the loud beating music that sounded like a repetitive loop. But it elated Lilly. She focused her eyes at whoever was speaking without understanding what was being said, a grin on her face and heavy eyelids that drooped almost to a close. *This must be what love feels like.* There was nothing else like it, and she couldn't believe her luck, that such an experience, complete with a brand new group of friends, could result from following her crush out of class that day. The pipe came back around, and she passed it on. She didn't need another hit, the first one suited her fine. The group chuckled again at her. Adam's eyes scanned the circle. When they landed on her, he asked if she wanted to join him outside for a cigarette break. She nodded in agreement, a smile still on her face, and lifted herself off the ground.

With daylight now gone, the outside stars were bright enough to dance against the beat of the music coming from inside, now muted behind the closed door. "So you having fun? What do you think about all this?" Adam asked.

Was he trying to make sure she was having a good time or just making conversation? She settled on a conclusion that he was genuine in his ask. "Dude! This is amazing! I don't know why I waited so long to enjoy this. I mean, this isn't my first-time smoking weed, I've done the drugs, this drug… is this really a drug?" She rambled as she struggled to save herself. "Weed is so cool, man," she said as the two of them enjoyed a friendly chuckle.

"You know what makes it even better? A cigarette! Here, try it." He handed over his lit cigarette. She grimaced and pulled her face back as if to say hell no, that's gross, I'm not touching that. Adam laughed again but didn't give up in his pursuit. "Trust me, you'll like it." She needed little convincing. Her face relaxed, and she reached out to grab his offering. She inhaled deeply. He was right yet again. Cigarettes after weed were delightful.

"Whoa, cool, so I smoke pot now and I like cigarettes."

"You poke smot," he corrected her.

"Yeah, yeah, poke smot. I'm a smot poker!" She laughed at her own joke and he smiled along.

"You know, you never showed me your new piercings…" Adam said, as if he knew the timing was perfect. And it would have been, but over that week since it had happened, rather than heal, her nipples had developed a severe infection that made them sore and swollen. Although she wanted to, it caught her off guard and because of this persistent infection, she hadn't put on her nipple chain that day. But this might be her last opportunity. She couldn't deny him now. *Maybe he won't notice the puffiness?*

Without saying a word, she lifted her shirt and bra, not realizing a crust had formed from the infection and dried itself on her bra and jewelry, connecting the two together. As she lifted her clothing the jewelry lifted with it, ripping itself right out of her nipple, leaving skin, blood, puss, and the surgical steel ring still attached to her bra. In the same moment she barreled over in pain, seething as her nipple throbbed and bled. A strong belly growl came from her mouth as she tried to fight back the urge to scream. Not knowing what to do next, she stayed there in a standing fetal position, suffering and hoping against all hope that Adam hadn't seen the gore.

"Uh, you okay?" Adam said, while still chuckling.

Lilly couldn't respond, she only nodded her head from its position next to her knees.

"Uh, okay, uh, you don't have to show me, it's cool," Adam said, now with a little more worry.

"Yeah, uh, I forgot that I, uh, took one out and it's

stupid if I just show you one." She strained her words as she tried to explain.

"It's okay, it's okay. Come back and smoke this cig with me?"

Adam, the forever gentleman, calmed her without making fun of her. At that point, she wasn't sure if he knew what had happened to her or not, but his sweet voice convinced her to rise back up and finish the cigarette as if what had happened never had. She squished her face in pain as she stuffed her breasts back into her bra, careful not to disturb them as much as she could. The awkward moment that followed lasted only that long as the front door creaked open. It was the rest of the crew coming out to join them in a cigarette. Lilly's attention refocused, and the mood shifted. The previous discussion inside the apartment continued on outside, and Adam and Lilly fell into it as the crew all stood around with their cigarettes.

Ryan looked at Lilly, who was hitting Adam's cigarette. "Oh, you smoke now too? What have we done to you?" They all laughed at his joke.

Back inside, Lilly tried her best to ignore the breast that was now beating like her heart. The crew listened to more music, talked, and poked more smot. Kyle took a particular liking to Lilly, as gay boys often did. A sweet, fat girl. Lilly found him easiest to talk to, and she liked him back. It had gotten late, and Adam announced it was time for them to go back to their subsequent homes. They all loaded back into Neil's van, The Experience, and made the journey back to the college campus, paired tunes to accompany them and the mood.

They pulled up to Lilly's car first and opened the door to let her out. As she climbed over Kyle to exit, he told her to make sure and come by the smoking section tomorrow. Her official invitation to keep hanging out. She said she would. Though elated, she still had a pressing matter to attend to, one that none of them knew about. Back home, she removed her shirt and, with extreme care, peeled back her padded pushup bra. Thank god she had worn that bra today because the extra padding was the only thing keeping the pool of blood inside it from seeping through to her shirt. A bloody nipple ring and chunks of skin mixed with puss still hung tight to the bra. Dried blood had crusted shut her now split nipple. Not knowing what to do, the first and only thing she could think to do was call her mother.

Her mother sounded annoyed. "What time is it? Why are you calling me so late? Somebody die?"

"No, no, sorry. So, I got my nipples pierced, 'cause this boy said he liked it. Anyway, I did it and I guess they got infected and one ripped out of my boob! I don't know what to do."

"Pfft," her mother scoffed, "serves you right for doing something stupid like that. What? You think you going to get your nipples pierced will make this boy like you? Stupid. What about your big, fat belly? Nipple piercings make that invisible or something?" Her mother laughed as she mocked her. "I don't know, call your dad, it's late, I don't have time for this." The line clicked off.

FIVE

The Tree

"Yo, yo, yo!" Adam announced his presence to the crew already waiting for him at the smoking section.

"Hi Adam!" Lilly was the first to greet him.

"You guys ready to go to The Tree?" The rest of them mumbled, nodded their heads, and stomped out their cigarettes as they gathered their belongings.

"What's The Tree?" Lilly asked, still new to the group and unsure about what was happening, or if they were inviting her.

"School's out. Time to find a new spot. Over break we go to The Tree," Neil answered.

The Tree, or the Poke Smot Spot, was a giant willow that sat at the back of a wooded ravine. It was a bit of a hike to get there, but not on any hiking trail. This was private property and inaccessible to the public. From the street it looked like an empty lot with a dirt mound in the back, but walk up to the mound and a secret entrance revealed itself. The entrance led down a path covered in brush and trees. Past the brush was a clearing, and in the distance sat the tree. Surrounded by small hills, the streets and buildings disappeared. "It's the perfect spot to smoke our illegal drugs!"

"Yeah, it's fucking cool, you coming?" asked Kyle, as he held out an arm for her to grab onto, offering her escort.

"Yeah, okay!"

"Ryan!" Adam said in a loud voice. Ryan's face pulled away from the conversation happening between Lilly and Kyle.

"Stop yelling, fucker! What?"

"Here's $40, take Kyle to get two separate sacks so we can poke at the spot. My sister needs one, she'll meet us there."

"No way, fucker. You know I can't take anyone with me."

"Ha!" Adam laughed. Neil and Kyle rolled their eyes as if to say, here we go again. "Oh, right, right, your super-secret weed connect that none of us can ever know about, ever. Ha! Okay, whatever. Just take the money and meet us there after you pick up." Adam handed the money to Ryan. Without another word, he took off on his bike while the remaining four headed for the parking lot.

"Ryan's gonna take forever. You guys wanna stop for munchies real quick?"

"You buying?" Neil asked.

"I buy fucking everything, you fuckers!" Adam shouted again, but joking. "Fine, I buy the weed, I buy the food, fuck it. I got you guys." Lilly laughed louder at Adam's jokes than anyone else. The crew, less Ryan, loaded into The Experience and stopped at the local Jack In The Box to order what Kyle coined The Stoner Combo. It comprised two tacos, a chicken sandwich, fries, and a coke, all for under $5. With greasy paper bags in hand, they continued on their journey to the new spot.

They arrived at the empty lot to find Ryan already waiting there, sweating and breathing heavily, cigarette in hand. *He must have just arrived.* When the four of them emerged from the van holding paper food bags and cold drinks, Ryan's face went white and his jaw dropped in disbelief.

"Where the fuck is mine?" he asked in a voice that sounded like a child complaining about fairness.

"I'll share with you," Lilly said when no one else offered.

Also there, waiting in the parking lot, was a silver Honda Civic. The window rolled down to reveal three high school girls, one much younger than the other two. "Hold on, guys, that's my little sister. Ryan, gimme a sack."

"Adam! You are not selling drugs to your little sister!" Lilly laughed and teased Adam as he walked over to the car.

"What?" he said in a playful tone. It was a sweet moment. She remembered back to her first experience, facilitated by her old best friend's brother, as she watched brother and sister engage in the act of drug transfer.

"Aight! Let's go smoke, fuckers!" Adam announced with arms up in the air as his sister and her friends drove off, the task complete.

They started walking down the path, playfully kicking rocks at each other's feet and calling out pretend spiders just to watch Adam jump. Lilly learned that day that he was deathly afraid of them. "Wait, for real, Adam? You're scared?"

"NO! I'm not, they're just fucking gross and disgusting and... I don't wanna talk about it."

"Adam's a little scaredy cat!" Kyle shouted, pointed, and taunted.

"Shut the fuck up, Kyle!"

"Oh, he's totally little bitch scared," Neil said as he laughed along with the others.

Ryan kept silent, distracted by the fast-food taco he was inhaling as they walked down the path. Lilly let her eyes gaze as the natural scene came into view and the rest of the city fell away. She had never visited a place like it, hidden within view. In the distance there was the willow, every bit as majestic as she had imagined it to be. A wooden swing hung down from one branch. They would not be the first ones to discover this place, but with no one else around, it would belong to them for now.

At the end of the walk, they arrived under the shade of the large willow. They plopped down in their circle to eat their food and smoke their pot. Ryan, having already eaten his share on the way, prepared the weed and rolled a joint. He didn't wait for the rest of them to finish eating before he lit the joint, took his two puffs, and passed it right to Lilly sitting beside him.

"What the fuck, Ryan! I paid for that shit!" Adam said.

"Puff, puff, pass to the right, motherfucker!" Ryan said, defending his choice. "Not my fault you're not sitting to the right."

"Fine, fucker, whatever, Lilly can have it next, but I was gonna offer it to her, anyway."

"Aw, you're so sweet, Adam, thank you." *Shit! Was that too flirty? Calm the fuck down, Lilly, just be one of them and swear a lot more.* Scared she had blown her cover after all the work she had put in, she turned to Adam for some sign of reassurance that he had taken it as a compliment and nothing more. He met her look with a soft smile and a chuckle.

This became the routine. In the off-school season, and

when it started again they met, they smoked, and they drove in The Experience, listening to Neil's music and trying to stump him. They never could. Lilly became more comfortable as she became one of them, all the while keeping her intentions hidden.

SIX

Candy

L illy was nine months into her invisible courting of Adam when he announced to the crew that his parents were leaving town and that he wanted to have everyone over at his place for a kickback. The small get together would be invite-only. He'd have beer, weed, and give them all a chance to relax away from their parents. This was it! This was the moment! It was going to be nighttime, there would be booze, she would be the only girl there. It would be the perfect opportunity for Lilly to slip in and seduce him. She had seduced no one before, wasn't great at flirting, and had still never had a boyfriend, been on a date, or even kissed a guy, but she was going to make this the night all that changed. Pumping up her ego, she reasoned with herself that he wanted this too, that he was playing hard-to-get. She used this logic to fuel her girlish excitement.

Each person had a task to complete before the kick-back. Adam wanted to make sure they had premium weed to smoke, the stress weed that Ryan handled wouldn't be good enough. No, this wasn't an everyday weed type of occasion. This was the first time Adam's parents had left for the weekend and would be the first time he invited them into his home. Adam requested Kyle visit their friend Shade to pick up some chronic, the strain of weed that was bright green with sticky white crystals covering the buds and orange hairs sticking out in-between purple leaves. This was the plant that hit smooth and sweet and didn't leave you with a headache or sore throat.

No seeds or stems in this stuff. Chronic came in a variety of strains with their own names and potencies, Lilly loved to listen to Shade list off fun names like Maui-Waui, Purple Haze, or Orange Crush. She couldn't tell the difference between them, but according to her more experienced friends, there was one. Being able to tell what flower came from what plant and how high one could expect to become from it was akin to being a wine sommelier; only someone with a trained palate could distinguish. This order wouldn't come cheap though, chronic was four times as expensive as their usual, stress, but for this event, it would be worth the cost.

Kyle didn't have a car so he and Lilly together became responsible for picking up the chronic from Shade while Ryan and Neil would pick up the beer and meet back at Adam's for the event. At school that day, they discussed all the logistics and Adam handed Lilly $40 for the order. He entrusted only her with the money and made sure she knew she would be responsible for it, thus ensuring the deal went down smoothly as he wouldn't be there to oversee. This responsibility was real, and she understood the importance of it. The last thing she wanted tonight was to disappoint Adam. Shade was a friend, and she wasn't too worried, but she had still only spent time with him in the

crew's company and Adam was always a force of confidence. She was never unsure of anything when he was
around. The first time without him though brought her
back to being that vulnerable 16-year-old again, doing an
illegal drug deal where anything might go wrong.

Kyle and Lilly pulled up to Shade's apartment. It
wasn't yet dark out, but dusk was setting in. Considering
what she was there to do, and that Adam would not be
there to protect her, she second-guessed herself. She felt
uncomfortable buying drugs, but Kyle assured her that
everything would be fine. Shade was outside with a few
other people, all hustling about and busy as he dictated
instructions to each of them.

"Yeah, Tank, over there. Load those in the truck."
Shade yelled over to a man named Tank and pointed at a
pile of audio cords. "Stuff, did you get the water? What
about the pancakes, don't forget the pancakes!" A woman
called Stuff nodded her head towards him as she carried
plastic crates of LED rope lights to the truck. It wasn't
until Kyle and Lilly were standing right in front of him
that Shade acknowledged their presence.

"Hey, Shade," Kyle said, as Lilly held a sheepish stance
behind him.

"Oh, Jesus, Kyle! You're late! Where have you been?
Whatever, we don't have time. Go grab the decks. They're
in the house." His demand was frantic and aggressive.
"And you," he pointed at Lilly, "go help Stuff with the
water. We only need two jugs. It's gonna be a small party."
Party? What party? Who were all these people? Lilly had questions, but gathered that the people surrounding him and
following his orders were planning some sort of party, and
by Shade's attitude, it was a big deal.

A whiteness drew into Kyle's face as his mouth opened
and his eyes widened.

"Oh... uh... okay," Kyle said as his spine slipped out of his back and onto the floor. He pulled Lilly in towards the apartment as Shade took a phone call. "Shit!" Kyle said to Lilly in an obvious state of distress. "I forgot Shade's party season starts tonight! I'm on the crew, I'm supposed to be here working!"

"Oh, well, it's just a party, I'm sure he'll understand if you tell him you had other plans?"

"No, Lilly, you don't get it! This is like showing up for your shift at The Sub Shop and then telling your boss you're not here to work, you're just here for the employee discount."

"But, why would I ever do that? It would get me fired?"

"Exactly!" Kyle growled as he balled his fists.

"What the fuck, Kyle! How could you just forget? How long have you been doing this with Shade? Forget?" Lilly furrowed her brow and pursed her lips. She couldn't leave him here; Adam expected the entire crew to be together, and she was going to make sure they would carry out his vision for the night. Kyle had, by accident or not, she wasn't sure, put her entire night with Adam in jeopardy.

"I don't know, I'm sorry! Say something to get us out of this."

"What?" Lilly shouted at Kyle, almost creating a scene and causing several of the other party crew members around them to glance over before focusing back on their task at hand. The air was thick with the weight of the evening they were preparing for. "Kyle! No! I don't even know this guy. He's supposed to be your best friend! I can't do it; tell him we're not coming and get the weed."

"Oh no, he won't sell to me if he thinks I'm not coming to his season opener. I can't. It has to be you. You do it. He'll listen to you cause you're new. Make something up, like your cat died or something and you need this time to grieve and you need the weed so we can remember the happy memories." Kyle said this with a smile and jazz hands, as if jazz hands could smooth out the rough edges of the encounter she knew she couldn't escape and was about to walk into.

"Oh, what the fuck is that shit, Kyle?" Lilly scoffed at how ridiculous his plan was. "My cat died. Really? Kyle!" She whispered at him aggressively so she wouldn't alert the worker bees hurrying back and forth from the apartment to the truck, only sometimes stopping to hit a pipe or puff a cigarette. Lilly shook her head at him and hung it down towards the ground while the reality of the situation sunk in. She had no choice; she would have to come up with something. The alternative meant falling through on her responsibility to Adam, and that wasn't something she could survive. Kyle wasn't doing anything about it, and she wouldn't let him ruin her night. This was now her burden. "Fuck!" she said out loud again, too loud, as she stretched her arms out over her head and shook them out, the way a fighter does right before a championship match. She walked over towards Shade, signaling to Kyle to stay back and out of the way.

As she approached Shade, he was still on the phone and from his tone and expressions she gathered the conversation wasn't going well. *Great. Perfect fucking timing.* She stood there in silence for a few moments as he ignored her presence.

He hung up the phone and smiled at her. "Hi," he said. "Sorry, they're trying to steal our spot for tonight and I told them, 'Oh hell no you're not! We've had that spot for years and no one else is throwing a party there except us!' But I handled it, we're all good. What's up?" Shade's tone relaxed and a calm smile ran across his face.

"Oh, uh, hi..." She struggled to find the words. "There's, uh, been a misunderstanding. We can't make the party tonight, I'm sorry. We just came over cause I wanted to pick up a sack from you? If that's okay? Adam sent us." As she spoke, the smile left his face, and she sensed his irritation with her. His phone rang again.

"Hello?" He answered in a harsh tone, while still staring right at Lilly. "I don't know, we just lost two people so, I don't know. Everyone's bailing on me." He flung his arms above his head and shook his neck and head in a violent and flamboyant display of displeasure. Lilly's throat tensed up and her stomach turned. She had never felt more guilty about telling the truth before. Shade turned away from her to finish his phone call, and she looked back to where Kyle was standing. She glared at him as if trying to send laser beams out of her eyes straight into his chest.

Kyle responded to her stare by hiding himself behind a bush that accented the apartment's front window. His shame caused him to sidestep his way right in between the bush and the dusty old window. Lilly, watching with everyone else, shook her head and rolled her eyes while also wishing she were the one hiding in the bush.

Shade took another minute on the phone, almost like he needed it to calm down a bit before addressing her. "Okay," he came back to face her, "did you know we had a party tonight?" he asked, looking down at her like a detective might and used his hands to stress his words.

"No, no, I'm sorry, no I didn't," she answered back with a crackling voice. She couldn't believe she was in trouble with the drug lord-kingpin she imagined him to be.

"Well, I guarantee you Kyle did, because he's literally..." Shade's tone switched from stern to screaming as he finished the sentence, "hiding behind a bush!" He shook his head towards Kyle. "Okay, honey, I'm gonna cut you a break this time, but if you're going to be coming around here smoking my weed and hanging out in my apartment, at some point you have to promise me you're going to help us with my parties too, okay?" His tone was condescending but kind, like he was speaking to a child too young to understand punishment. Lilly let out a sigh of relief and a nervous chuckle.

"Yeah, no problem. I promise." She would have said anything in that moment to ensure she could get out of there unscathed and with the weed.

"Alright, see you next time." Shade turned to walk away.

"Oh, uh…" Lilly stopped him. "Can I still get that sack?"

Kyle slunk down further behind the leaf line. Lilly knew Shade would not appreciate being asked for such a favor after he had let her go with his version of a warning. She gritted her teeth in preparing for his response. Drug dealer etiquette wasn't something she had a firm grasp on. How was this any different from a transaction at Target— he had a product and was in the business of selling that product, any business was business? Right? This was the first time she'd ever attempted to buy drugs since the last first-time and she was lucky to have such an understanding drug dealer. She didn't realize that she had offended Shade when she showed up at his house, unannounced, refused to attend his first party of the season, and then asked him for drugs instead, because that was all she cared about. She didn't know that drug dealers had egos that needed stroking. It would not be the last of her missteps in this underworld.

"Oh, for fuck's sake, kid. Sure. What the fuck, yeah, hold on." Shade answered, more annoyed than the first time, and red in the face. His reaction wasn't great, but it was still more preferable than showing up at Adam's house not having completed her assignment. Shade walked towards his apartment and opened the door to step in. As he did, Kyle slinked out from behind the bush, neither of the two acknowledging the other. Kyle kept his eyes averted like a beta in a pack of wolves where Shade was alpha. He ran up to Lilly while Shade was in the house. Lilly stood looking at him, arms crossed with eyes that would have sliced right through him if eyes could do such a thing.

"Hey! How'd it go?" Kyle asked with an upbeat pep in his voice, as if nothing was wrong and they hadn't insulted a local drug-dealer.

"Fuck off," Lilly replied.

"Cool, okay, I'm gonna go wait in the car. Bye!" Kyle said as he walk-ran to Lilly's car. The others working all watched him as he entered the car and converted the back all the way down until he was laying out of sight in the flattened passenger seat. They shook their heads, smiting him for leaving like this. Below the window line he stayed, as if they couldn't all see, with laser beam eyes that struck right through the thick metal car door, him hiding there in his shame.

Shade emerged from the apartment with the sack of weed and they made the exchange, a sharp frustration on his face. She apologized again and promised she'd make it up to him as she also hurried off to her car, slipped inside, and drove hard and fast away from the scene. The mood changed from tense to relief, and again to joy as they relished in defeating their obstacle. They were on the way to their evening at Adam's. Nothing further would stop her from the fantasy rendezvous she had planned in her head.

They arrived. Lilly walked up to the door of Adam's

home with a self-assured step. She had completed her mission, despite present company, and would deliver to him the product of the task he had entrusted her with. This would please him. An impressive start to the evening. As Kyle rang the bell, she pulled the sack of bright green buds out of her purse. She couldn't wait to hand it to him, her trophy and access to his good graces.

Adam opened the door. Lilly was already holding out the bag to him. A grin came across his face and she knew she had done well for him. They exchanged pleasantries and Adam praised Lilly as he took the bag from her hand.

Ryan and Neil were already present and had a beer in each hand. His little sister was also in attendance, talking to the guys in the kitchen.

"Lilly, you remember my Sister?" he shrugged in her direction, unenthusiastic about introducing her, but obligated to.

"Hi, I'm Sasha."

"Hey, Sasha, you partying with us tonight?"

"No, no! She's leaving! Right Sasha?" said Adam, a stern look in his eye.

"Aww, come on, Adam. Let her party a little bit?"

"Yeah, come on, Adam! Let me stay, please!" Sasha held her hands up in a prayer pose with puppy-dog eyes that begged for his approval.

"Fine, whatever. For a little bit! And you have to be silent, the whole time." They all laughed at Adam's joke, and Sasha bounced around in excitement.

Being a proper host, Adam offered both Lilly and Kyle a beer and a tour of the home. Settled in her accomplishment and refocused on the night's festivities, Lilly scanned her surroundings. The house was monstrous and gilded with expensive adornments. His parents had an affinity for the arts as classical paintings and marble sculptures covered the walls and hallways.

"A'ight, you guys bored with this yet? Can we go party?" Adam projected his voice into the air as Kyle and Lilly explored the third living room they came upon.

"Okay," Lilly said. Her focus was back on him and she was ready to comply with whatever it was he was ready for.

Kyle continued to scan the room, almost like he was searching for something small enough to fit into and go unnoticed in his fat pants.

"All-right!" Adam shouted. "Let's get this party started! Follow me!" The group refreshed their beers and followed Adam outside to the deck overlooking the grounds. They arranged the furniture in a circle to create a mock smoking circle. Adam loaded the pipe with the flower and took Greens for himself before passing to Lilly, sitting to his right. The group sat for a while, smoking, drinking, laughing, enjoying the evening. Lilly kept herself in a powerful position, sitting next to the party's host. Each of the guests looked up to him and her right next to him. They acknowledged his every word and agreed with every statement he made. He controlled the conversation. Everyone was quick to jump at his suggestions or requests, and he could convince any of them of anything, even if it was only for his amusement.

"Ryan, Ryan, dude, do that thing you were telling me about earlier." Adam interrupted the conversation to make a request of Ryan. Several beers in and a few bowls got the party relaxed and loose as the voices got louder and jokes a little dirtier.

"Haha! You mean this?" Ryan laughed out loud as he jumped up from his seat, turned around to bring his back facing into the circle, bent over, lit a lighter to his ass and let loose a flatulence so grotesque it sent a ball of fire outward into the center of the gathering as the lighter ignited in a putrid inferno. After the initial shock subsided, the entire group bowled over in a fit of uproarious laughter. Neil fell out of his chair. Lilly, unamused and grossed out, couldn't believe she had witnessed that, but when Adam laughed at it, she joined in.

Adam leaned into her ear to explain. "He was talking shit in the car about how him and his brothers used to do stupid shit like this when they were kids, so I called his bluff and he said he would prove it later. I couldn't let him forget. Sorry if that offended you, I had to call him on his shit."

Lilly, still grossed out, but was also impressed by Adam. She was sure he knew what he was doing, and that he had a reason for calling upon Ryan to perform for them in that moment.

"Alright you disgusting fucks…" Adam announced the group, but turned back to Lilly to motion to her he wasn't calling her a disgusting fuck, just the boys. "Let's go back inside, I have a surprise for you." Still laughing but intrigued, they all stood and followed Adam back inside the house.

The group followed each other back inside and into the kitchen. They all stood around Adam as he began his announcement. Ryan came and stood next to Lilly, obviously, like his action had purpose. This caused her to step to the side, still squeamish about what had happened on the deck. Next to Ryan was the last place she wanted to be in that moment. She refocused again on Adam and caught him looking straight at her and Ryan. Was that a hint of satisfaction on his face? No, she reasoned with herself; she was high, she must have been imagining things.

"Hey! I got a present for you assholes," Adam announced. "I brought you some candy." With that, he pulled out a small plastic baggie filled with a soft white powder. Lilly couldn't be sure, but assumed it was a drug. It must have been, but she didn't know what. "Here fucker, rack um up." Adam tossed the baggie to Ryan and pointed to the kitchen table at the other end of the room. Adam positioned himself right next to Lilly as Kyle and Neil followed Ryan to the table.

"What is that?" Lilly asked Adam.

"It's just candy, nose candy." Adam shrugged his shoulders, as if to say it was no big deal and sniffing drugs was as normal as buying a candy bar at the grocery store checkout. He put his hand on Lilly's back and led her over to the table with everyone else, a reassuring smile on his face.

Lilly, intrigued, observed as Ryan poured the powder out onto the glass tabletop. He pulled his college ID out from his wallet and held it against the powder in a scraping and chopping motion. He knew what he was doing and had done this before. She listened to the comments from Kyle and Neil that told her they had all done this before too. Comments like 'Careful, don't cut them too thick, we gotta make it last,' or 'Dude, make sure you get those tiny rocks.'

The mood changed. No one was laughing anymore, the environment was no longer relaxed, in fact an air of tension circled around them. Lilly's shoulders tightened with the change and she became uneasy. *Another beer might be good.* She walked away from the table to the fridge on the other side of the kitchen. She sipped her beer while she looked back at the group huddled around the table. Sasha followed her over to the fridge and grabbed a beer for herself.

"You like my brother, don't you?" Sasha asked Lilly.

"Huh? What? Pfft! No, no way. He's weird. I… uh. No.

I don't." Lilly stumbled over her words and looked down towards the floor.

"It's okay, I won't tell. But I know. Everyone likes my brother." Sasha rolled her eyes and swigged her beer. "You into this?" Sasha nodded towards the table and what was happening.

"No. I don't even know what that stuff is. I'm just gonna chill over here."

Sasha nodded.

"Okay, stop!" Adam shouted to Ryan. "They're perfect."

Ryan had cut the powder into five straight and even rows. He backed away from the table as Adam pulled a one-hundred-dollar bill out of his wallet and rolled it into a small tube. "Who wants to go first?" Adam asked to the group. All of them raised their hands in unison with a palatable urgency. Lilly stood back with Sasha, feeling the pressure of a college student praying the professor wouldn't call on them to discuss the previous week's reading assignment. "I think…" Adam scanned the room as if he were choosing the worthiest candidate, each of them staring at him with begging puppy eyes. "Lilly! You. Come here." The focus of the room shifted to her, and their eyes pulled at her. Adam motioned for her to come.

"Huh? Oh, no… I'm good. You guys enjoy."

"Come on, Lilly," Adam insisted.

"Go, Lilly!" Sasha nudged her shoulder.

"No, really… I'm so drunk, I don't think I can." Lilly laughed through her nerves. Her legs started shaking as her heartbeat increased. Internal panic took over as her thoughts raced with objections.

"Oh, okay. I thought you were cool. No problem, no problem." Adam kept his eyes fixated on her.

The rest of them watched her. Her chest sunk into her

belly and crushed the butterflies into a nauseous goo. *Oh no, he hates me now. What have I done?*

"Come on, please?" Adam smiled at her and waved the rolled bill in her direction. All their eyes burned through her body. *Oh, my God. This isn't going to stop until I go.* Her feet brought her towards the table. Encouraging words and smiles from the guys kept them moving forward until she was standing in front of Adam.

"What do I do?" Lilly asked as she looked at Adam with wide eyes.

"It's okay, it's not scary. It's fun." Adam rubbed her back in a gesture of support. His hand sent a tingle of relaxation through her tense muscles. At the same moment, the beer kicked in and she felt inspired. She was ready to sniff an unidentified white powder up her nostril through a one-hundred-dollar bill, how classy. "Here, like this," said Adam as he went through the motions of what it involved, showing her the mechanics of how drug sniffing worked. She understood what she had to do. Adam handed over the rolled-up bill.

"Don't blow out!" Kyle added with a sincere worry. His eyes stretched open as she took a deep breath in and held it.

"Shut up, Kyle, she's got it." More reassuring words from Adam.

The white lines came into focus in slow motion. Her heart thumped in her chest. She grabbed the bill from Adam, holding its seam to ensure the roll stayed tight. She bent over so that the tip of the rolled bill was the only distance between her nose and the table and took a sharp inhale while following the line of powder as it disappeared before her.

As the powder vanished, she felt a rush overtake her. It started with a burning sensation in her nose that turned cool and soothing. It stuck to the back of her throat and made turned it numb before continuing down her spine, around to her breasts, and onward through her torso, down her legs and arms, and out the tips of her fingertips and soles of her feet. An electric euphoria hummed through her body and provided her with an energy that made her more awake than she had ever been. Her eyes popped open wide as she lifted herself back up and stretched upward. A wave of bliss roared through her.

"WHOA!" she said out loud. "Holy fuck, that's crazy!" They all laughed at her with love as a piece of her innocence disappeared.

"Haha! That's right! See, candy for your nose, I told you," Adam said as she handed him back the bill and the gang focused their attention back on the remaining rows of white powder.

The wave flashed through and out of her as quick as it had come. She stepped away from the table as the rest of them remained fixated on it. She became dizzy and felt like her head was floating above her body. Something wasn't right. Panic overtook and that good feeling left her. The next wave was one of nausea and aching muscles. Was she dying? Was this what an overdose was? Oh my God, what had she done? How stupid had she been? This was how she was going to leave the world, another statistic in a fucking footnote.

Unable to scream out for help, she sunk to the ground and huddled in the fetal position on the floor. This was it. She wished she could apologize to Adam for killing herself in his kitchen. This was not how she had envisioned the night going, not her own death. There was no sense in fighting it. There was nothing anyone could do for her now, they weren't even paying attention, and she wouldn't have wanted them to end their fun on her account, anyway. It wasn't their fault she couldn't handle sniffing drugs. She would go now, close her eyes and drift off into the abyss. She closed her eyes and relaxed into it as she slipped away. Their voices trailed off until all she could hear was her own breath. She waited for it to stop. *Stop, stop, stop*, she repeated in her head over and over to help herself fall into her demise.

"Lilly?" someone called out.

That must be God, or maybe the other one.

But it was neither. She opened her eyes, expecting to find a bright white light, or the burning flames of hell, but looked up to find the gang all huddled around her with puzzled faces. "What the fuck are you doing on the floor?" Adam asked. "We heard heavy breathing and then saw you down here." He didn't sound concerned, more like he was holding back laughter. They all looked at her with slanted eyebrows and cocked heads.

"Huh? Oh, uh, I... got... tired..." She searched her brain for any words that might help her explain and those were the best she could come up with.

"You're tired? Okay, come on, you can lie down in a guest room."

A guest room? Why not his room? Ugh, she had done it again. Ruined another perfect opportunity to prove to Adam that she was more than a friend. *Damn it!*

He led her away from the powdered frenzy happening at the tabletop and down the hall to a decorated room. "Alright, buddy, here you go. See you in the morning." He flicked off the light and shut the door.

Buddy? Oh, for fuck's sake. All she was to him was his buddy. She had taken a giant leap backwards, securing her footing deep in *the friend zone*, escape from which she knew would be difficult. But she wasn't ready to give up yet. She'd come up with something else again, but for now she would focus on not dying in her sleep. How embarrassing would that be if they had to call the coroner to come lift her big, heavy body out of his fancy sheets? Oh God, that would be a nightmare. *Don't die tonight, Lilly*, she told herself as she drifted off to a sound and restful sleep.

SEVEN

A New Habit

D espite her initial fears, Lilly still wanted to win Adam over. His interests became her interests. The cocaine habit hadn't started off as hot and heavy as it became. In the beginning, she still tried her best to shy away from it, or ignore completely, the hazardous white powder poured out on the table. Adam coaxed Lilly into this new habit in the way one becomes addicted to cigarettes. Like a smoker who starts off casually trying a hit off a friend's cigarette one drunken night at a bar who then smokes a whole cigarette the following week, that graduates to the person who buys a pack of cigarettes to bring with them to the bar to hand out and enjoy with friends, until that person is running late to work on Monday morning because they're out of smokes and can't get through the next several minutes without stopping at the local 7-11 to pick up a carton for the week.

After that first night, Lilly was eager to get back to their normal routine of smoking weed, driving around, and hiking up to The Tree. It was time to regroup and assess the damage she had done with her little I-think-I'm-dying episode. But back to normal didn't exactly happen the way she'd hoped it would. Talk of cocaine amongst them was no longer an unspoken taboo. Albeit the substance was illegal, they instead referred to it by code, their own half-baked attempt at respecting the gravity of law. With affection Kyle named cocaine Pearl, as if personifying a substance made it less ominous. Once someone said the name Pearl, the conversation wouldn't likely switch back to anything else until they found, purchased, and used. This became the new normal.

The months following were a cascading rollercoaster of chemical catalyst as the group lost interest in the staple of weed and replaced it with the new allure of something a little more dangerous, a little more daring.

It was here that Lilly introduced the crew to her garage studio apartment. The living quarters held a desk with a computer she used for schoolwork and downloading music, an oversized chair, a queen-size bed that was three mattresses tall, and a 6-drawer dresser with a glass top that her mother had bought for her as her first piece of *big girl* furniture when she was thirteen. The glass top came in handy and would prove to be the most useful thing her absent mother had provided for her. Lilly liked a high bed, and this one was so high she had to hop onto it every night or time she wanted in. Her friends thought this was novel, as whenever anyone came over it was the first thing they did, ignoring the oversized chair or desk of much easier access. Here they could hide away and sniff their drugs, all cramped together while the smoke from their cigarettes yellowed the walls. Daily afternoon hot boxing sessions in Neil's van fell away in lieu of nights like this. Her dad pretended not to notice, or so she assumed, never hearing a peep from him. Lilly became more familiar with the drug as the lines she sniffed became bigger and more frequent.

. . .

"HEY GUYS," Adam said as he approached the crew. All were in attendance at the smoking section, waiting for his arrival. The crew acknowledged his presence and waved at him as he walked up, already holding a cigarette in his lips. "Are you guys down to come with me to run an errand real quick? My homie Jose needs me to pick something up for him and we can chill with him at his place after."

"Now, when you say pick up, what are we picking up and why would we want to hang out with this guy that none of us knows?" asked Neil, the ever inquisitive one, using a tone that showed apprehension and unwillingness to comply. No one ever failed to comply with Adam's requests; he wasn't used to being questioned. This would become the beginning of the end of Neil's run with the crew, and had he known that, he might have asked a different question, or maybe none at all.

"Trust me, Jose is cool. He's the one who hooks us up with Pearl. If you guys wanna see her again we gotta go, that's why we chill afterwards."

"Naw, man, I'm cool. I'm gonna smoke my weed and hang out here." Neil was out, not interested in burrowing down into this hole with the rest of them.

At this stage, the crew was playing with Pearl, but still only enough that she didn't have her claws in any of them yet. They all could have walked away at that point, Lilly especially as her usage was lightest amongst the group. But she didn't take the option when Neil did. Everyone else was in. They left Neil behind and went on their way, following Adam wherever he was going to take them.

The four of them walked through campus and into the parking lot. The Experience sat off to the side. Each of them looked over at it, silently recognizing a symbolic death of the former smoking section crew. Leaving Neil behind was a moment they all silently revered as the conversations stopped and their heads turned down towards their feet, one by one, until the van was again out of view. A few rows over, Adam's Rav4 waited for them. Once again the energy rose and they excited themselves for the adventure to come. The new crew piled themselves in, and Adam told Lilly to sit shotgun. A sense of power and status rushed through her.

On the drive, Adam adjusted the dynamic and allowed Kyle to play DJ for the first time, Neil no longer in charge of the music. He pulled out a CD wallet from his fuzzy character backpack and leafed through the sleeves, landing on a burned CD titled, in black sharpie, "BEST TRANCE EVER!" Kyle insisted Adam play the CD and instructed him which track to skip to. Adam complied, and the car filled with happy, silly dance music. Kyle called it rave music. Lilly rolled her eyes and groaned in annoyance, but Adam showed his excitement for it by bobbing along and even screaming out the window in excitement. His exclamation got the entire car excited as their energy ticked up to meet his. Adam joked and told Lilly to relax and passed her a joint. As the weed smoke filled her lungs, she relaxed into the repetition of the beat. She concluded that maybe she did like dance music after all when she found herself fist-pumping and screaming along with her friends. The palm trees lining the streets waved their fronds, dancing along with them as they drove.

They danced through several tracks before arriving at a gas station. Lilly wasn't exactly sure where they were, but they had long since left their familiar bubble and were instead surrounded by rundown businesses and trashed streets. They pulled into the pump and waited, but Adam wasn't getting out of the car or even fiddling with his wallet.

"Uh, are you getting gas?" Lilly asked him.

"Shh, hold on..." Adam had an expression on his face and tenseness in his body that screamed urgency and focus.

"Are we doing a drug deal? Really, Adam?" Kyle crossed his arms and pointed his head down, his condescension emanating from the backseat. "Ugh, so trashy..." He trailed off and lifted his chin so that his nose pointed upwards as he looked away.

"Oh, what's the matter, Kyle? Is this beneath you? You? The dirty finger-nail hippie?" Lilly said with a snap, daring anyone else to question Adam's intentions again.

"Yeah, Chill out, Kyle!" The sternness in Adam's voice brought silence. Adam's response offered no additional information. He cut the music and turned off the car. Each of them sat and waited, not knowing what for. "There!" Adam shouted in a bout of excitement as a brown Cadillac coupe pulled into a parking spot to the side of the station. He started the car to pull up beside it. The other driver stepped out and popped the hood. Engine troubles had him fiddling with little bits and pieces inside the mechanical workings of the car. Adam told everyone to stay in the car and hopped out to lend a hand.

"It giving you trouble?" Adam said to the man looking at his engine, a chuckle in his voice that said, "Wow, what a fun role-playing scenario were doing here." Subtlety was not his strong suit.

"Yo, I can't seem to figure out what's wrong with it," the man said. "It's onions, man."

Onions? What in the world do onions have to do with anything? Lilly hadn't the slightest clue what was happening. Was this a drug deal or was Adam being a good citizen to someone crazy about vegetables?

"Oh, onions? Well, onions go great on tacos, man."

Did Adam just say tacos? Lilly had to roll down the window to be sure because her brain wouldn't let her accept that this was an actual conversation. The man laughed, shook Adam's hand, and gave him a half hug as if the two were old friends. Adam reciprocated and offered the man a cigarette. The two took a couple steps back from the car to smoke their cigarettes and chat. Interest in the Cadi's engine had waned. Lilly watched the two, not paying any attention to the conversation between Kyle and Ryan in the back seat. Did Adam know this guy? Was this in fact a drug deal? Or were they two hungry dudes, and this was how hungry people talked to strangers? Before Lilly could listen in enough to answer any of her questions, the conversation was over. Adam stomped out his cigarette while the man shut the hood on his car. The man then opened the back seat, driver-side door, and grabbed a small package wrapped in butcher paper and tape.

"Okay, homie, fresh order, Carne Asada. Enjoy your tacos!" He tossed the package at Adam.

"Aight, dawg, coo, coo, hope she does okay back on the road," he said as he popped the hatch on the back of his Rav4 and tucked the package away in the trunk.

"Yup, definitely a drug deal," Kyle said, rolling his eyes as all of them watched Adam fumble around with the package, seeking an appropriate hiding spot.

"Shut the fuck up, Kyle!" Adam said in a harsh but quiet voice, so as not to alert the Cadi man, who still hadn't pulled away. Kyle flashed back a face that said, "What? I didn't say anything," when he had said something.

Done with the exchange, they were back on their way to Jose's house. Whatever was in that package, Lilly wanted to push out of her mind. It must have been Carne Asada, like the Cadi man had said, and perhaps he was a friend

who worked at a butcher's and had some extra he gave to
Adam as a gift for helping him with his car. This was the
story Lilly told herself to cope with the reality of what
might be in that package and how deep of a situation
Adam had involved her in.

No, she didn't want to think about that. Doing something like thinking, in a moment like this, might have
pushed her into a mindset of logic and good judgement.
She didn't want to end up like Neil. Her place was here
beside Adam and she knew that to keep her place she had
to fall in line with what Adam wanted to do and who he
wanted to involve them with. She didn't want to be like
Kyle either, asking questions and getting yelled at. She had
learned enough about Adam to know that he was not the
type who appreciated being questioned about anything,
and certainly not when it came to his intimate business
dealings—whether they be with Butcher shop employees or
drug dealers. The story she told herself was enough to
keep her at Adam's right hand, and that was all she cared
about.

Back on the road, Adam pumped up the music again
and they danced to the same songs, the CD now repeating
itself. Adam drove faster, bobbed along to the music harder,
and spoke stronger. He drove them further away into a
corner of Los Angeles Lilly had always tried to avoid,
South Central. They came upon a neighborhood of old
and worn houses with sidewalks of cracked concrete, and
front lawns of patchy yellow grass over hard dirt. The
houses were all hidden behind gates and chain-link fences,
with iron bars that shielded the windows and front lawns
adorned with rusted cars or broken pieces of furniture.
Large barking pit bulls patrolled some of them. It was a
place that felt uneasy to an upper-middle-class girl like

Lilly, and a place that a rich boy like Adam had no business being.

"We're here!" Adam exclaimed, almost bouncing out of his seat with eagerness. They pulled into a driveway attached to a lopsided house with cracks running up the outside walls. Lilly scanned her surroundings and especially the address. *422 121st Street, 422 121st Street,* Lilly repeated it to herself over and over in her head. She had questions, but it was probably better not to ask. The repetition of the address enough to keep her distracted. *It's still daytime. We'll be fine, probably.* The four of them exited the car and waited for Adam to retrieve his package of meat from the trunk before following him through the gate and up to the security-screen front door.

"What up, what up!" said a voice behind the screen.

"What up, dawg! I got your tacos right here, man!" Adam said with a laugh. The screen door opened, and they were invited inside. Adam handed the butcher's paper-wrapped package over to Jose, a tall Mexican man with a black bandana tied around his head, an oversized white t-shirt, black Dickies pants, and house slippers.

"Coo, coo man, you met with the homie? What'd you think of that Cadi, though?"

"Tight, tight, yeah, it was all good, man," Adam replied as he greeted Jose and nodded to the other men standing silently in the house. There were at least five others, all in the same uniform as Jose. Lilly felt her palms sweat and a tremble build up in her chest, but it didn't last when Jose greeted her and was warm in his offer to get her a beer and a place to sit. He wasn't intimidating when he spoke to her, he was kind and respectful, and his friends were too. Over the next several minutes, Adam and Jose walked out of the room to talk while Lilly, Kyle, and Ryan all sipped their beers and kept to themselves.

Some of Jose's friends tried engaging in conversation but they spoke with thick gangster accents, not an accent that came from a specific country or region, but one that came from a particular lifestyle of living in the rough world of thugs and gangbangers. She'd never met anyone who spoke like that in actual life, but she was as familiar with it as anyone who's ever watched a television. They offered to smoke a blunt with her and her friends, and finally found something in common they could all connect over. Lilly smiled and accepted the offer. The tension loosened as they all became friends.

Halfway through the blunt, Adam and Jose came back into the room. "Hey! I see the party already started without us!" Jose announced to the room as he entered. His tone jokey. The room shared a polite laugh. "Well, let's keep it going! Tony, hit the beats!" A man named Tony turned on the stereo, bumping hard gangsta-rap. "Ay yo, rack um up!" Jose yelled to a man from across the room as he tossed over that same butcher paper-wrapped package. It was all happening so fast. Before she knew it, Lilly found herself surrounded by friendly gangsters that appeared from other rooms or came in from outside, all introducing themselves and asking her and her friends how they were and what they did for fun. Pleasant small talk coming out of the mouths of men with tear drop tattoos and bullet hole scarred arms and legs. It was surreal, but it was better to be friends with these people than enemies. There was a full-blown party happening now, at the drop of Jose's request. The environment transformed when music and drugs emerged for an impromptu afternoon kickback with several dozen of Jose's closest friends.

A few of the gangsters huddled around the kitchen table, a scene she was now familiar with. *Oh my God, it's mid-day! It's way too early for this.* Lilly kept to her conversation on the opposite side of the room with her beer and her friends, trying to ignore it. She maintained eye contact with the man she was talking to but didn't hear his words, all she could think about was how she was going to manage staying away from that table and out of Adam's eyesight, her only defense mechanism that hadn't worked yet, not in the many times she had tried it since that first time at Adam's house.

It wasn't until Adam called out her name that she pretended to be interested in what was happening over there. She couldn't ignore Adam's call. That would have been suicide in a room full of men who, if movies and TV had taught her anything, lived and died by the code of respect. Sure, they all acted friendly, but she had seen enough cops and robbers' movies to know what would happen the second a woman disrespected a man in a house full of these guys. *Okay, fuck, okay, you gotta do this, Lilly, it's for Adam.* Adam was elevating Lilly to a seat of power within the crew. And this is what it meant. If she wanted to sit by him, it meant supporting him and answering to him in whatever he got them into. Today it was a major drug deal at a gang leader's house. Tomorrow, who knew? Regardless, she accepted it as she headed the call and made her way over to the table.

"Okay, Lilly, Adam tells us you're a pro! It's your line!" Jose said as he made room for her at the table and handed her a rolled up one-hundred-dollar bill. Several monstrous-sized rails of cocaine were all laid out in front of her. At Jose's request, the men surrounding her took a step back, in a sign of respect, so she could have space. She turned to Adam, who gave her a face of encouragement and a nod, asking her to take the offer, while saying no words. *Oh my God, these are the biggest lines I've ever seen. What if it does kill me this time?* With nowhere to run and no other options, she bent down over the table and closed her eyes so she didn't have to watch as the cocaine disappeared up her nose.

She sniffed hard and lifted her head in synchronicity with the electric wave of euphoria she expected would follow. Her nose and the roof of her mouth numbed, she felt a ball smash into the back of her throat, and that familiar rush exploded into the rest of her body. As she rose from the table, there was cheering and chanting from everyone surrounding her. She'd never experienced such praise before, not from anyone in her life, ever. But more than anything, she felt the warm touch of Adam's hand on her back, a gesture she recognized as pride and appreciation for her. Her cheeks flushed and her heart jumped in her chest. *He loves me!* she shouted silently to herself, reassured and safe in her decision to pursue this man. She was getting closer.

Shit, that was a huge line. She waited for an adverse reaction, but it didn't come. She didn't die this time; she wasn't anxious or sick. Her heart was racing, but in a way that made her feel alive and uplifted. She felt powerful and unstoppable, like she could fly if she could find the courage to step off the roof of a building. A million words to say swirled around in her mind, waiting for anyone who would listen. These people were her friends. She was happier than she'd ever been, and she didn't want it to end.

"Oh, Chica, you like that, ay?" asked Jose, Chica, her new nickname, she guessed. She nodded with bright eyes and a wide white smile. "Okay, okay, you wanna go again?" he said as he offered her more. She flashed him the same toothy grin before bending back down to hit another line. Adam smiled and held his shoulders high and back like a proud father watching his kid make the first pitch at a Little League game. She was fitting herself into his alternative lifestyle. This plan, the doing-drugs-with-gangsters plan, wasn't how she had pictured it happening, but it was working and that was good enough for her.

It only took that one enjoyable experience to make this a regular thing for Lilly and Adam and the crew. They were no longer casual users that paid pocket money for small amounts. They were running errands for their supplier, which meant bigger sacks and freebees. Still, doing pickups for Jose wasn't a frequent enough of a thing to satisfy their growing habit. Still employed at The Sub Shop, Lilly began budgeting cocaine into her monthly expenses, $80 a month for her phone, $90 a month for car insurance, $189 for the car payment, and $160 for a ball of cocaine when it was her turn to buy, Adam or Ryan would buy the other times, and Kyle was always invited to join.

Where and when they could get their hands on more cocaine became the primary motivation for how the crew planned their days and nights. Lilly enjoyed talking about Pearl now. The name itself brought a residue of the rush back to her, enough to excite her and motivate her towards finding it. The crew planned out Fridays as their party day and started calling it FriYay—Yay was the shortened name for Yayo—what the gangsters called Pearl.

Class got out at 4 pm, the soonest they could pick up a sack was 5:30 pm. They drove around, an anxious pulse coursing through them, and tried to calm their nerves with weed until the time came and they could pick up their sack, sniff it gone way too fast, and repeat the whole thing over again the following week.

The nights alone were difficult. Keyed up from cocaine, and her friends gone, Lilly spent the pre-dawn hours pacing her room, unable to relax or lay down. Her thoughts circled around Adam. How well the night had gone, what she could have or should have done differently, what she was going to do the next time. The intensity of her obsession brought her to tears as she had no other way of coping with them. There were no friends she could talk to, no one to listen to her lament over him. Instead, she found solace in the glow of her computer screen.

The nights she couldn't sit still or calm herself, she sat at her desk, a restless leg hopping continuously up and down, and typed out letters to Adam. Letter after letter, professing deep and undying love for him. The rambling words would have made no sense to anyone else, but the moment moved her to action. Letter writing became the outlet she used to purge her feelings so that when she was with him again the next day, because she would be, it was easier to pretend like she hadn't just spent a sleepless night exhausting herself over her obsession for him. She remained vigilant in protecting her hidden feelings, always deleting and never saving the scrambled letters to her underhand lover.

Instead of studying, her textbooks began collecting the dust of cigarette ash as they sat, unopened, on top of her desk. Her nose dripped liquid most days now. She carried toilet paper and tissues around with her in her purse. The lights in her bedroom stayed on most hours of the nights, a feature her father could see when he peered out through the living room window and across the garden back yard. None of this was a problem for her until her father and the child-bride spoke up. The once laissez-faire attitude they had for Lilly and her lifestyle was no longer acceptable. They had discovered her grades were slipping, she was calling out sick from work all the time, she was staying up late or possibly not sleeping at all, and there was a pile of tissues in the corner of her room that reached up to the window. A quick peek through revealed she wasn't even trying to hide it, there's only so much tissue a common cold could be responsible for.

The evening they confronted her, it was five pm on a FriYay. She got home from class and was going to grab a quick bite to eat before meeting with Adam and the guys for the 5:30 pm pickup. Eating at home meant more money for coke. Her father cornered her in the kitchen as she was gnawing on a slice of bread and waiting for her Easy Mac to finish in the microwave. The child-bride stood close behind. He asked her what the deal was with all the tissues in her room and presented a mound of parapher-nalia as evidence, which included an empty birth control pill pack, an empty cigarette box that reeked of marijuana, a pack of rolling papers, and a few spent lighters. There wasn't enough though, and she knew they knew it.

"What?" she said to her father. "There's nothing here except sex pills and cigarette trash. I'm an adult and I can do with my body as I choose!"

"There's more here than just cigarettes. This empty pack smells like marijuana. Are you high right now?"

"Oh my God, Dad, seriously? Just stop, you got noth-ing, and I'm late." She ended the microwave time 30 seconds early, grabbed the hot cup, and stormed out of the kitchen.

"What about the tissues!" her father yelled at her as she left the house and was already halfway through the backyard.

"I have a fucking cold!" she yelled back, without turning around or slowing down. Minus genuine evidence, she could walk away from the situation, angry at them for invading her privacy. She took it as a warning that she and her friends needed to be more careful and less casual about their evolving habit.

EIGHT

Adam Goes Away

"Hey guys, , look, I know it's FriYay, and we're fine to stay here, but this is gonna have to be the last time." The crew all looked at Lilly with intent, waiting for an explanation. "My parents started asking questions. They're getting suspicious."

"Don't trip, we're just hanging out. It's Friday night, this is what college kids are supposed to be doing anyway," Adam reassured her and laughed, bringing the party vibe back into the room. "A'ight! Music!" He shouted as he sat down at her computer and pulled up LimeWire.

"Oh, let me pick! Let me pick!" Kyle hopped down off of Lilly's bed and stood behind Adam, peering at the computer screen.

"Yeah, I guess…" Lilly said, averting her eyes and tapping her foot on the floor. Kyle and Adam began fighting over the music for the evening, and Ryan approached her with a popped beer.

"Don't sweat it too much, they can't see what we're doing in here. And Adam's right, this is exactly what college kids do on Friday nights, and they're probably happy you're doing it here instead of out driving around and being unsafe... or some other shit that might make you feel better?"

Lilly smiled at his explanation and relaxed into the sensation of sudsy beer in her mouth as she took a sip.

The evening began with the four of them together, drinking beer, smoking cigarettes, talking loudly amongst themselves and listening to music.

"Okay, fucking Kyle! Fuck!" Adam, now fed up with arguing about music selections, got up from the computer and let Kyle take over. "Here! Since you wanna be a little bitch, you can rack 'um up too!" Aggressively, Adam tossed the baggie of Pearl at Kyle.

"Okay! Sure!" This was no insult to Kyle. It meant the festivities could begin. Kyle drizzled out a small mound of cocaine on the table and pulled out his California ID card to prepare the lines. Once the cocaine took hold, the mood changed. The music turned itself down, and the beers went unopened. There wasn't enough beer in the world to help them catch a buzz now. Cocaine overpowered the ability of beer to provide them with anything.

Of the four, two broke off into their own conversation, as with the other two. The pairs stuck together like this for the rest of the night. Their conversation was meaningless, but in the moment, felt profound and significant.

There was an energy pulsing through Lilly that created a desire for an anxious burst of words from the mouth. Like she had a million important ideas all jumbled up inside her head and getting them out was the only way to save herself from spontaneous human combustion. It could be compared to that of what happens when two people newly fall in love. There's an electric spark that courses through them and connects them to each other. Except here, the connection was happening within herself and she was simply using the other as a facilitator to participate in the conversation. A coke conversation was no more meaningful than one person spewing the words and the other person holding theirs at bay only long enough for the first person to finish. The words did not relate to one another, and the topics had no consistencies. It was the pause each person allowed the other that gave the impression of a conversation.

Every FriYay started out the same. She learned to place herself in a position that put her closest to Adam to help the transition from party to pair, the easiest way for her and Adam to connect. Most of the time this worked, but sometimes she ended up attached to Ryan or Kyle. However, being the ever-diligent observer, Adam developed his own little habit that kept him watching Lilly when it would occur that she paired off with Ryan. And when that happened, Adam would break up the pairs and bring the group back together again. Once Lilly recognized he was doing this purposefully, she would try to pair herself off with Ryan to force Adam into breaking them up to bring the party back together. It worked every time, except on the off chance the crew were at a coke party with Jose and his gang. During those meets, Adam was far too involved with Jose. It was the only time Lilly recognized Adam as being beta to anyone.

THERE WAS no hiding the fact that Lilly's father was onto them. Although they remained uninvolved in her life, she knew that a drug habit would not be something he would support happening under his roof, or in his garage rather. She told Adam again that they would have to find a new place to party for a while, that she needed to lie low. This didn't surprise Adam who assured Lilly that he would brainstorm and find a new party spot, safe from the watchful eye of her father, but that it would have to wait because Adam was being sent away for the summer to visit family in the South of France.

The news stunned Lilly. So much so that she couldn't find any words to respond.

"You okay? Hello?" Adam said to her frozen face, playfully shaking her shoulders.

"Huh, oh, uh, yeah. Wait, what did you say?"

"Oh, I'm going to Southern France for the summer. To visit family. My parents send my sister and I there every couple years."

"Your sister…" Lilly was repeating words to give herself a chance to soak in the information.

"Yeah, Sasha?" Adam laughed, trying to soften the blow he was now gathering this caused her.

"Right… your sister…" Lilly felt her chest tighten as her eyes welled up. *He's leaving me? Is he coming back? Is there someone else? What am I supposed to do without him? Everything's falling apart. I can't handle this!* Her mind trapped itself in a loop as she panicked in silence with herself. She had become accustomed to spending time with Adam every day and looked forward to their FriYay parties.

"Hey, it's all good. I'll be back. We're only going for three weeks." Adam spoke without having to know what she was thinking. Her lip quivered and her chin went into spasms. "Look, look, you should still hang out with the guys. They'll take care of you. Don't trip, chocolate chip."

"But what about Fri-Yay!" Lilly got out the words before tears burst from her eyes and she collapsed into a deep sob.

Adam laughed at her ridiculousness. "Dude! Dude, it's fine. Ryan can get you guys weed, Kyle has lots of other friends he can get stuff from too. Listen to him. But don't go to any parties without me. I know he's been talking about raving a lot, but you have to wait for me, okay? I'll be back soon, and we can all go together."

"Okay…" She kept her gaze down, embarrassed at creating an emotional scene.

Lilly did as Adam said and continued spending time with Ryan and Kyle. School was out for summer, there was plenty to of time to be spent. Without a coke connection, and only Ryan's connection to shitty weed, the crew spent most of their time hanging out at the local coffee shop or The Tree, or with other pot friendly friends, poking smot and talking about nonsense like they used to. FriYay would remain on hold for now, something Lilly became aggravated about as the days passed and it got closer to Friday.

That first Friday of Adam's departure, Lilly, Ryan, and Kyle were all together, hanging out at the coffee shop when Lilly sparked a conversation about how lame it was, that they were all missing FriYay because stupid Adam left her… left them. That she missed her friend Pearl and couldn't believe the injustice Adam had inflicted upon all of them, being gone for so long and thus blocking their access to her.

"Okay, but isn't this so lame that we can't get high just because Adam isn't here? Like, I have money, I wanna talk to Pearl! This is dumb! Fuck Adam! He should have left us his hook up or something," Lilly said to the group. They nodded along and agreed with her, but then Kyle, with a face that lit up as if a light bulb had popped on over his head, grabbed at the opportunity and spoke.

"You know, if you really wanna party tonight, we could hook up with Shade and go to his party? He's throwing a local tonight, it's gonna be wild!"

"Fucking Kyle!" Lilly yelled back, half-joking. "You're

always trying to get us to go to these dumb parties, I don't wanna go, I just wanna get high!"

"All I'm saying is there will definitely be party favors there, and you already like the music now, so you can't keep using that as an excuse. Plus, you promised Shade that one time…"

"I had to promise him because of your fuck up, you asshole!" Lilly was being playful now, already half convinced.

"I don't know. It could be fun," Ryan chimed in. "I mean, just because Adam's not here doesn't mean we have to sit around with our thumbs up our asses waiting for him to come back."

"Oh baby, don't threaten me with a good time!" Kyle mocked Ryan and made kiss faces at him.

"Fuck you, dick. I'm agreeing with you!" Ryan bit back.

"Alright, alright, shut the fuck up, both of you. Let me think about this…" Lilly took a moment to compose her thoughts while she puffed on her cigarette. She mulled over her options. Adam had left her behind, meaning she was now without access to a high, or his presence. Going to the first party, without him, would be a passive aggressive message to him. She knew only days before he had demanded she not go to any parties without him. This would serve him right. If she did this, she would assert herself over his dominance. Maybe it would make him a little jealous? Maybe it would teach him a lesson to not leave her again? At the very least it would get her high and that was enough of a justification. Kyle and Ryan observed her face for any sign of what her final decision might be. She scanned their faces, and from their intent focus knew she was the ringleader in Adam's absence. The final decision was hers. "Fuck it. Let's go," she blurted.

"Yes!" exclaimed Kyle.

"Fuck yes!" shouted Ryan. Pumped, they were ready to experience the night.

The three of them arrived at Shade's apartment. The scene was familiar with active bodies hustling about, loading up the truck, organizing the equipment, and following orders, all while Shade stood in the center and supervised, taking frantic phone calls and running around in a haste. Lilly had avoided Shade's place since the incident. It had been months since any of them had stopped by for a smoking session. She remembered how things had gone the last time they met each other. Staying away for a while was the best course of action, and she was right.

As soon as the three of them exited her car, Shade shouted over to Lilly. "You better be here to party!" He caught the attention of all the moving workers and drew blood into Lilly's cheeks.

"Yes, sir!" She answered back, diffusing the tension. "Where do you want us?"

"Cool, go inside and grab a crate!"

That was easy. Not a word from Kyle or Ryan. The three of them walked inside and started the work of loading equipment and supplies onto the truck and cars that would follow along in the caravan. During the loading time, Lilly met the rest of the party crew.

She was first greeted by Stuff, the tall redhead she had only seen in passing before, but who this time greeted her with a warm embrace and offered to smoke a bowl with her. Stuff introduced her to Tank, another raver she remembered from last time but hadn't met officially. Next she met Connie and Eric. Connie was a sweet raver girl who was the best-friend type and told Lilly her rave name was Care Bear. In the few minutes they sat with Stuff smoking, she had told Lilly her entire life story and how she and Eric had been raving with Shade's crew for several years and loved what 1 Earth 1 Rave stood for. Another couple of kids stopped in to say hi and introduced themselves as James and Stan. They were brothers and had been partying with the crew since the beginning. Kyle chimed in to include that sometimes he stayed with the brothers when he was couch-surfing the city. Lilly wasn't sure about how often that happened, or if it was a permanent situation.

"There's more of us too," Connie said as she took a deep inhale of the pipe and passed it along through the circle. "Cuddles. She's no longer with us, but she was family. Once you're family, you're always family."

"Rest in Peace," the rest of them mumbled in unison as they bowed their heads in remembrance of their friend. The moment brought a coldness to the room, but lasted only that long. Sooner than the pipe switched hands again, the mood brightened as they talked about the night to come and the festivities that awaited them all. Lilly didn't want to ask questions and bring up a sore subject. She gathered they had all lost a good friend, and that was all she needed to know.

These people would become her newest friends as her circle grew to include the most important people at the rave, the people responsible for throwing it. What she didn't know then was that some partygoers try for years to infiltrate the party crew that call themselves the family, and they never even make it close to the inner circle. Being included in this circle was an honor in the underground subculture of the rave scene, something that wasn't easy to achieve, but revered. It was like being adopted into a genuine family of caring and compassionate brothers and sisters, a band of misfits living in their own little world that they created every weekend at the rave. They were in charge and made the rules. To be part of them was the most glorious symbol of status amongst all in attendance. Lilly didn't understand then, but her being there, loading crates into a truck, made her royalty within rave culture. She was about to immerse herself into a world that would pull her in deep and hold her tight, all while being embraced by a group of people who would make it safe, loving, and fun for her.

Dusk was setting in, and it was time to roll out. With cars and trucks full of supplies and equipment, the caravan was ready to go. Lilly, Kyle, and Ryan loaded in her car and followed second in line behind Shade in his truck. As was always his responsibility, Kyle set the info line. The info line was a phone number posted on the back of every flyer for every party. This number did nothing most of the time, until the night of the event, when the party crew recorded a message to voicemail giving partygoers directions to a map point. The map point was a gas station or fast-food parking lot close by where the party was. Ravers called the info line on the night of the event, followed directions to the map point, where they would meet a couple members of the party crew for screening. These family members would do a quick profile to make sure they weren't undercover cops or whatever (not like they could tell; they were just a couple kids wanting to be part of something bigger) and gave potential partygoers directions to "the gate."

The directions were something like "exit the gas station left, go 2.3 miles to the dirt road turnoff, reset your odometer and go another 3.6 miles, turn left at the fork, reset odometer and go another 1.6 miles, turn right at the orange cone, reset odometer and go another 1.2 miles until you see the flashing light guide you to the gate." The gate was the entrance, only a short drive down a dirt road to the beginning of the party. "By the time you hear music, you'll be pretty close to the gate."

As they drove off following Shade's truck, Kyle borrowed Lilly's phone to set the message. He spoke clearly and gave directions to the map point. The map point was a commercial gas station with a McDonald's attached to it right outside the city, where buildings and structures fell away and were replaced with rolling hills and valleys. They, however, wouldn't have to stop at the map point. They would follow Shade right into the party spot and begin setup. In the rearview mirror, one car from the caravan pulled off the exit.

"Where are they going? Are we supposed to exit?" Lilly asked Kyle.

"Huh? No, no, don't worry about them, they're map-point tonight, they stay here. We go with Shade." Lilly's excitement rose as they continued to follow Shade's truck off the exit, down a dark road, and into a dirt turnoff. They drove for miles into nowhere until they were nestled in a desert valley surrounded by protective hills. There was not a house or structure in sight, a haven where they would romp around all night without care or consequence.

Because it was Lilly's first party, they spared her the responsibility of any major jobs. She would not have to work map point, gate, security, searching, or regulation and was only asked to help set up and enjoy the party. They reserved the roll of security for the big guys, as was necessary in case a couple of crazy kids might get a little out of hand. Searching was the job for crew members that would search cars or individuals entering parties. This was a protection against weapons to keep their parties safe, and drugs to help the regulators. Regulator was a job reserved for the top-level party crew who would police the drug dealings at the party and make sure only the approved dealers were selling, and who would also collect all taxes. The party crew required all approved drug dealers to give up a small portion of their drugs as party favors to crew family members. This ensured a good time for all family members at no cost. Failure to comply with selling or taxing protocols resulted in a forever ban from attending any future parties, and was a big deal, especially for the big party crews that attracted hundreds or thousands of raver kids every weekend. Shade's party crew was this exactly.

The set up was long and difficult. Shade was a perfectionist that wanted everything to be right and felt his particular brand depended on it. The lighting had to be bright, the decorations immaculate, and party crew had to be working their assigned posts with no screw ups, no questions asked—as was imperative for the safety and well-being of all the party kids and crew. No one ever questioned Shade, only followed his lead. He was supreme lord of the rave and everyone else fell in line. By the time the music started, it was well past dark, and they needed flashlights to complete hooking up the equipment.

Lilly met the DJ's who would perform that night. The DJ's were rock stars of the parties and had the groupies to prove it. Some of them were residents of Shade's crew and others residents of a sister party crew, with their own family structure, called Sound of The Underground, or SOTU for short. This crew, unlike Shade's crew, was a Junglist crew. These guys were a little more hardcore than Shade's Trance music loving, Kandi kid crew. There were no Kandi bracelets in this crew (the plastic beaded bracelets were a relic of rave culture that Lilly had seen so many times before but had no idea what they were or meant), no trance, progressive, or house music like in Shade's crew. These DJs spun the genres of Jungle, Drum'n'Bass, Break Beats, and Techno, wore dark camo prints and black bandanas to shield them from the outdoor dust. These guys filled the role of the too-cool-for-school kids of the scene and worked side-by-side with Shade's crew that acted as the peppy, popular kids. When the cool kids and the popular kids got together to throw a party, it was something special.

While all of SOTU DJ's were nice and friendly to her, they were also intimidating as Lilly grasped the depths at which the culture held in the hearts of these guys. SOTU founder and lead DJ, Shade's counterpart, was a man named Strange Guy. His brother and co-founder was Bass Man. Not only was Lilly intimidated by their status, but by their physical features. These guys were kings for a reason. Their good friend and resident DJ Freestyle was the big brother of the group, and best friend to anyone in the family. The last resident, a DJ named Sunrise, was the most aloof of the group, more interested in the groupies and attention from the sexy girls in their underwear than being a team player. Although he was part of the family, he was more likely to be found flirting with his followers than helping set up or get the party going. When referencing him, the crew members rolled their eyes and shook their heads.

Among the top crew of SOTU was a girl named Jungle Jen. She wasn't a DJ, but a family member who made a name for herself as right hand to the crew leader, DJ Strange Guy. JJ was to Strange Guy what Kyle was to Shade, a very important person and someone you didn't want to mess with in the scene. If it weren't Shade's party, she would have been Strange Guy's regulator for the night.

Towards the end of setup, Lilly was helping the DJs by holding a flashlight over them so they could finish up with plugging in and getting going. As she stood there, Jungle

Jen, being the friendly, outgoing personality that she was, introduced herself.

"Hey, I'm Jungle Jen, but you can call me JJ. I haven't seen you around before."

"Oh, hi, I'm Lilly. This is my first party. I came with Shade and Kyle."

"Cool! So you're part of the family now? Sweet. You're in with a cool crew. We'll take care of you."

"Hey thanks, I appreciate that. Yeah, I don't know much about parties or anything, so it should be interesting."

"Interesting is for sure. You let me know if you need anything, and come find me later, we'll hang out, okay?"

"Yeah, totally. That sounds great. Thanks!" Lilly was pleased with this interaction and how easy it was to make friends with these people. She was already part of Shade's family, which she guessed got her honorary membership into the SOTU family? Maybe? She was only beginning to understand the significance of that.

Once the crew finished set up and the first DJ was spinning, a word they used to describe a DJ performing, she went off to find Kyle and Ryan, who were also finishing up with their assigned set up tasks. "Kyle, Ryan!" Lilly called out when she found them. "This is cool so far, everyone's been so nice. I already met all the DJ's and someone named Jungle Jen."

"Oh shit, you met JJ?" Kyle said. "Dude! That's your in! JJ loves coke, and she takes care of her homies. Definitely go find her later."

"Oh, no way! This is fucking awesome already!"

"See, bitch! I told you! Listen to your rave momma!" Kyle said as he joked. "Hey, so, you guys are gonna be on your own tonight. Is that cool? I'm on regulator duty so I'll be working all night, but as soon as I collect some tax, I'll find you guys and hook you up."

"Tax?" Lilly asked. Kyle explained the tax and the responsibility of policing the dealers. Kyle was a skinny, unintimidating guy, but everyone knew who he was here and that was enough to force compliance. She already felt like she had plenty of new friends to hang out with, was interested in getting to know JJ better, and in the meantime she and Ryan would hang out and check out the party. Kyle left Lilly and Ryan, and the party was underway.

Ryan, who had also never been to a party before despite having a great familiarity with recreational drug use, walked with Lilly around the party making unfamiliar discoveries. There were flashing lights and strobes, people dancing with glow sticks in their hands and in front of other people's faces. There were puddles of people all cuddled up on the floor together. Lilly pulled a random kid aside to ask what was happening. They called it a cuddle-puddle and said it was a favorite pastime of rolled-out partygoers. *Rolled-out?* Whatever that meant, Lilly kept asking questions. It was a phenomenon that occurred when a bunch of kids, all high on ecstasy, or rolling, would cuddle together for the sake of nothing more than connecting with strangers. *Ecstasy must be a much harder drug than cocaine.* How in the world could someone become so high that they would cuddle with strangers on the moist, dark ground? It was an oddity that intrigued her, although she would never make herself the fool who would take part.

There were four separate stages, each hosting a different genre of electronic music. DJ Shade was on the main stage, as it was his party, playing trance, house, and progressive. The second stage also hosted 1 Earth, 1 Rave DJs with more of the same. SOTU, the sister crew, headlined by DJ Strange Guy and his brother Bass Man, hosted the back two stages. Deep jungle sounds of Drum'n'Bass, Techno, and Break Beats filled the air, and Lilly appreciated the vibe as being much cooler than that of the Kandi Kids. The Kandi Kids exchanged their beaded bracelets and hugs while the Junglists danced under the moonlight. She liked it here and wanted to find JJ.

JJ wasn't hard to find, hanging out behind the DJ booth with the other DJs. A sacred place reserved only for DJs and family members. With no experience in the culture, Lilly knew this was a special place and only select people were invited to be there. Lilly approached with Ryan in tow, but stayed on the audience side of the booth, and waved to get JJ's attention. JJ motioned for her to come back and into the sacred space. She was being invited inside. Knowing how special a moment this was, she turned to Ryan and told him to wait for her, that she would be right back.

Behind the booth, JJ introduced her to the other DJs and crew members. She had met them during setup, but being re-introduced by JJ had a special significance and they accepted her in as easily as Shade's family had. These were the cool people, the party people she wanted to be hanging out with. JJ held a small vile up to her nose and sniffed from a detachable spoon. Lilly knew what she was doing but had never seen such a cool contraption before.

"You blow?" JJ asked her as she held out the vile for her to take.

"Oh, yeah, thanks!" Lilly said as she took the tiny spoon and dipped it into the vile. After she sniffed, she passed it back to JJ, who then handed it over to the next person as it made its way through the group. JJ and Lilly hit it off, and Lilly got the feeling that they each considered the other a friend after only a short time together. Lilly stayed behind the DJ booth long enough to get a good high going from the communal vial of coke that was still going around and being refilled. But with fresh energy she wanted to go explore the party more. Lilly thanked JJ for sharing and said her goodbyes. Ryan was still waiting right where she had told him to wait—she had almost forgotten about him. She asked what he wanted to do next, and he told her they should go back over to the trance side. He liked it over there more. Lilly agreed and off they went.

The party had grown significantly by now. There must have been at least 100 cars surrounding it and 300-400 kids in the center, all dancing and hugging and having the time of their lives. There was an energy in the air that was peaceful and uplifting. Strangers became friends, and friends became lovers. By accident, this happened to Lilly that night. Still high off the coke JJ had shared with her, she and Ryan walked around and observed the Kandi Kids and their unapologetic raver behavior.

"Hey fuckers!" Kyle shouted at them in a playful tone. "Got something for ya!" Without even approaching them, he tossed a tiny little baggie of crushed up cocaine at Lilly. "It's pre-sifted, so all you gotta do is sniff!" This implied that they wouldn't have to crush or prepare it. There were no little rocks that would stick in their nostrils, it was all smooth powder—a convenience considering dirt surrounded them and no surfaces were available. As soon as he tossed it, he was off again, into the darkness. It elated Lilly to open the baggie and dip their fingers in. It was good.

"Hey, give me a cigarette," Lilly told Ryan, who handed over his pack. Another trick she had picked up was using the recessed filter of a particular brand of cigarette, to scoop cocaine with. She used it like JJ used the spoon in her vile and scooped out a bump of cocaine and then scooped one out for Ryan. The two of them walked around and fell into a deep connection as they paired off into their own little world, as is customary for cocaine users.

As the night wore on, Lilly suggested they go to the car to get out a little more cocaine than a bump could offer. She wanted a full line. Once in the car, Lilly poured a small amount of powder out on a plastic CD jewel case from the center console.

"Lilly, there's something I've been wanting to talk to you about."

"Yeah? What's up?" She answered without stopping what she was doing with the coke, her eyes never leaving the task.

"Well, it's uh..." he let out a laugh and grabbed at the back of his neck. "I guess, I kinda, like... I like you. Like more than just a friend." Lilly stopped cutting the coke and married her eyes to his.

"You like me? Like, like me, like me?"

"Uh, is that okay?" His eyes averted down like he was preparing for the sting of rejection.

But Lilly smiled at him. "Really?" Her smile deepened as she nudged his chin upwards, lifting his eyes up to meet hers.

"Yeah!" He sounded excited now. "But I mean, I couldn't say anything because Adam asked me to stay away from you. But he's gone now, so fuck him." He chuckled through his words.

She was dumbfounded! Adam had asked Ryan to not talk to her? *That must mean he has feelings for me too!* Was all that she got from that conversation, disregarding that Ryan had poured out his heart to her. After soaking in this fantasy, she snapped back to Ryan. He had presented her with the perfect opportunity. She would date Ryan and make Adam jealous! That had to work! It was perfect! Lilly leaned in and kissed Ryan. Her first kiss.

"So, does this mean that we're together now? Like, do we tell people?"

"I guess so." Lilly giggled and bent her head down to the CD jewel case that was waiting for her. As the sun rose on the party, Lilly introduced herself and Ryan to Kyle as the new couple they had become.

Lilly was eager to get back home and wait for Adam to call, like he did daily, to tell him the news. But the party wasn't over yet. Part of being in the family meant taking part in the after party. The decompression celebration of a party well done where the crew leader, in this case Shade, would congratulate his crew and dote on them with left-over party favors and a private spin session. The afterparty always took place back home in a familiar place, away from the elements they had braved throughout the night. Back at Shade's house for the afterparty, Lilly and Ryan found a spot on the floor next to Kyle and Shade. As if they had been together for years, their two bodies laid on top of each other, advertising their closeness and Lilly's seriousness about her new relationship. The spent crew members littered themselves all over the floor, sitting, lounging, sleeping as they occupied every available inch.

"Okay guys," Shade said, "you all did such an amazing job, and we had such a splendid party, I have something special to share with you all. Hold on." The room sat with their anticipation at what he was going to retrieve. He left the room for his bedroom and came back out holding a giant, dark blue, metal tank that resembled one she'd seen at her dentist's office. When he revealed the tank to the room, it was instant fanfare. The crowd went wild with applause and cheers. Lilly waited for an explanation and turned towards Kyle.

"Oh shit! He filled the tank!" Kyle said, his eyes wide like a kid walking into a candy store. "It's called a NOS tank. You fill up balloons with the gas and inhale the balloons. It's like the opposite of helium, the dentist calls it laughing gas." She was right, she had seen something like this at a dentist before, although she had never experienced it there, she was interested to try it now. Shade threw handfuls of balloons out over the floor of bodies and arms reached up to grab them as they fell. He sat back down next to Lilly and fit the mouth of a balloon over the spigot of the tank. When he turned the nozzle, a loud rushing sound filled the room as the balloon inflated. Once full, he took the balloon off and put it right into his mouth and held his hand out for the next person to hand him a balloon to fill.

Tanks had one operator, their owner. Tank owners were very protective over their tanks and didn't like anyone else touching them. More culture, she observed and understood. Lilly waited as several other people filled their balloons. They took bottomless inhales and spoke in voices altered into deep, almost sinister sounds by the gas. Shade stared right at Lilly sitting next to him.

"Give me your balloon," he said to her in a voice that was not his own. He filled her up and as he handed it back to her, said, "Careful, don't fish out." She didn't understand what that meant, but didn't care to ask. She took a deep inhale in and was transported to a state of intense yet mellow bliss, like the moments before falling asleep when the body sinks deep into the mattress and almost sticks to it. It was as if she disassociated from her body, and it was hilarious. She laughed out loud. The voice was not hers, but one of a cartoon character's father shaming his children for being naughty. *Hilarious*. The moment was fleeting though, and only lasted a few seconds longer than it took her to exhale and inhale fresh air. Her new boyfriend watched her inhale the balloon, his eyes pointed up and his face down like a puppy begging for a treat. She knew what he wanted, but she wanted it more. Instead of offering to share, she turned herself away and focused her attention on Shade.

"Whoa, this is cool," she said as she handed him her empty balloon.

"Oh, you like that?" She nodded in agreement. "Here, give me your hand." She held out her hand, and he pulled a purple Magic Marker out of his fat pants. "You.. get.. a multi-pass," he said, his voice staggered, as he wrote MULTI-PASS on her hand in purple ink. His voice mimicking Lelu from The Fifth Element as he said multi-pass. "That means you get as many balloons as you want, anyone tries to say anything to you, you just hold out your hand and say multi-pass!" Shade giggled at her giggle and filled her balloon.

"It's purple!" Stuff shouted and pointed at Lilly. "It's purple! I love purple! I want the purple!" Lilly learned in that moment that Stuff was a fan of purple and the slightest inkling that the color purple was in her sightline was enough to make her shout it out loud. Lilly laughed; the crowd laughed.

"Oh Stuff, here! Take the marker!" Shade said with a laugh as he tossed the purple marker over to Stuff sitting a few inches away. She caught it in both her hands while a balloon stuck out of her mouth. "Back to the multi-pass… everybody shout for MULTI-PASS!"

"MULTI-PASS!" The mass of family members shouted almost in unison as they all acknowledged Lilly and laughed in tune. She felt like an official part of the crew now, and she couldn't wait to tell Adam all about it.

NINE

20-Sack

A s Lilly predicted, Adam called later that day. The same day her new family gifted her with an honorary multi-pass and made her an official family member, in that same 24-hours she had been to her first party, secured her first boyfriend with her first kiss, and hit her first balloon of NOS. She played the events over and over in her head so as not to forget any details. Her phone rang and sang Adam's special assigned ringtone to the tune of "I Got 5 On It" by Luniz, a favorite song of Adam's that reminded her of him without being sappy or revealing.

"Hello!" Lilly answered with enthusiasm.

"Hey, It's Adam, how's…"

"Hi, I know, oh my God, I have so much to tell you!" She cut him off before he could finish a complete sentence.

"Cool, what's up?"

"Oh my God, so like, first we were all like kinda pissed that you had left without giving us any hook up, cause like, duh, it's FriYay…" Her tone was so overzealous it was obnoxious. She was giddy and bubbly and couldn't get the words out fast enough.

"Okay." Adam laughed.

"Anyway, so then Kyle was like, let's go to Shade's party, and I was like, um, I guess, fuck it, let's go. So we went! And it was so cool, dude!"

"What the fuck!" With a playful tone, Adam yelled into the phone. "You went to a party without me? What the hell! I told you to wait for me!"

"Oops, I know. But, hey! You went to France without me, so this is what you get!" *Oh shit, was that too forward?* Her new boyfriend was standing right next to her. *Maybe he didn't catch it?*

"Okay, okay, so what happened?"

"Dude, it was so cool! They had lights and music and people doing this thing called a light show and I met so many cool people and they're basically all my best friends now."

"Nice! Did you take E?" Asking her a direct question now, making sure she hadn't also tried ecstasy for the first time, again without him.

"No, no, we just talked to Pearl, like I said, FriYay."

"Okay, good. Don't do that without me!"

Wait, is he flirting with me now? She glanced over at Ryan, half expecting to find an expression on his face that said, "I fucking see what you two are up to," but there was none. Nervous about where the conversation had turned, she took a quick turn to change the tone.

"Okay, but there's something else."

"What?"

"Ryan and I are dating! Yay!" She laid it on extra thick, wanting him to hurt for it. She delivered the news as if she had been pining for Ryan for ages, and she finally got her shot with him. But it was not her relationship with Ryan that she was waiting for, but her being able to tell Adam about it. The symptom of jealousy, merely the possibility of it, excited her.

"What the fuck? I haven't even been gone a week and you guys are hooking up? Fuck!" Adam tried to keep a playful tone, but Lilly could tell there was a hint of something more there that he couldn't hide. Her plan was working. Jealousy was exactly what she wanted from him. She kept up the charade, hoping it would only further enrage him, leading to him professing his love for her so he might whisk her off her feet and into the sunset on his white horse.

"Haha! I know! Isn't it great? We're so happy, and we can't wait till you get back to party with us!" There was now an *us* that didn't involve him. She imagined that stung a bit, or at least she hoped it did.

"Okay, fuckers, whatever. I'll be back soon, Don't do ecstasy without me! We'll all do it together when I get back. Okay?"

"I promise. Have fun, call me later."

"Bye."

Lilly hung up the phone elated and halfway turned on. She forgot to tell him about the NOS, dang it! Oh well, she would tell him the next time he called, tomorrow. Only he didn't call tomorrow. He didn't call the next day either. In fact, he didn't call again until right before he headed back home, and the conversation was short. It was information to let her and the gang know he was heading back and when and where to meet him when he arrived. It would be right back to business as usual. In his three weeks in France, she and Ryan and Kyle continued hanging out and partying and Lilly developed legitimate feelings for Ryan. The two of them, being horny 18-year-olds, fell deep and fast into a sexual relationship.

Lilly lived only walking distance from campus while Ryan lived an hour by bus. Without Adam around to come between them, they fell into a routine that revolved around their budding relationship. Each morning Ryan would bus to Lilly's home and wake her up with a fresh bowl and a bang. The two would get ready and go to school, and spend the entire day together in class or at the smoking section. When classes completed for the day, they, with Kyle, would go to one of their several smoke spots, either the coffee shop, Lilly's apartment, or The Tree, or now that Lilly had an "in" with the 1 Earth, 1 Rave party crew, they made a habit of spending time with Connie and Eric, Stan and James, Shade, and Stuff. In Adam's absence, the focus shifted back to poking smot, cocaine less of a motivation. Neil had even resurfaced amongst them, and Lilly introduced him to the party crew. He mentioned that he had taken a liking to Stuff. It became one big happy family again, and Lilly overflowed with love and adoration for each of them. It was a privilege to have such an enormous circle of best friends. She understood why Connie, upon first meeting her, was already so open to being friends, because that's how the culture worked. When accepted into the family, they became a legitimate family. Loved and cherished and respected and like they always had been.

Lilly caught herself falling for Ryan. He provided to her an intimacy she had never had. Endless lonely nights of crying herself to sleep became a distant memory. He was there with her: affectionate, compassionate, and giving. She had no experience of being sexually giving in a relationship, but accepted every gift he gave her openly. Two weeks into the relationship, they exchanged the words "I love you"; Lilly didn't know if this happened so fast because Adam was coming back or if this was how love worked. All of it together was confusing her now, her true desires for Adam colliding with her new feelings for Ryan, but she brushed it off as a normal part of a new relationship as she had no former experience to compare it to.

ON A TUESDAY AFTERNOON, Adam called Lilly to tell her he had landed at LAX. She and Ryan were lying in bed together, smoking and cuddling under the covers. In an instant, Lilly jumped up from her relaxed state, ready to receive the information Adam had for her. She was to gather the crew together at The Tree and wait for his arrival. Lilly spent the next hour hurrying through phone calls and coordination efforts to bring the guys together, making sure everyone was ready, that they had weed to smoke, and they were on time. Ryan squinted his eyes at her as she paced around the room, planning. She was breathing deeply, prodding at her clothing, and fidgeting with her face.

"Babe? What's going on? Why are you freaking out over Adam, all of a sudden?" he asked, still lying on the bed while she was a few feet away, staring into the bathroom mirror.

"Huh? What do you mean? I'm not. I'm just making sure it's all good."

"Why does it matter so much?"

"It doesn't, just hurry up. Get up. We gotta go get Kyle."

Ryan begrudgingly followed his order to get up and put on his shoes. He was silent in the car to retrieve Kyle. She stayed silent herself and stared at the road ahead.

"What's up, bitches!" Kyle announced himself on the porch as they pulled up to the home he was most recently couch surfing at. He exulted an energy that met Lilly's excitement.

"Whoo hoo! Let's go!" Lilly screamed back at him, free in the company of others to express her excitement. An evil-eye from Ryan scorched through her. She ignored it.

When they arrived at the empty lot that held the hidden entrance to their favorite poke spot, Adam's car was already waiting there for them.

"Yo, yo, yo, mutha fuckas! You miss me?" Adam shouted into the open air as his friends approached.

Ryan didn't react. Lilly and Kyle both jumped to offer him a warm greeting.

"Oh my God, dude! You've been gone forever!" Lilly said with a smile on her face so tight, stretched any further, she wouldn't have been able to speak at all.

That poke session at The Tree was awkward at first, made tense by Ryan's budding jealousy, but the group readjusted, each of them eager to get back to their FriYay sessions even though the dynamic had changed. The difference being that Lilly had a little more power in the group, now being connected intimately to an original member. She had gone to a couple parties now and was 'in' with the party crews. She had made Adam's best friend her boyfriend and was confident in her place in the rave family.

With this new sense of authority in the group, Lilly exercised her right to test Adam's reign. The two began bickering over coke—whose turn it was to pick up or pay, who got the first line, where they would party at, etc. Anything and everything relating to party-time, where Adam used to have the final and only say, Lilly took an opportunity to speak, making sure Adam considered her opinion. This annoyed Adam, but he accepted it. They both understood Lilly had a place in the group, and she tested how far she could push it. Adam allowed this to a point. It was playful at first until it wasn't.

In the weeks after his return, the crew had shifted their attention towards the summer party season. Adam made attempts to hold the group's focus on Pearl. He motivated Lilly by allowing her to have Jose's number, and would share responsibilities with her regarding picking up the coke for the evening's festivities. This was a big deal, and Lilly understood the context surrounding it. Programming Jose's number into her phone meant she was now one of the select people in touch with the dealer.

One FriYay, both Adam and Lilly, put in a call to him for a sack. It started out as a fun game between the two of them. A who-could-get-it-first type of friendly competition. More of a pissing contest than anything, but they found the fun in it, anyway. Jose told both of them he would pick up a sack that evening after making a trip out to his dealer, the big guy. Neither Lilly nor Adam nor anybody wanted anything to do with this guy. The crew watched way too many classic gangster movies like Blow and Scarface. The picture they painted of him became the image of the scary drug lord type they were better off not knowing.

That day, Lilly and Adam were not together. Lilly had picked up an extra shift at work instead of going to class. She had come up a little short on her weekly coke allowance and needed the extra paycheck, and Adam was in class. They had planned to meet up later, after they secured the sack for the weekly FriYay sessions.

While Lilly was at work, she got a call. It was Jose telling her that his dealer was dry and all he had was a small 20-sack, and that she could have it if she wanted it. A 20-sack was nothing, enough for two people to get three to four lines out of. With Lilly's current habit, that would only get her high for an hour, at most, less if she had to share it with another two heads. She also knew that Adam would want to get his hands on that same 20-sack and keep it for himself. Jose confirmed this when he told her Adam wanted it too, and whoever got him the money first could have it. He refused to choose sides. This made it serious. There were sides. Lilly had to hurry and make a move. She told Jose that she would get him the money and coordinated a meeting. In a fit of anxiety, she left work without clocking out or telling anyone where she was going. Acting like she was suffering an actual emergency, she was frantic and left quickly, saying she would be right back. She hurried to the ATM for the money, met up with Jose, and secured the sack. She had won. The tiny sack belonged to her, and Adam couldn't do anything about it. She returned to work to finish her shift.

Less than an hour later, Lilly received a slew of text messages from Adam, demanding she relinquish the sack to him. When she refused, he called her to reinforce his demand. Knowing what he wanted, she didn't answer. This only enraged him and he left voicemail after voicemail demanding she give him what he wanted or she would not be part of the crew anymore in a final and aggressive ultimatum. But Lilly stood her ground. He wouldn't kick her out, she was calling his bluff. After about twenty minutes, the constant phone calls and voicemail notifications stopped.

She finished the rest of her shift walked out to the parking lot. When she arrived at her car, she found scratch marks on the door seal, like someone had attempted to break into it! A closer glance revealed the dents and scratch marks made of two thick, parallel lines like the head of a crowbar, and the pile of glass on the ground and smashed in back window revealed someone had vandalized her. With hyper speed, she opened the driver door and searched the secret compartment for the sack. It was still there. Relieved, she brushed the beads of broken glass out from her back seat and called Ryan to tell him what had happened.

"Hey babe, you off work?"

"Fucking Adam broke into my car to steal my shit!" she yelled at Ryan through the phone, not acknowledging his greeting.

"What? Did he get the sack?" The sack was at the forefront of both of their minds.

"No! 'Cause he's a fucking asshole and didn't check in the hiding spot. But he smashed my fucking window, anyway!"

"Aww fuck. Are you sure it was him?"

"Yes! It was him! Nothing else is missing, my laptop and backpack are still here. He was looking for my coke!"

"Shit."

"Whatever, I'm on my way. See you in a few minutes." Lilly went to pick up Ryan and bring him back to her place, continuing to bitch and complain about Adam and her car. How dare he try to steal from her! She was angrier about him attempting to rob her than the fact that she now had to drive around and deal with a busted window.

Coked out and wanting to be brave, Lilly called Adam to confront him about what had happened. She instigated a verbal altercation, intending to force him into admitting to what he had done, but her plan backfired.

"Adam! What the fuck? You broke into my fucking car!" She started off strong in her accusations.

"Lilly, watch your fucking mouth. You forget that this is my fucking crew, my coke connect, and if I said so, this would all end for you. In one fucking second. Do you hear me?" His response became louder and more aggressive as he went on.

"Dude, you didn't have to smash my window?" Lilly's rebuttal was a little more subdued.

"Hey!" he screamed so loud she had to pull the phone away from her ear. "You listen to me, bitch! If I tell you to do something, you do it. That's how this works. You're nothing without me and my crew. All I have to do is tell them all that you're a cokehead and you're out!"

"But…" Adam cut her off.

"That's it, we're done. This is done. Don't ever fucking call me again!" With the click off of the line, Lilly felt the pieces of her heart fall into the soles of her shoes. She had never been crushed before, but she understood now what it meant and why it had such a name.

How would her new rave family friends take this? Coke was not something that the loveable 1 Earth, 1 Rave crew appreciated. They had seen it tear friendships apart and wanted nothing of it in their crew. They were a bunch of fun-loving, pot smoking, rolly-polly, raver kids that loved ecstasy and wanted to live a life of Peace, Love, Unity, and Respect. PLUR-life was their motto. He was right, if Adam told them she was a cokehead, they would outcast her. The realization of what had happened left Lilly in tears. Ryan attempted to comfort her, but then questioned why this upset her so much.

"Babe, it's okay. We don't need him or any of them," Ryan said to her softly.

"You don't understand, you don't get it." Her tears choked up her words.

"What don't I get? He's just a fucking asshole. Why do you care so much?"

"This is everything! You don't know. No one knows."

"Are you fucking in love with him or something?"

"Jesus fucking Christ, Ryan! No!" She paused to think. "I just mean, that, like, our friends. It's all gone. It's over, he… they hate us now."

Ryan stopped asking questions as she continued to cry.

Lilly moped around for three days as the group remained broken. She was sure Adam had by now followed through on his threat, and that's why no one was calling her to come hang out and poke. Until Kyle reached out and asked Lilly why she hadn't been around, hadn't called, or shown her face.

"Hey girl! Where you been? It's almost FriYay again, and we missed you last time." Kyle's voice a welcome change from the lament she had been fighting in the wake of her fight with Adam.

"Adam didn't tell you?" She waited for his reply.

"Tell me what, Chica?"

"He hates me now. We got in a big fight last week about a stupid sack of coke and he doesn't want to be my friend anymore, so I don't think we can be friends anymore."

"What? That's some bullshit. Hold on, I'm gonna three-way this mutha fucka in right now. Be quiet." Kyle always had a way to cheer Lilly up when she needed it. She would stay silent on the phone while Adam and Kyle talked. He was a good *girlfriend* like that and followed the girl code, despite not being one.

The phone rang. Her heart sank at the sound of Adam's voice.

"Hello?" His voice was deep and scratchy, like he had just woken up, despite it being the middle of the day.

"Adam? It's Kyle."

"I know, what's up?" Adam said.

"What the fuck is this bullshit I hear about the *I-hate-Lilly* shit? Where's Lilly?!" Kyle said in an angry and demanding tone.

"Nothing, nothing, it's nothing. I'm gonna apologize to her. I have to call her."

"Okay, good. You can tell her right now, because she's on three-way."

Fuck! He had exposed her! But considering the context, maybe it was a good thing.

"Hi, Adam" she said, self-consciously.

"Hi, Lilly. Look, I'm sorry about the other day. I didn't mean to say those things. Can we talk about it later, just the two of us?"

"Yeah, okay," she replied, still shy and reserved. She would not risk overstepping again. Adam was giving her another chance, and she had learned her lesson well.

"Okay, great!" Kyle added with exuberance. "It's Monday, so everyone better be at the smoking section today, normal time. Okay?"

"Yeah," said Adam.

"Yes, see you there," said Lilly.

Crisis averted! Lilly breathed a deep sigh of relief upon ending the phone call.

Ryan, right there with her, as he always was these days, squinted and pursed his lips. "Babe. Do you have feelings for him?"

"Ugh, oh my God, shut up. No. I told you no. Stop asking me." Lilly rolled her eyes and shrugged him off. Instead, she focused on what would happen next, and hoped that everything would return to normal and the group would mend itself back together. There was an extra pep in her step. That one-on-one talk she would have with Adam later acted as an energy shot. She made sure not to bring it up to Ryan—that was for her and Adam only.

TEN

Feels Like Wow

L illy got to the smoking section before Ryan, as he was still in class. Adam and Kyle were already there. Lilly gulped air as her heart jumped into her throat.

"Hey, where's Ryan?" Adam asked, making sure it was safe to pull her away. Although it was obvious that he didn't approve of the relationship, Adam respected his friendship with Ryan and wouldn't try to apprehend his woman while in his presence. Lilly knew this, and she wanted her one-on-one talk as promised, so she went to the smoking section without waiting for Ryan to get out of class.

"He's still in class for like another 10-15 minutes," Lilly responded.

"Can I talk to you?"

"Sure," she said, and the two of them walked off together, away from listening ears.

"Look, I told you I was sorry about how I spoke to you on the phone the other day, and I'm glad that you accept my apology, but the reason I had to do that is because my girlfriend was listening on the other line and she's gotten kinda suspicious of me and you lately, so I had to."

"Girlfriend?" Was what she said while stopping herself from screaming it out loud. What girlfriend? Her mind reeled, her cheeks flushed. When did he get a girlfriend? Who was this girl? How did she not know about this? Why had Adam kept this a secret for so long? Why was he telling her now? A million questions whizzed through her head and made her dizzy as Adam continued his explanation.

"Yeah, look, she and I were a thing in high school. She went away to college, and I stayed local. We've been doing the long-distance thing, but she has my voicemail pass code so she got to my voicemails a couple times before I could, and she heard a few from you. It became this big thing, and she told me I had to say those things to you, or she was going to breakup with me. And it just happened that I was on the phone with her when you called, and I clicked over to do three-way just to get her off my back. So, I'm sorry, but you understand now."

"Right, okay." She had no words, but now a broken heart. An unmistakable sting crept into her chest as she understood with certainty that he would never be hers. An entire year of trying, waiting, shot down in an instant. A lump in her chest grew off the sting and developed into a tightening as she snuck in subtle gasps for air, shaking as she released the breath. She didn't want to accept this news. Her head went hot, her palms a cold sweat. *Get it together. This doesn't have to be a big deal, he's just your friend, you have a boyfriend.*

"Alright, so I was thinking this weekend we do something different?" Adam blurted out, changing the subject and lightening the mood. "I still haven't been to a party with you guys, and Shade's been bugging me about coming. So, you down? There's one coming up this Friday."

It was back to business as usual. The conversation that Lilly had been looking forward to turned out to be a dagger to the heart, but she could pretend like everything was fine. "Yeah, for sure. Let's do it."

"Cool. Wanna poke?" Adam asked as Ryan was walking up. The three of them walked back into the heart of the smoking section to gather Kyle for an afternoon hot boxing session.

Lily remained silent throughout, her mind caught up in the new information she had received. With a silent understanding, Adam distracted the rest of the crew from her withdrawal, allowing her to have her moment in her head.

FRIDAY CAME AROUND AND, instead of picking up their weekly coke sack, the gang agreed to go to a party. This weekend, the drug of choice would be ecstasy. It would be Lilly's first experience and she was excited to share it with her new boyfriend, whom she had taken the week to convince herself was the love of her life. The scene was the same as it had been the first time around. The party started at Shade's apartment, loading crates and equipment, scrambling to meet his demands and get off on the road before dusk. It pleased Lilly to see Neil in attendance this time, holding tight to Fluff's side, the two of them a couple now, a handsome one at that.

They skipped past the map point and headed straight to the gate. Again, no one asked Lilly to work during the party and this time she understood it was because all jobs had been long since assigned by the existing party crew and no one wanted to give up their task or share. There was a sense of pride in having an assigned station, a responsibility for the entire night. Lilly was happy with setup and tear down as it meant she was free to enjoy herself during the meat of the night.

Adam was not new to the crew or the family, Lilly learned they had made him an honorary member long before Lilly joined the crew, but he hadn't gone to any parties yet as he "joined" during the winter previous to Lilly's arrival. Shade threw parties during the spring and summer, with few exceptions, as he enjoyed the openness of outdoor venues in the outskirts of the surrounding deserts and woods. The fall and winter months were reserved for warehouse parties that took place in the back alley, industrial complexes that all but became ghost towns in the off-business hours, free for kids to roam, run and play. These parties interested other party crews, but 1 Earth, 1 Rave and SOTU were two of the vast network of party crews that preferred to keep their parties outdoors, under the stars, and away from any evidence of civilization. Adam was already friendly with Shade's crew and the sister crew of Strange Guy and Bass Man. Lilly now felt a little silly for being so excited to experience this with him. She had fooled herself into believing that she held a key for him. But she had nothing he didn't already have. She was no gatekeeper to the rave scene. To her embarrassment, she discovered she had no power over him, the scene, or his introduction to any of it. Adam was still in charge and knew his way around better than she did, despite never having been to a rave, an advantage she never had.

At the party Adam took on the role of regulator with Kyle. He was a natural leader and intimidating while still being friendly. The dealers handed over their tax to him without asking who he was or who he was working for—he picked up the position with ease and fell right in as if he had been doing it for years. The confidence Adam exuded was enough to force compliance. He was at home at the party; it was a new and exciting domain for him to conquer, and he did. Working the gate, he moved through the line of cars, making sure all sanctioned dealers paid their tax and that no other dealers could sell. When he and Kyle gathered enough party favors, they came to meet Lilly and Ryan, who were waiting off in the distance to join their friends. Adam and Kyle approached. This would be the start of their night together.

"Are you fuckers ready to party!" Adam yelled at them while Lilly skipped and hopped around in excitement. "Come here, look." He pulled four little pressed pills out of his pocket. One was green with a pressed image of a smiley face on the surface, another was pink and oval-shaped pressed with a rhinoceros head, the other two were dark blue with a diamond press. She had seen nothing like them. Who knew pills could look so... fun!

"Okay," Kyle chimed in, acting as the group's resident medicine-man, the one who had the most knowledge and experience in what was about to happen and thus qualified to explain the options. "So, we have a Green Smiley, a Pink Rhino, and two Blue Diamonds. From what I hear, the Diamonds are the most roll-y, the Smiley is super amp-y, and the Rhino is the best of both. I think you and Ryan," pointing to Lilly, "should take the Diamonds because they're the same and as a couple you wanna be on the same level. Adam can take the Smiley and I'll take the Rhino." He finished up.

"Fine, what the fuck ever, Kyle. Let's go!" Adam said, it was obvious to Lilly that Kyle had used strategic wordplay to reserve the best pill for himself, and from Adam's reaction it wasn't lost on him either. He handed out the pills to their assigned user and pulled a water bottle out of his back pocket.

Lilly held the little blue pill in her hand and revered it for a moment. What was about to happen could be the best night of her life, or it could kill her. It was a roll of the dice, one that a year ago would have never even crossed her mind as an option, but today, at this moment, she was excited to take the opportunity. She put the pill on her tongue and cringed from its bitterness, almost gagging.

"Haha," Kyle remarked, "that's how you know it's good. Hurry! Swallow!"

She chugged the water and washed it away. She looked at Adam for some kind of reassurance that what she had done was the right thing, not noticing that her boyfriend was looking to her for the same.

"Cool! Good job," said Adam, knowing what Lilly needed from him in that moment. "Alright, so you two lovebirds go have fun, you'll feel it kick in, in the next 30-40 minutes. Kyle and I have to keep working but come find us when it kicks in and we'll poke some smot, okay?"

What? He isn't coming with us? Lilly couldn't believe it, but she nodded, grabbed Ryan by the hand, and led him off into the party.

Lilly and Ryan disappeared into the dance floor made of compacted sand underneath the desert sky. Cacti and desert shrubs littered the valley of sand dunes that surrounded them. The sky lit up under the moon next to the stream of stars in the Milky Way. A small rumble of nerves in the pit of her stomach awakened her as she observed the beauty in the sky above. *Is this it? Is it starting?* It had only been a few minutes, but she wasn't sure.

"Are you feeling it yet? I think I'm feeling it!" she asked Ryan.

"No, no, trust me, you'll know. You're probably just excited. Let's poke a bowl, that'll help." Ryan pulled out a pipe from his pants pocket and packed a fresh bowl of stress for his lady. They smoked. It didn't bring on the high any faster, but it helped to relax her so she wasn't so tense. She let it go. It was still early, the party had only recently got going and was still light as far as attendance. They occupied themselves on the dance floor to happy trance music during resident DJ Sniper's early set.

The music slowed and deepened, almost to a stop. *When did that happen? What's happening to...* her inner monologue stopped itself as she fell into the experience. Her body followed the sensation as her movements slowed in-time, a wave of electric euphoria rushed through her, almost knocking her down. It was so intense it made her eyes wobble and her teeth grind themselves shut. *This... This was IT.* She turned her head towards Ryan and watched neon visual trails of everything in her path along the way. It was like the images her eyes took in were being pulled and stretched with her movements, leaving behind thin and bright lines of light. Once centered on his face, her eyes deceived her and showed him intensely shaking, but it was the eyes in her head that were shaking, not him. Every molecule of her body pulsated through the wave. Every inch of her, down to the hairs standing up on her neck, screamed in pleasure, like the peaking moment of orgasm, happening all over her, as if every piece had its own clitoris, climaxing together in unison through this symphony of ecstasy. She brought her hands up to her face for evidence that this was real. The sensation of her hands touching her skin created a fresh wave crashing upon her and pulling her out to sea.

"Hoooooo, it feels like wow!" The breath it took to speak only intensified the wave, and she could no longer continue speaking and remain standing at the same time.

"Yup, wow is right," Ryan said as he grabbed her and pulled her into him. His touch another new wave that collided with the others, creating a deeper and more challenging sensation of being swept away. The feelings were intense but welcome as they came with an unexplainable sensation of love, adoration, happiness, and elation mixed with an unending gush of energy and enthusiasm. But was it Ryan's touch that brought these new feelings into light? Or was it the drugs? *Where was Adam?* She would test it out on him, for scientific comparison.

"This is WAY better than coke! Why haven't we been doing this for way longer? Oh my God, let's go find Adam!" Lilly said out loud in Ryan's general direction, but she wasn't sure she was having a conversation, more so she was talking because it felt good to speak. Ryan, also high, made no opposition and followed her away from the dance floor and through the desert night that was brighter now. Her pupils dilated to grab at all available moonlight.

In the distance, her eyes were of no use as they were trailing and shaking too much to make out actual faces or people, but she heard his voice yapping at people, "Hey you! You pay your tax? NO dealing allowed! Unless you give me drugs…" He sounded like he was having a ball, rambling at strangers and ordering them around, laughing while he did it, a shit-eating grin on his face, she guessed.

"Oh my God, shut the fuck up, Adam. You're so stupid," Kyle said. That must have been them up there in the dark. Two figures in the darkness, outlined by the neon shine of a few cracked glow sticks, looked as if they were in the general direction of where the voices were coming from.

"Adam!" she shouted, taking a total shot in the dark. Her jaw and teeth chattering as the noise escaped her.

"Who's there!" he shouted back, a flashlight now pointed in her direction.

"It's me!" She didn't specify who "me" was, but figured he'd get the idea.

"Lilly?" The flashlight bobbed in the darkness as it rushed towards her. Adam appeared in front of her and rushed to give her a great big hug. Her face lit up at what was happening. The waves again rushed through her, crashing inside her chest and exploding out through each follicle of her skin. She held onto him and didn't want to let go. When she did, a scowl on Ryan's face screamed jealousy. Kyle walked up after. She gave him as big of a hug, diffusing the situation.

"Hi ya!" said Kyle in a happy baby voice. He tussled her hair and giggled at her. She giggled back.

"Are you guys having fun?" Adam asked, that shit-eating grin across his face that Lilly had imagined.

"Dude, this is the BEST thing I've ever done in my life! Why didn't you tell me?" Lilly said, her voice animated and alive.

"I know, I know!" Adam laughed. "I couldn't tell you, I had to show you."

"Shit, man, I never want this to end," Ryan chimed in, trying to make himself part of the conversation.

"Ya know what?!" Kyle was still using the same voice. "I think it's time for your rave mama to give you your rave name!" He spoke to Lilly as he bestowed upon her a glow stick necklace, placing it around her neck.

"Really!" Lilly gasped as she looked up at Kyle with puppy dog eyes, her face illuminated by the glow of her gifted necklace. "What's my name? Tell me!"

Kyle took a minute and looked at her with fond eyes. "You are… Glow Girl!" As the words left his lips, the rest of them awed and oohed, the group all hugged each other as they celebrated the significance of what had happened.

"I'm Glow Girl! I'm Glow Girl!" Lilly shouted to the sky and twirled around in pure bliss.

Adam laughed lovingly for a moment before he caught himself and shook off his grin.

"Fuck it, we're done working for a while, let's go party," he said.

Lilly's face flushed. Getting to spend this time with him was all that she had wanted. The crew sauntered off back to the party, where they enveloped themselves in pure rave culture. There were light shows and cuddle puddles, Kandi trading, and endless free hugs. Lilly partook in these activities this time instead of only observing. She made friends with what must have been 100 ravers, and added their phone numbers in her phone, as if that made it real. They danced and danced until their legs turned into Jell-O and the sun rose over the valley. It was a night she swore she'd never forget, surrounded by strangers that became friends, her new family, her new boyfriend, and propelled by a chemical catalyst that turned her black and white world to shades of bright neon colors she never knew existed.

This became the new normal as the group shifted yet again into an alternative form of recreation. Lilly, who had fought against attending raves for so long, became the quintessential party girl. For the rest of the summer weeks and into the fall, Shade and Strange Guy threw parties almost every weekend. Every party was an opportunity to let the drugs take her to a place where overwhelming love and affection was warranted and encouraged. She waited patiently for her pills to kick in and for Adam to come searching for her. Their hugs were magic. The drugs also made it easier for her to ignore the side-eye that came from her boyfriend, always standing right behind her while she and Adam engaged in their party peaking rendezvous.

ELEVEN

Break

After learning about Adam's girlfriend, Lilly allowed herself to become closer to Ryan. But as the party season wrapped up, Ryan's love grew into a paranoia that poisoned their relationship. It started small, Ryan and Lilly would hang out with several friends, poking smot, like they always did, sitting in a smoking circle in a backyard under the Autumn sun. A few trips around the circle Ryan's face would change. Lilly came to recognize this as a decent into suspicion and desperation.

Soon Ryan's accusations became verbal and he would allege that Lilly was touching the leg of, let's say Tank, sitting next to her when she passed over the pipe, this would escalate to him condemning her for cheating on him, out loud, in front of their friends. Outbursts like this would ruin the moment and made everyone embarrassed for both of them. It became hard to bring Ryan around their friend group once she discovered they had nicknamed him Buzz Kill behind his back. But Lilly persisted, she wasn't ready to leave behind her family friends for something as unimportant as her boyfriend's honor. She found a home among this misfit family of hers and couldn't fathom walking away from it. She tried to keep it together for as long as she could until everything came to a head. But the moment came that forced her to make a choice between her relationship and her friends.

It was her birthday, November. Invited for a kick back at her place was Adam, Ryan, Kyle, JJ and the couple from Shade's crew that she had become close with, Connie and Eric. With these people Lilly spent the summer bonding at raves and under the influence of ecstasy. Connie and Eric had become close enough that they knew about her cocaine habit in the background but didn't judge her for it. It would be easy for Lilly to host this kickback because her parents were out of town for the weekend and there were no parties worth going to, it being the off season.

Lilly was heart set on hanging out with Pearl that night. She was excited to invite JJ over for a coke party as JJ had shared so much of her own coke over the summer each time they met up at a party. The guests all arrived, except for Adam, who was off securing the sack for the evening. The party waited with beers in hand for his arrival, when Lilly's phone rang.

"Hello? You getting my friend, Pearl?" Lilly asked, her voice bright and cheery in front of all their friends.

"Lilly." Adam's voice said on the other end, not so bright and not cheery. "Look, Jose doesn't have anything. He's dry."

"What? That's impossible! He's never dry!"

"I know, I know, it sucks. I'm sorry."

"Oh my god, this isn't happening! No!"

"I'm so sorry, Lilly. I know it's your birthday." His voice soft and sincere.

"Damn it! Pearl's not coming, guys," she announced.

The guests grumbled and sighed, most of them

anyway. Connie and Eric smiled in secret to each other as tension released from their shoulders. But for Lilly, it was more than disappointment; it was a strong angst, a heaviness that swept through her.

"I mean, whatever. We have beer at least, you on your way?" she asked Adam.

"Listen, I'm sorry, but I can't make it after all tonight. Something came up at the hotel. My dad needs me there."

"What!" Lilly screamed, a lot louder than she meant to.

"I'm sorry, I know, I'm sorry. I'll make it up to you, I promise. Okay? You guys just have fun and I'll call you tomorrow." He hung up without saying goodbye, or giving her a chance to argue. In a room full of people, she couldn't let herself cry, but her eyes filling with water gave her away. With nowhere to run or hide, she brought her hands up to her face, in complete cover and wanting to escape.

"No, no, no! GG! Don't be sad! I have something for you!" Kyle said, comforting her and pulling her in for a hug.

"I just wanted to have a good time with all my friends. Coke is the best for a kickback, and now my birthday is ruined!" she said in full cry-blubber. Maybe if she pretended like the missing coke upset her, they would believe it. A glance over to Ryan revealed he didn't. His face stayed stoic as he kept his eyes averted towards the ground, looking up only to glare at her from across the room.

"GG, look," Kyle said, calling her by a nickname he coined and was special between the two of them. They all called her Glow Girl at the rave, but only Kyle called her GG. He laughed at her as he pulled out a sandwich baggie full of stale, dry mushrooms with long white stems and small brown caps.

Her mood changed, and she pepped up.

What she didn't know was that Kyle had a special evening planned that night. Surrounded by their closest friends, the conditions were perfect. Lilly had been asking Kyle about Magic Mushrooms for quite some time. She was interested as her introduction to the world of psychedelics had been positive with ecstasy and pot, although not hallucinogenic, usually, but both substances fell under the umbrella classification of psychedelic. Knowing this made her comfortable taking the next step into a more hallucinogenic territory of stronger potency.

"Oh, my god! You got me shrooms?"

"I got you shrooms!" he responded in a tone that matched her newfound enthusiasm. Kyle saved the party as he distributed the dried caps and stems amongst the group. Lilly bit into a long white stem. It was like plant jerky in her mouth and tasted like dirt and the shells of dried pumpkin seeds. It was dry, so dry she needed several gulps of her beer to wash it down, a few more to rid her mouth of the flavor that stuck behind. Kyle disclosed to her it would take a while to kick in, but she had become accustomed to reaction wait times by now. The guests sat and talked and smoked and waited for the shrooms to kick in.

Within an hour, the others began wandering around outside in the garden or down the back alley behind her house. The group walked down that alley together, looked up and stood underneath power lines that stretched as far as their eyes could see on either side. Sensations and visuals exaggerated themselves. Lilly disappeared into fantasy when the cords turned into wire strings, and she found herself standing on the nape of a guitar neck. Music played from inside her as she drifted through the illusion. It was a magical experience. She looked over to Ryan, looking for someone to share the moment with, but he was standing alone, off to the side, that same stoic expression, uninterested in engaging with her or anyone.

Further into the evening, the guests all separated and were exploring their own worlds. Kyle and Lilly were standing outside alone, smoking a cigarette when she experienced an onset of an intense connection to the earth and its beauty, a bohemian moment that resonated with her.

"Shrooms!" Kyle said. No context, no follow up, except for a fit of laughter that spiraled into a barrel and pulled her into it. The two of them both laughing in a fit and gasping for air. It hit her. Her reality disappeared, and she tried to make sense of it through kaleidoscope eyes that shone bright floral and paisley patterns and colors that she was sure weren't there before. Kyle, still laughing with her, but his body now hidden behind a flood of colors and patterns, all spinning and twisting and tying themselves up in knots. This, she understood, was the lifeblood of the earth, the heartbeat that was always invisible to her before, now colored so bright and more vivid than anything she had ever experienced in her waking life before. She was part of it, she was being shown a gift and got to experience it in pure joy with one of her closest friends.

Ryan broke through the heartbeat and destroyed the vision when he came outside. Interrupting a beautiful moment, he looked Lilly right in the eye, and said, "Do you want me to leave?" He had a pathetic and desperate face that enraged her. How dare he impede on this gift she had received from Mother Earth herself! How could he have done that to her? Inside her, she felt her blood boil as she visualized tiny bubbles in her veins, bursting through her skin in a rage fueled by Ryan's inconsiderate interruption of her beautiful birthday moment.

"What? No, I don't want you to leave. What are you even doing right now?" she said, giving him a chance to calm himself.

"Whatever, I'm leaving," he said as he turned away and walked back into the house to grab his backpack.

It was well after midnight, there were no busses, and his house was at least six miles away. She couldn't let him leave like that. It worried her he might get hurt or lost. He was high and having a bad trip. Her moment was over, and she wasn't getting it back. The best thing to do, the PLUR thing, for the safety of her boyfriend, regardless of how angry she was with him, would be to help him through this.

"Ryan, stop. Come back. You're not going anywhere." She ran after him.

Kyle, wanting to help, followed. "Ryan, you're having a bad trip, we can help you through this," he said. They followed him back inside where the rest of the party also was still off in their worlds, now interrupted by Ryan's abrupt and heated entrance as he ran away from Lilly and Kyle.

"No, fuck this! Lilly doesn't want me here. I just wanna leave. She doesn't love me, she never has. I'm fucking done with this shit!"

"Hey, hey, hey." Connie added her soft voice to the commotion, offering calm and peaceful tranquility. "What's going on? We're all cool here, brother. Let us help you."

"She hates me. I can't be here. I have to go." Ryan had slunk down and brought his knees into his chest, holding onto himself for any comfort he could find. The guests all looked around the room at each other and settled on Lilly.

"I don't hate you, Ryan. We're all just having a good time. It's my birthday, this is supposed to be fun."

"No, no, no, no. If you cared, you would tell them all to go." Ryan, now crying, rocked himself back and forth in his own arms.

"Okay, guys, I think it's time for us all to go. Let's let them figure this out," JJ said.

"No, I don't want you guys to leave, please!" said Lilly, worried that they would abandon her.

Ryan screamed. So loud, and for so long, the rest of them drew back and covered their ears before running outside of the house to the safe serenity of the outdoors.

"Look, I'm sorry, but I think we're all gonna go. You've got some shit to deal with here," JJ said, speaking for the entire group who nodded in agreement and refused to look at her. There were no goodbyes as they left. Lilly watched them go, listening to the sound of Ryan screaming her name, beckoning her back inside.

THERE WAS no real recovery after that night. The group withdrew from her and Ryan, and Lilly responded by clinging harder to Ryan. Lilly reasoned it must have been what Ryan wanted, because he relaxed in their solitude together and things felt peaceful. The two became inseparable. Ryan began bringing Lilly along on his pickups with his weed connection, the one he had always been so secretive about.

"Okay, look, I have to tell you something, don't freak out," Ryan said to Lilly on the day he first felt comfortable inviting Lilly in with him to the house where his weed connection lived and sold from. She was about to meet the mystery man.

"Yeah, okay, what?"

"So, you know I have to keep this guy a secret?"

"Yeah…" Lilly responded, now annoyed, wanting to tell him to get to the point.

"His name is Milo, he used to work for Shade in 1 Earth, 1 Rave. He was one of the original family members. There was a big falling out. They accused him of stealing money, but he didn't. No one can know we pick up from him. It has to stay a secret, just between us."

"Yeah, well, thanks to you, none of our old friends are even talking to us anymore, so, okay, whatever, let's go!" Lilly hurried him along, eager to smoke.

A large Mexican man with neck tattoos greeted them at the door. It was Milo. The four of them sat around in his tattered living room and passed between them a joint of shitty weed. Lilly stopped listening to their conversation as the two of them talked like old friends. Instead, she lost herself in her mind full of Adam and her friends, and when, if ever, she might see them again. She missed them. She missed being close to a large group of people. But could their friendship ever go back to how it was before Ryan pulled her away?

"Fucking Shade, serves him right for letting that bitch Cuddles attack me…" She heard Milo say.

"Wait, what about Shade, and did you say Cuddles?" Lilly asked.

"Oh, did you know Cuddles? Stupid bitch turned up dead! Serves her right for accusing me of stealing. I'm not a thief. Fuck all of them."

"Dead how?" Lilly exclaimed. She was flustered as her mind reeled with the possibilities of what might have happened to a girl she didn't know but had heard her friends talk about.

"Well, the bitch accused me of stealing $500 from the gate money. And Shade, oh fucking Shade… I had been with that mother fucker since day one! Since he was still wearing G-strings and purple fucking eyeshadow. Then some bitch comes along and he takes her word over mine? Na. Fuck all of them. Serves them all right for what happened to her."

"So, what happened to her?" Lilly persisted as beads of sweat gathered on her forehead and her breath became loud in her ears. The face of her boyfriend, sitting two feet away, was sweating as his eyes screamed at her to be silent.

"Bitch turned up dead in the fucking LA River." Milo stared right into Lilly's eyes. "I'll teach a bitch a lesson for accusing me..." The second part of his statement trailed off into a mumble as he turned away from Lilly and his eyes fell into a blank stare at the TV in front of him.

"Shut the fuck up," Ryan mouthed to her, now eager to collect his purchase and leave.

Oh my God. Oh my God! Her heart thudded so hard it hurt. The pains in her chest caused her to grab at it. She pulled at the piece of shirt and bra that sat on top of its skin. Her collar felt tight, despite it not touching her throat. She pulled at it anyway, gasping at the air as her cheeks flushed and the beads of sweat turned into rolling streams that fell down her face.

"Get me... the fuck... outta here," she whispered to Ryan, taking pauses in between words to catch a fast breath.

Milo stayed still in his chair and focused on the TV as they hurried themselves out of his home.

TWELVE

New Friends

T he winter months were full of warehouse parties with other party crews, not friends, but something to do at least. Not having Adam or Kyle around, Lilly needed an alternative to satisfy her growing demand for cocaine. Lilly didn't enjoy being alone with Ryan, it aggravated her need for her friends further. As luck would have it, at one of the winter warehouse parties, they met another couple, Sly and Tom. Sly was a super sexy, sassy drug dealer and Tom was her boyfriend that Lilly knew from high school. The two hadn't been friends back then, but it made their introduction to each other now smooth as they had something in common. Sly and Lilly became fast friends. Not only did they have a common love for cocaine and ecstasy, they both had annoying boyfriends that they, deep down, were looking for any excuse to get rid of.

Lilly and Ryan spent the rest of the winter hanging out with Sly and Tom at parties or the random hotel room Sly and Tom checked into for the evening. Sly, only 17-years-old to Lilly's 19, was still living at home and couldn't manage selling drugs from her mother's kitchen window.

Instead, the couple did business out of seedy motel rooms that they often invited Lilly and Ryan to as the couples became closer. The girls never spoke about it out loud, but there was a consensus that both of them were becoming fed up with the constant, nagging insecurity from their boyfriends. Tom was like Ryan and accused Sly of cheating on him with her customers. The boys wanted to have the full and undivided attention of their girlfriends, without having to share any attention with friends or family or anyone that might get in the way. That wasn't something the girls could give them. The girls were only interested in partying and having fun, meeting new people, and making forever friends. Worrying about their boyfriend's feelings was becoming an arduous chore.

Lilly experienced a moment of clarity at the end of a party that she and Ryan attended alone. Sly and Tom were at a different party that weekend and Lilly, despite knowing already it wouldn't work, tried and got none of her old friends to attend with them. At the end of the party, still high from the ecstasy and wanting to find an afterparty, Lilly tried to make friends with a few strangers and ask if there was something they were doing afterwards. These strangers would have invited only her, but with a boyfriend in tow, were less likely to want to party with him too. This boyfriend of hers was adding nothing to the party lifestyle she wanted to live. He wasn't getting her access to parties or after parties; he didn't have a supply of drugs for her; she was the one who supplied and purchased the drugs for the both of them. He was dead weight and adding nothing to her good time. She lost all respect and affection for him, and the energy she gave off told him this, which only exacerbated his insecurities and made matters worse. Despite knowing it was over, she tried to hold on to it for reasons she couldn't articulate.

As the spring months approached, Lilly missed her old friends more knowing that Shade's party season would start soon. After months of being confined to dark warehouses, she longed for a night under the stars in the safety of the deserts and forests, surrounded by people she still loved. She was excited to introduce Sly to that world too, as Sly had only experienced warehouse raves. Lilly hadn't planned it, but the day came when the pressure Ryan placed on her would become too much, freeing her to reconnect with the world she left for him. The relationship was meaningless, and she had lost sight of why it started. Adam was no longer in her life, and Ryan was doing nothing but adding unnecessary stress and discomfort.

On the day it became enough, she was taking a shower while Ryan was sitting right there on the toilet waiting for her. His insecurities became so pressing that he couldn't even leave her side long enough for her to shower alone. The pressure bubbled, and she ended the relationship, right there in the steam-filled bathroom.

"I just don't understand why you need to walk to class alone. Why can't I come with you? I always come with you? Are you trying to get away from me?" Ryan asked.

"Oh my God, Ryan! I can't do this anymore. It's too much. You're always right up my ass! I'm done, this is over," Lilly said as the water hit her face.

"I knew it! I knew this was coming! It's Adam, isn't it? I know it is! You're cheating on me!" Ryan screamed from outside the shower curtain. She couldn't see his face and she didn't want to. It was easier this way.

"What? Fuck, dude! No! You're just psycho. I can't do this. You need to leave."

"I fucking knew it!" Ryan cried and screamed as she heard him run out of the bathroom and slam the front door.

The water became a stream of relief that washed over her. She was free. The release was liberating. The first thing she did after stepping out of the shower was call Sly to share the news.

"Hello?"

"So, I just broke up with Ryan," she said right away.

"Oh my God, are you okay?" Sly asked.

"Yes! More than okay, I'm relieved! He was too much, I just wanna have fun, and he's making everything so serious all the time, constantly accusing me of shit, I just can't do it anymore."

"Oh girl, I get that… You know what, hold on…" Sly began speaking to someone else in the room while staying on the line with Lilly. "Hey… Hey! This isn't working anymore. I need you to leave. We're done."

"What the fuck, Sly!" Tom yelled in the background.

"Hey, you there?" Sly said back to Lilly without responding to Tom.

"Uh, yeah…" Lilly tried to hold back her laughter. Was this happening right now?

"Wanna hang out? Come pick me up, I gotta get away from this asshole."

"Okay! Be right there!" Lilly said in a fit of laughter as she hung up the phone and rushed to go meet Sly. The end of an era and the beginning of a much grander one. Perfect timing for what was going to be the perfect party season.

Key moments like this developed this new friendship and bonded the girls closer together. At parties they had discovered it was fun to hide from their boyfriends and watch from the corner as the boys searched for them. Now that the girls had broken up with their boyfriends and replaced those relationships with each other. To celebrate, Lilly and Sly got a hotel room, as Sly often did, to sell drugs and party with each other or any customers that might come by. Because Sly was only 17, Lilly put the room in her name. The girls paid for one night, but the following day were too tired to checkout and forgot to call the front desk to ask for another night. They slept past check out, ignored the various phone calls coming from the front desk, and instead woke up to the sound of the Fire Marshall breaking through the front door justified by a "wellness check."

THIRTEEN

Party On

"Hello?" Lilly answered the phone when Adam's name popped up on the caller ID. She thanked God that the interaction was happening by phone when a nervous tick developed in her eye. *But why?* She asked herself.

"Hey, buddy!"

"Um, what's up?" She said as a smile ran across her face and her cheeks warmed.

"Nothing, nothing, just wanted to check in. I just got off the phone with Ryan, he said you guys broke up?"

"Yeah, fuck that guy, I couldn't handle it... I'm surprised to hear from you though, I thought he was like your best friend. For sure, thought you guys would be all buddy, buddy again."

"Best friend?" Adam laughed at her suggestion. "No, no, that was a long time ago. I called because I care about you, you're a cool chick and I wanna reconnect."

No way, this isn't happening. He's being way too nice... care about me? Cool chick? A slant crossed her face as she squinted her eyes at her thought. "He also told me you've made a new friend?" *There it is.*

"Oh! Yeah, Sly. She's super cool and has really good coke." Lilly laughed and let out a tense breath. It made sense now. She had something that he wanted access to.

"Cool, cool, well, we all really missed you. It's been too long and boring without you."

Was Adam begging for her to come back to him? After she had shunned him and all their friends for the sake of a demented and misguided relationship? The words he spoke didn't feel genuine, even so, she felt her heart pounding in her chest, and an old, stifled spark reignited. She had only broken up with Ryan a couple weeks ago and was ready to jump right back in with Adam.

"Really? Aww, I missed all you guys too! And the season is starting again! We can party again all summer, like last year!"

"That's right, we can!" Adam said back, squeezing his vocal cords to match her tone of excitement.

The conversation went on for hours. The two caught up and shared stories about their winter season. At Adam's request, Lilly went into detail about her newfound friendship with Sly and bragged about the morning the Fire Marshall broke into their motel room. She woke up to the commotion in time to stop the invasion, meeting the Marshall and two uniformed police officers at the other side of the door. Luckily for the girls, this prevented the authority's entrance into the room where they would have found a full-size mirror lying flat on a bed corner, removed from the wall and used to cut cocaine all night, loose ecstasy pills on the dresser, a weed pipe and ash on the bedside table, and the non-smoking room still hazy from an over saturation of cigarette smoke.

She convinced the Marshall that they were okay and

would stay an extra night. The following morning, when Lilly and Sly entered the lobby to retrieve their $100 deposit, the hotel desk clerk denied the request because the maid reported to the front desk the state in which the room was in. Neither Lilly nor Sly had had the wherewithal to at least put the mirror back on the wall and wipe the cocaine residue from it. After being threatened again with the police, the girls gave up their deposit and left. This, she cited as the true bonding moment that made the girls inseparable.

"Wow! That's crazy. So, you guys are like best friends now? Does that mean you just do her coke for free all the time?"

She knew what he was looking for and she wanted to give it to him. "Oh yeah, dude. All the time."

There was more to talk about too, like why she ended the relationship with Ryan. She told him, and added in a little jab by revealing the truth behind his secret weed connection. Adam became interested in this as it offered an opportunity. This information would exile Ryan from the rave family, allowing space for Lilly to come back with her new coke connection.

It was like nothing had changed between the two friends, and it was still so easy to talk to each other. Adam spoke about how he was spending more time with the Junglist crew, SOTU, and had become close to the crew leaders, Strange Guy and his brother Bass Man, that Jungle fit his personality better than Shade's Kandi crew. He mentioned that FriYay had evolved into weekends at JJ's house with the DJ brothers, Freestyle, sometimes Sunrise, and a sack of coke. They would plan out the upcoming parties and spin Drum'n'Bass music. Saturday they would go to the parties, and Sunday they would relax and decompress again at JJ's. It was way more chill than before, he explained, because JJ had her own house, all to herself, and it was clean and well cared for; her parents were wealthy business owners that had three houses, this one they gave to her without interruptions or check-ins. Lilly was excited about the prospect of having a more chill party spot instead of the single room garage studio.

After discussing all topics, Adam invited Lilly and her new friend to the upcoming FriYay at JJ's house. This would be the first time Lilly had seen Adam since last year. Lots had changed, but Lilly held a new ace in her hand, Sly, a drug dealer who offered the one thing the DJ's and party crew couldn't.

The relationship between dealers and DJ's was symbiotic. The DJ's throw the party at which the dealer sells their favors. They are kings and knights of the rave. In a metaphorical sense, placed on a pedestal and worshiped with an almost religious sanctity as if the rave was a church they built with their own hands, the party kids its disciples, and the dealers the spiritual healers. Without the party, the dealer is nothing more than a two-bit criminal helping addicts kill themselves by slow death. At the party, the dealers are the revered keepers of fun and amusement, respected and acknowledged. On the opposite hand, without the dealers, the party is nothing more than a bunch of dudes getting together in the desert to play music. Something about the emotional power of psychedelic drugs mixed with the repetitive beat of electronic music created the perfect atmosphere for a sacred experience.

Lilly hung up the phone, validated in her decision to breakup with Ryan. He was the only thing holding her back from enjoying her life the way she wanted to. If this relationship taught her anything, it was that she didn't need strings or attachments, all she wanted was to surround herself with friends and her party family and all the party favors she could get her hands on. Dating Ryan to make Adam jealous had backfired, her biggest one yet, and took almost a year to recover from. But she was back in Adam's graces, and they were already planning to spend the party season together. She couldn't wait to introduce him to Sly and get her involved in the scene too, in with the family. If Lilly could be the person to bring a new and reliable dealer into the scene, that might be her restitution with the Junglist crew to get her accepted back into their family.

FRIYAY WAS HERE. Lilly had mentioned to Sly that a few of her old party friends were getting together for a little kickback and they had invited her to come along. Interested in the prospect of new customers, Sly smiled in delight that they asked to include her. Sly even brought along a sample sack of coke to share. The girls arrived at JJ's house for the evening's festivities. It was a large house on a secluded cul-de-sac, in the quiet outskirts of the LA suburbs. Adam's silver Rav4 was in the driveway. The two girls walked up to the front door and rang the bell. Lilly was nervous but played it off as excitement to see her friends and blow some rails.

"Hey! Lilly! Lilly's here, everybody!" JJ exclaimed when she opened the door. So happy to see her, Lilly threw her arms around JJ and jerked back and forth for a few seconds in a show of her own excitement. It shouldn't have been so easy, this re-entry, considering how things ended at her birthday party last year. But Lilly came back bearing gifts that could benefit all of them in the upcoming season. With summer so close, having something to offer the party was all that mattered to any of them.

"Yay! Hi! Oh my God! Thanks for inviting us!" Lilly said through the hug.

"Yeah, we're so happy you're here. Hi, I'm Jungle Jen, but you can call me JJ." JJ said as she offered a hug to a stranger.

"Hi, I'm Sly," Sly said and hugged her back. The three of them walked inside to meet the rest of the crew who were in the kitchen. Waiting for their arrival was Adam, the brothers Strange Guy and Bass Man, and resident SOTU DJ's, Freestyle and Sunrise. This was the Junglist party crew and the people Lilly wanted to be friends with again. Adam had already made himself a prominent family member, leaving Kyle behind with the Kandi Kids, and Ryan out of the way thanks to Lilly's information regarding his connection to Milo, a scene enemy.

Lilly was more at home with the jungle kids than the Kandi Kids. This could be her new crew, the summer party crew to rival all others. This crew was smaller than Shade's 1 Earth, 1 Rave crew, but attracted as many, if not more, partygoers. The jungle crews didn't need to be as large because they had a more minimalistic philosophy with throwing parties. Unlike the Junglists, the Kandi crews put a lot of effort into decorations and services like free water and pancakes, LED lights, banners and neon paints, and Kandi-making stations. Junglists remained much more connected to the music and put little effort into anything else. Less setup meant a crew could sustain itself with nothing more than the resident DJs and sound equipment. The parties were darker, but this was in line with the general feel of the night, the music, and the jungle color uniform.

Inside the kitchen, they all exchanged pleasantries and introduced Sly to the group. Lilly looked at Adam. There was a glow on his face when the two walked in.

"Lilly!" Adam said as he walked toward her. She loved hearing her name by him. Her face gleamed a bright white smile as she prepared for his embrace.

"Hi, Adam." The two collided in a hug to end all hugs. It was so tight, it was so strong, she lost herself in it and took in a deep whiff of his hair. *Fuck. Did they see that? Oh, my God.* Lilly recoiled back from him with flushed cheeks.

"This must be Sly? Hi, I'm Adam," he said to Sly, grabbing her for a hug too, a much less intense one than what he and Lilly had shared.

"Hi, hi. Nice to meet you," Sly responded, and that was all it took as Adam's focus shifted over to her.

Fuck! It's the nipple photo all over again! What should have brought extra attention onto her, Lilly had transformed into yet again a distraction for Adam. It pulled him towards the prettier, skinnier, bustier friend by her side. Shit! She would come up with something to keep the two away from each other, but for now she needed Sly there. It was her ticket back into the group, as she had no other real offerings to gain their reacceptance. Three of the four guys were single. Maybe Sly would be more interested in one of them instead? She would figure something out. For now, it was an annoyance anchoring into her night and distracting her from enjoying the social interaction she had been craving and starved of since being with Ryan.

Sly offered her samples to the group, and they all enjoyed it. It had a clean taste, no cut. The group bonded together over coke and conversation. Lilly, who had only met the brothers during a brief introduction and hadn't seen or spoken to JJ in quite a while, learned more about them and who they were outside the party scene. Strange Guy and Bass Man were both in their 30s and had been partying since they were teenagers. They became DJs as they learned the culture of the scene and understood that the role of DJ meant they could dominate it. Freestyle and Sunrise had a similar story. Also in their 30s, being a DJ also meant they never had to grow up, embodying the true spirit of Peter Pan. To Lilly they were gods, prodigies of the decks who deserved the utmost levels of respect and adoration.

"So, Sly," said Strange Guy, the leader of the crew and final decision maker. "We really appreciate these samples, you got good stuff and we all love good coke!"

"Oh, thanks," Sly responded with grace.

"Listen, I know you're new to the scene and don't really know how it works, but if you wanna get involved, we can help each other out."

"Yeah, okay. How does that work?"

The rest of the group listened with intention, like they had stepped into an important business meeting.

"Okay, so, on your end, you come to our parties, all of them. You don't pay gate, you don't have to worry about any other dealers, and you get access to all our customers, free rein, all night, and obviously you can take numbers to grow your hustle. Our parties happen basically every weekend and we see anywhere from 500-2,000 kids, depending on location. And we never have cops. We keep it super underground."

"Okay, so what's the catch?"

"Well, you have to come to all our parties, you'd be part of the crew, and you have to pay your tax. We don't charge you to come, party, or play, but you have to pay the crew tax for the privilege, which we will accept in coke, after the party is over."

Sly took a moment to think about it. The rest of them focused on her face for any sign of an answer.

"Um, yeah, okay. I mean, I guess I'll have to see how things work out after the first couple parties, but that sounds pretty good. What about security? Do you have protection for me or how does that work?"

"We police our own parties, and Adam is our regulator, so he'll make sure no one tries selling under you. If you come across any trouble, you can come to any of us and we can handle it."

"And all I have to do is give you guys free coke?"

"And pills, you can get pills, right?"

"Oh yea, I do pills too. And whatever else you guys want."

"Good. But if you wanna do this, we have to be able to rely on you. You wanna be official supplier, you have to supply. How many pills can you get at a time?"

"Oh, that's not a problem. I have access to boats."

Lilly's eyes widened. She knew a boat was 1,000 ecstasy pills and filled up an entire gallon size Ziploc bag. She looked over to Adam, who was holding in his cheers. The rest of them squirmed in their seats or used their fingers in a soundless drumroll an inch above the kitchen table. Sly smiled at the acknowledgment and sat up a little straighter, held her shoulders a little higher.

"Well, welcome to the family, Sly. And welcome back, Lilly," Strange Guy said first to Sly and then turned to Lilly and winked. The rest of them all clapped and cheered, business settled.

"Aight! Let's celebrate!" Adam shouted as he grabbed at the plate of cocaine. By the time the night was over, after bonding over copious amounts of free cocaine, and Lilly and Sly now official family members, the plans for the summer season were in full swing. Lilly's plan had gone off without a hitch, except for that annoying insignificant fact that Lilly couldn't take her eyes off of Adam, who couldn't take his eyes off of Sly.

Lilly knew she had to do something about Adam's

potential infatuation with Sly. The best course of action would be to open up to Sly about her genuine feelings for Adam. She had done such a good job, for almost two years, of keeping her feelings for Adam a secret in her silent pursuit of him, but now she needed help, an ally that could steer Adam towards her, the perfect role for a new best friend. Lilly gushed the details to Sly. She talked about how they first met, how they spent an entire semester passing notes to each other in English class, how she had followed him to the smoking section, her various schemes trying to win his affection, everything.

Sly listened as Lilly revealed her belief that Adam was coming around and their relationship kept bringing them closer and closer, despite her almost ruining all her progress when she chose Ryan over him. She was so close to winning him. All she needed was a little help from a friend to push it over the top and finish the pull of Adam into her. Sly, wanting to be a good friend, listened with open ears and a warm heart. She would help Lilly in any way she could and promised to not hook up with Adam. She promised also that she would keep quiet about the fact that Lilly was in love with him. This eased Lilly's worries as she trusted Sly. Confident in her vulnerability, it brought the two of them even closer together as friends, now having a secret to share.

FOURTEEN

Coke Doctor

T he party season was in full swing, and Lilly and Sly were at its epicenter. Lilly, Sly, and Adam were in attendance at every party, sometimes hitting several a night across all surrounding cities, deserts, and forests, Adam's Rav4 taking them as far as it could manage across the terrain. Sly rose as official dealer amongst not only Strange Guy's parties, as they had invited her to be that one FriYay, but also among Shade's parties as Lilly could vouch for her there too. This gave Sly exclusive access to the drug market at the parties and blocked all other dealers from treading in her territory. Sly went from holding twenty pills of ecstasy to over 1,000 and from one to two ounces of cocaine to over a kilo in a few short weeks. Weed, shrooms, ketamine, and acid followed in her menu of party favors and in all of them the demand increased as the season wore on and she became the only trusted source at the rave.

. . .

DURING THE NON-PARTY DAYS, Lilly and Sly spent almost every waking minute together. Lilly took advantage of Sly's generous tax payments that flowed over into the weekdays. She soon dropped out of school and quit her job. There wasn't enough time in the day to run around with Sly, sniff coke, party, and work, and go to school. She had to make a choice, and the options were clear. Adam continued school and work, but as he worked at his parent's hotels, work stopped being a priority and he often made excuses to get out of a shift. The three of them became the new crew outside of their involvement with the weekend party crew. The days became routine, Adam attended school and Lilly spent the day with Sly selling drugs and smoking cigarettes until Adam finished school, when the three of them would meet up and sniff coke.

"Hey, Adam can't meet up today, wanna go back to my place?" Lilly said to Sly after they delivered their final sack for the day.

"Can we invite some people over?"

"Yeah, sure, as long as they don't mind chillin' in the studio." And off to Lilly's they went. The girls were exhausted from selling all day and ready to relax, not take any phone calls, and unwind with a few lines of their favorite white powder. It was after five o'clock when they arrived and Sly pulled out a plastic sandwich bag full of white cocaine rocks mixed with powder. No side eyes or second glances. Pulling out a bag full of cocaine was as commonplace as pulling a bag of bread out of the cupboard during lunch time.

"Hey, hand me that scale, I wanna weight this before we break into it," Sly asked while pointing to a scale sitting on Lilly's dresser. Lilly complied, and Sly sat the bag on top of it. "Exactly an ounce. Cool."

"Well, I don't think we'll need all that for just the two of us, 28 grams is kinda steep, even for us," Lilly said.

"Yeah, but Eric and Bobby hit me up and they might wanna come hang out for a bit."

"Oh, yeah, cool."

The girls didn't wait for their guests to arrive before breaking into the bag. They racked their lines and sniffed them as soon as they locked the door behind them. The conversation circled around nothing, as is common within the cocaine experience. The early evening sun had long gone before their first guest arrived, Eric.

"Ladies, ladies, what's up?" he said as he entered the apartment, arms stretched out in open greeting.

"Hi!" Sly said, a smile ear to ear. Her crush's best friend had arrived. "Where's Bobby?" she said, asking about the whereabouts of the person she was interested in.

"Oh, he's on his way, he'll be here any minute." Greetings exchanged; they didn't wait. They got right back to what they were doing and what the boys were looking forward to, too. It wasn't until a few more lines in that Bobby arrived. Sly gravitated towards him and embraced him. Inhibitions lowered by the catalyst, she clung to him hard and giggled at his every word. Bobby flirted back, and sniffed up all the free lies she was offering.

"Hey sexy, you wanna try?" Sly said to Bobby as she sat on his lap.

"Hell yeah, I wanna try, you gonna hook me up?" he said back with a grin on his face and his hand on her thigh.

After gifting several lines, Sly showed off her sack and danced around the room with it. The boys oohed and awed and asked for more freebees. Lilly sat back, letting Sly revel in the attention, and stayed focused on preparing the lines for all of them. Lilly saw that Sly was enjoying her status as a sanctioned dealer, and Lilly benefited from it too.

It became quite obvious that these boys, while they were regular customers of Sly, did not indulge all that often. The boys could not match the rate at which the girls were sniffing. Within an hour, Eric had to stop. He was shaking with eyes that almost popped right out of his head. His skin flushed, and he tapped his chest in a repetitive motion, explaining out loud (no one was asking) that if he didn't, his heart might stop. The girls giggled at him. He paced around in a tiny circle inside that little studio, stopping only to peak out the blinds for suspicious activity. Through her giggles, Lilly mocked him that the only suspicious activity was happening right here in this room. Eric decided he would make his escape. He left without saying goodbye and sped off down the alleyway.

"Whoa, what's your friend's problem?" Lilly said to Bobby.

"Don't be mean, he's just yakked out. He'll be fine," Sly said, not wanting to offend her crush or scare him off as well. Bobby also looked a little shaky, but held it together for the time being. "Well, now that he's gone we can have some real fun!" Sly slinked over to Bobby and climbed up on top of him, straddling his waist and dangling the now smaller coke sack off the tip of her finger.

"Oh, I'm good for a minute. My heart is, like, pounding." Bobby's face showed a lack of confidence in himself to handle much more.

"Oh, come on, you guys have been here for what? An hour? We started like three hours before you guys even got here. Don't be a pussy," Lilly said, very matter-of-factly. She knew Sly was having a good time with him and didn't want some lame ass dude ruining their night.

"Aw, I don't know…" Bobby trailed off.

"Please! Please! We're having so much fun with you!" Sly begged in a puppy dog voice. He didn't respond with words but motioned his agreement, which prompted Sly to pour out more cocaine.

It was three am. Hours had passed and Bobby was now the one pacing around, peeking out the windows, acting paranoid and taking big, deep breaths in. He reasoned that taking deep breaths made it easier to breathe, that his throat was closing up and he couldn't take in oxygen otherwise. The girls more or less ignored this behavior. At this stage in the night, they we no longer flirting or giggling, just sniffing.

"Time for birthday lines!" Sly exclaimed. "Bobby, how old are you?"

"What?" Bobby responded, not stopping his pacing.

"How old are you?" Lilly repeated in a more harsh voice than Sly had. "She wants to know how old you are to make you a birthday line, hurry." Lilly didn't like how he was acting. He was moving around too much and making it uncomfortable for her. Sly's happy attitude suggested she remained unaware and in awe of him.

"Huh? Oh, uh, 22, I'm 22, 22."

"Cool. I love writing two's!" Sly said expressing her overt excitement as she sat down and prepared a line of coke for Bobby shaped like the number 22. "Here you go!"

Bobby, without even considering the amount of cocaine sitting before him, leaned down towards the table and sniffed. To Lilly's surprise, he had taken it all in one shot. He rose to take a huge breath before collapsing on the floor.

"Bobby? Bobby!" Lilly shouted, as if shouting at him would help him hear her.

Sly screamed. Lilly rushed to his body. He was clammy and cold, his face already white as his circulation failed. She slapped him and shook him with vigor. There was no response. She tried prying open his eyelids and found cloudy, dilated pupils that sent a chill through her body.

"Oh my god, what do we do? What do we do?" Sly said, her first instinct to bend over and take another line.

"Okay, calm down, okay, look, we're gonna get him up and put him in the car. We're gonna go to JJ's house, she'll know what to do."

"Okay, okay," Sly said as she let out a deep breath. "Here, take a line real quick."

"Oh yeah, good idea." Lilly sniffed. "Okay, let's go."

The girls grunted and grimaced as they heaved his large, cold body into the back of Lilly's car. She didn't check his pulse; she didn't bother listening for his heart rate. If she didn't confirm what she already knew, it didn't have to be real and she could instead burden her friend JJ with the gore.

They arrived at JJ's house to the sound of her angry barking dogs. The lights were off, but they turned on and she opened the door for them.

"Hey, guys? What's up?" JJ said, wiping her groggy eyes.

"We need help. Fuck. Let us in," Lilly said as she and Sly lugged in the heavy, 22-year-old body.

"What the fuck?! Lilly, I'm not a fucking coke doctor!" JJ shouted.

"He just collapsed. We don't know what to do. Can you help us?!" Sly said while Lilly reexamined him and slapped him a few more times.

"Fuck! Did you check his pulse?" JJ said.

"No, no, I'm not doing that," Lilly said.

"Why the fuck not? Check his pulse!"

"No, he's fine, he's just… no way, that makes it real."

"Well, if he's really dead, you better get him the fuck out of my house!"

"He's not dead, chill out! This shit happens all the time," Lilly announced to the room while flailing her arms and pacing the foyer, trying to assure herself. Sly trembled in place and chewed on the nubs of her nails.

"God damn it, Lilly… Oh, try splashing water in his face!" JJ's eyes widened and a faint smile came to her face, like she was pleased at her own genius.

"Oh! That's a good one, we didn't try that." Lilly raced off to the kitchen. She came rushing back to where his body lay and dumped the full glass on his face. All at once the body gasped for air as if it hadn't ever savored it before. His eyes jolted open, and he shivered in place.

"Bobby!" Sly yelled, as she laid her body on top of him and embraced him.

"Oh, for fuck's sake!" JJ exclaimed in pure relief.

Lilly wanted to speak, but the words wouldn't come. It was like she was still processing the entire situation and what the consequences could have meant if they hadn't saved him.

"What the fuck happened? Where am I? I'm fucking cold," Bobby drawled through chattering teeth.

"You're okay, it's okay, baby, you're okay," Sly said in a soft voice. An energy of relief spread throughout the room.

"Alright, you guys good now?" JJ said, not questioning or criticizing why they had come to her in the first place, only relieved that the ordeal was now over.

"Yeah, we're good. Thanks, JJ. You're the best," Lilly said as she threw her head back and placed her hands on her hips, in the same way a spent athlete does after a sprint.

"Oh my god, thanks so much, JJ, you're so cool! Here, you can have the rest of our sack. You're a badass," Sly said to JJ as she helped herself off of Bobby and pulled a sack out of her jeans.

"Shit, that's hardly anything! You guys owe me more than that after this shit!" JJ joked and laughed, trying to lighten the mood.

"Oh fuck, Sly! Are you serious? Is that the rest of the sack?" Lilly said, pointing to JJ holding a dusted sandwich bag but addressing Sly.

"Yeah, there's like half a gram left. I know it's not much. Sorry, I'll hook you up more next time for sure. Promise. Just, thank you, so much!"

Lilly's mind reeled at the fact that they almost killed a man that night, and that they tore through almost an entire ounce of cocaine by themselves and were still standing. *What was Adam going to think?* But she couldn't let that in her head right now. She had to get Bobby the fuck away from them before he died again.

All of them had a red face and bloodshot eyes, watery full tears streamed down their cheeks. Lilly's nose went from numb, to swollen, to shut. Breathing through her mouth became paramount. Her throat was full of dripping mucus that tasted like chemicals and as the night ended, it closed up too. The only way to breathe became through cough, forcing air in and out. The thuds of her heart in the chest were hard and slow and her body trembled with an electricity that changed from feeling amazing to unpleasant mini shocks all over that wouldn't stop. By the time they reached home and sent Bobby away, her mind was racing, and she couldn't relax or turn down, despite how tired and worn out she was. Everything in her body and mind screamed "go to sleep" but neither could do it. It was an aftermath Lilly loathed, yet not enough to make her stop.

FIFTEEN

One Drunken Night

As the summer wore on, the parties and hotel after parties all faded into one another, separated only by brief moments of sobriety. One party stuck out, because it was the one when Adam became vulnerable with Lilly and told her something she had been waiting to hear for a long time.

"Lilly!" She heard Adam's voice call out to her over the thumping bass flowing from the wall of speakers she stood in front of. Her pills in full peak, it was time for the two of them to disappear for their special rendezvous. She turned around, searched the dance floor for the source of his voice. "Over here!" She found him a few feet behind her, waving his hands above his head, seeking her attention. She smiled and pushed her way through the crowd of dancers to meet him.

"Hi, Adam!" She embraced him in a heavy hug.

"Hi!" His voice pitched up. "Come poke with me?" She nodded as the two of them walked away from the floor and found themselves under star cover of the desert night.

"Oh my God, I love this!" Lilly said, looking up as

Adam packed pieces of chronic bud in the bowl of a glass pipe.

"Yeah, pretty cool." He handed her the pipe. "So, I wanted to tell you something. It just happened and I'm pretty broken up about it. You're my best friend and I thought I should tell you." *Best friend? Oh my God, he's in love with me!* Lilly focused on his face, waiting for the words to come. "Well, me and my girlfriend broke up. She said the long-distance thing was too hard, and I agreed."

"Oh, gosh! I'm so sorry, Adam." Lilly offered forced condolences, but inside she was screaming in delight. "Is there anything I can do? Are you okay?"

"Yeah, yeah, I'm fine. It's better this way. We've been growing apart for a long time and we're different people now."

Lilly pouted her lips at him and leaned in to rest her head on his shoulder. He responded by giving her a half hug and a sweet chuckle.

"Well, if you think of anything…" Lilly remained calm on the outside, her responses sympathetic.

"Oh, yeah, thanks. I'm glad I have you. You're really special to me, Lilly. Thanks for always being there."

"Of course! Always," Lilly said with a deep smile as she pulled back from the hug to stare into his eyes. *He's gonna kiss me, he's gonna kiss me!* Lilly pursed her lips and leaned forward, readying herself.

"Uh, well, thanks for the poke session. Come on, I'll walk you back to the party."

Lilly's eyes jolted. She straightened up and took a step back.

"Okay, uh, yeah!" she said without looking into his eyes but holding her head down and kicking her foot at the desert sand beneath her.

This opened up a door for them, though. Both now

single and always high, Lilly and Adam became closer. They cuddled and hugged at parties, under the guise of intoxication, concealing their true motivations—or so Lilly came to conclude. But he had to have feelings for her. *This couldn't just be about ecstasy, could it?* Lilly's mind reeled with the back and forth—did he, didn't he? Would he, could he? Her only refuge was pouring her thoughts out to Sly, who listened without complaining most of the time. Cocaine fueled conversations between the two of them always revolved around Adam and how much Lilly pined after him. It was no surprise to Lilly when the day came that Sly told Lilly to stop talking so much about him. She was tired of it, and all Lilly did was talk in circles.

"So you know last weekend when Adam pulled me aside on the dance floor just to give me a hug? Wasn't that crazy?" Lilly said.

The night was young, and the girls had only begun the evening's coke binge.

"Lilly, oh my God… Okay, I'm not in the mood to listen to this all night," Sly said, a tone of annoyance in her voice.

"What? What did I do?" Lilly asked, not ready to have this conversation but unable to avoid it.

"All you do is talk about Adam! Like every time! I wanna be there for you and I support you, but you just talk and talk and talk and never do anything about it. Why don't you do something already? The next time you talk about Adam, it better be because you guys hooked up or something 'cause I'm over this." Before allowing Lilly to offer a rebuttal, Sly said that if Lilly couldn't stop talking about Adam all the time, she would cut off her coke supply because it was the coke that made her talk so much. That was enough to shut Lilly up.

She flashed back to the fallout of The Sub Shop Hoes

and how they all cut themselves from her over this exact subject. She didn't want to go through that again, not with a friend who supplied her addiction. The threat of her drugs being taken away scared the word Adam right out of her vocabulary. The conversation shifted, and they enjoyed the night anyway, Lilly now put in her place and given a task. Sly was right, it was time for her to do something about it. Going into the third year of her infatuation with him, she had to act now, or shut up.

IT WAS A THURSDAY. Sly wasn't feeling well and wanted to stay in for the evening, leaving Lilly and Adam to themselves. This was not unusual. They spent plenty of time alone together at parties or at the smoking section before Lilly dropped her classes. To waste the night, they would visit a mutual friend's house where they could smoke weed and drink beers.

Steve and Crazy Joe were a platonic couple of men they had met at the local coffee shop who had become customers of Sly's. The men were closer than brothers. They fought with each other, wrestled with their shirts off, shaved each other's heads in their bathroom, and worked together in construction. This Thursday night did not differ from any other night. The evening began with innocence as the four of them smoked and drank beers, played video games, and listened to Crazy Joe ramble on about nothing.

"Hey, Lilly," said Crazy Joe. As the beers went back, the group became loose and Joe, only out of prison a few short months and not having smelled a woman much longer, looked at her with slanted eyes and a devilish grin. "You and I should hang out more often, ya know? I can never get you away from this guy, though." He gestured towards Adam, who laughed along at the joke.

"Oh... uh, yea, I guess I could do that sometime. I'm just always busy with Sly, I don't mean anything by it." Lilly ignored his forwardness. Adam had stopped laughing and watched Lilly and Joe interact. Adam's shoulders tensed as Joe moved in closer to her. Lilly tried a subtle escape as she sat further back in her chair and looked towards Adam with wide, screaming eyes.

"Alright, alright, calm down, dude." Adam spoke up as he stood, laughed, and shoved Joe back in his chair, breaking his sightline to Lilly.

Joe shot a stare at Adam, like an instinct to fight surged into his bloodstream, but he caught himself and relaxed into a playful response. "What? I'm just fuckin' around, man."

Lilly stayed silent and swallowed the rest of her beer.

"A'ight, Lilly, you done with your beer?" Adam gestured towards her. She nodded. "Cool man, so, we're gonna take off. I'm too drunk and I gotta get home before my mom calls."

"Oh, you're already taking off? Well, it's still early, Lilly you can stay and party with us and crash on the bed. I'll take the floor," Joe said to Lilly with those same slant eyes.

"Uh..." Lilly said before Adam cut her off.

"No, no, no, she's not staying. I gotta take her home," Adam said while laughing. "Thanks, man, we'll see you guys later. Come on." Lilly and Adam said their goodbyes in half hugs and took a swift exit.

They were both drunk, too drunk for Adam to be driving, but that was never an obstacle for him, and Lilly always followed his lead. At the car, Adam pulled on Lilly's hand before letting her walk around to the passenger side door. "Let me get that for you," Adam said as he walked around with her and opened the door. *What in the world was happening?* He never opened the car door for her, before. He must have been a whole new level of drunk. The car ride back to Lilly's house was exhilarating. There was a sexual tension so thick that it almost scented the surrounding air. They exchanged no words, but Lilly's heart raced and an electric warmth traveled down from her chest to her inner thighs. Too much alcohol had made her brave. Tonight would be the night. She sat in the car in silence, imagining all the things that Adam might do to her when they arrived back at her house. It was a quick ride, and she snapped back into reality when they pulled up to her garage, the front door of her converted studio apartment.

"I think I'm too drunk to drive all the way home, can I come in?" Adam asked in a slurred speech that wasn't there when they were saying goodbye to Crazy Joe and Steve.

"Yeah, come on." Lilly had a grin on her face so wide, she looked insane.

The two walked into her apartment. It was the first time the two of them had been there together, alone, this late at night, and as intoxicated as they were. Adam tripped over an extension cord and the two of them laughed and giggled. The tension was still there, but Lilly was uncertain if she was the only one feeling it or not. Adam was his normal self, nothing out of the ordinary, just a little more drunk. Was she reading too much into the car door thing? She had let her imagination get away from her and reasoned with herself that she needed to calm down.

"I'm tired!" Adam yelled. "Come sleep with me." He said this with a giggle. Should she interpret it as flirtatious? No, she stopped the thought when he laughed it off as innocent.

"Oh my God, you're so drunk, shut up," Lilly replied,

not knowing any other way to respond. She followed Adam over to the bed and they both hopped up into it. As they leapt, Adam, being as drunk as he was, slipped, causing them to knock heads at the top. They both fell onto the bed in a hysterical fit of laughter and rubbed their sore spots as they rolled back and forth. This was a different side of Adam that Lilly hadn't seen before. He was playful and silly, sweet and fun. She was used to his hardened demeanor, but he softened when high on intense love drugs like ecstasy. She enjoyed seeing him in this new light and let her guard down again as she let the warmth build up again in her chest.

They got under the covers to cuddle. This was familiar and normal for them, as they had practiced several times while high at parties in various cuddle puddles. Never had it been under the covers of her bed, but being intoxicated made it ordinary. As they held each other, they rubbed their hands down each other's backs and shoulders. Petting became more intense as Adam incorporated light squeezes. Lilly held her head tilted down to rest on his chest, his head above the top of hers. *What would happen if I tilt my head up? Our lips would face each other, then what?*

Self-doubt gave her pause, but the moment was too perfect. The petting was heavy, and that electricity over-flowed from her thighs into her panties. With reserve she tilted her head up, only an inch at first, then another. Until her head faced fully up, and with her eyes still closed, his lips meet hers and grasped on hard and tight. A breath of release let itself out of her throat in a light moan as the tension exploded into a manic episode of tangled tongues and lips. Their hands grabbed at each other as they tried to pull each other closer in with a heaviness that felt almost desperate. Adam ripped at her clothes and Lilly tore through his belt. Fire poured out of her as the intensity grew to match the heat between them.

It all happened so fast and the passion was so forceful, like they had both been saving a pent-up energy for one another, that they abused each other in the process of its release. Lilly sucked on Adam's neck hard enough to leave bruising, her territory now marked, and Adam smacked her ass long and strong enough to leave behind welts in a shape that outlined his hand. They grinded their hips on each other as if they had an itch deep enough inside themselves, no amount of surface friction could touch it. Adam inserted himself into her, and she counted three thrusts before he let out the heavy grunts that completed his climax. It was everything she had been waiting for and more than she could have dreamed of. Three years had culminated in the ultimate sexual experience and she now had him right where she wanted him. It had happened; it had finally happened. Her challenge met, and Adam was now hers. She fell asleep in his arms with this thought, in the bed they had made of pure bliss.

SIXTEEN

Secret

_____

Lilly rose the next morning, glowing inside the tender embrace of Adam, his naked body draped around her, a verification that she hadn't dreamt it. She stirred him to rise. It was late, and he had class that day.

"Morning!" she whispered into his ear. He didn't much respond, but groaned as he re-snuggled himself next to her under the covers. "Oh my God, dude," she said, giggling, "you have class today, get up."

The next most important thing to Lilly in that moment, besides reveling in the aftermath, was getting over to Sly's house to tell her what happened. Lilly had kept her end of the bargain and hadn't mentioned a word about Adam to Sly since she was told to shut up about it, but now that something happened, that social contract was void. Adam stretched and opened his eyes, looking up at Lilly who was lying on her side with her head propped up on a wrist and elbow, staring straight down at him.

"Listen, Lil" he said in a serious tone. "What happened last night, you can't tell anyone."

"What? Why?" Why did this have to be? The sex changed nothing about their relationship, and she demanded an explanation.

"Just because I said so. We're friends, I don't want this to change anything between us." As the words left his lips, Lilly's heart broke into pieces and fell into the crumpled sheets. He must have read her face because he laughed at her and tried to offer reassurance. "Look, it's fine, I'm glad it happened, it was fun, I've been wanting this to happen for a long time and I think you're a super cool chick. Let's just keep it on the DL for now."

Lilly nodded and not having anything else to say got up to take a shower. She thought about was whether she was going to disobey his order and tell Sly. Back and forth her mind went, twisting up thoughts and tumbling down and around on itself. She wanted to obey, because she wanted to stay in his favor and secure her opportunity to allow this relationship to develop. This had taken so long, and she had worked so hard for this. But then again, Sly was her best friend and would be so proud of her for making it happen. She was going to disobey Adam because she needed someone else to hear her story. Sly was the only one who knew the depths of her obsession with him. No, she couldn't, she had to stay loyal; he was the most important thing in all of this. Without loyalty to him, everything would end. She stayed underneath the heat of the water stream to calm her beating heart.

"Lil?" Adam yelled from outside the bathroom door. It was almost like he knew something was wrong or that this caused her an internal struggle.

"Yeah?" Lilly answered back.

"I guess you can tell Sly."

No words ever spoken had brought her such relief. She had his blessing; the weight lifted off her as she let out a sigh that almost stole her consciousness underneath the steam.

"Oh my God, thank you!" she exclaimed with enthusiasm. "I need someone to talk to about this, you don't understand."

"I know, I get it. She's your best friend, and she's trustworthy. But that's it! No telling JJ or anyone from the crew, got it!"

"Yeah, yeah, I promise, I promise." Lilly repeated herself to cement not only for him, she would keep her word, but to remind herself of it.

"Okay, I have to go to class, I'll call you after and you can come meet up with me to poke."

"Okay, bye!" Lilly said as he left. Lilly jumped up and down a few times and stomped her feet while letting out a muffled, excited scream. She still could only half believe what had happened, and she couldn't wait to call Sly. Talking about it with her would make it real. Lilly half-rinsed her hair out and had soap still on her ears when she turned off the shower and grabbed her phone.

"Hello?" Sly said as she answered the phone.

"Dude!" Lilly replied, still dripping wet and half-soaped. "You're not going to believe what happened last night."

"What?"

"Me and Adam had sex!"

"Ahhhhhhhhhhhhhh!" Sly screamed and squealed into the phone, Lilly responded in kind, both girls jumping up and down in their subsequent homes, apart from each other but together in spirit.

"Oh my God, shut up! Are you lying? You did not!" Sly shrieked.

"I did! I swear, I did!" Lilly squealed. Lilly explained every detail, down to the girth of his penis and the sound he made when it released; she left not a single element undiscussed. The girls giggled back and forth like school children whispering about a playground crush. At the end of the conversation, Lilly and Sly made plans to hang out and sell drugs for the few hours before Adam got out of class and the three of them all went over to JJ's for FriYay. Tonight was a big one as they were planning the upcoming party, Visualize III, the third installment of SOTU's roster of annual flagship events. Visualize was the largest and the one to close out the summer. Anyone who had even the slightest connection to the underground rave scene would be there. This was the party to end the summer before the kids were all forced into the refuge of the winter warehouses. There would be lots to talk about, and Lilly needed to get all her "Adam" talk out now, before showing up, because at JJ's, it would be back to business as usual.

Less than two hours after Lilly and Adam separated, her phone rang and his name popped up on the caller ID. Lilly bounced up and down and shoved the phone in Sly's face to show her who was calling. Sly laughed and nodded, encouraging her to step away to take the call. "Hello?" Lilly answered, as cool and collected as she could pretend to be.

"Hey. What are you doing?"

"Oh nothing, just slangin' with Sly. Trying to fill some orders so we can be free tonight for FriYay."

"Okay, cool. I was gonna tell you to meet up with me to poke, but you guys are busy. Finish up and meet me at five at your place and we'll all drive together."

"Okay, see you later," Lilly said as she hung up the phone and walked back over to Sly, standing outside the driver side window of a customer driving through to pick up a sack.

Sly and Lilly had a system for delivering drugs to

customers. Sly lived on a corner house with a side street that ended in a cul-de-sac. The side street was not visible from the house, and only a few steps walk outside from the front door. The calls rolled in all day long. Sly took orders while Lilly weighed, packaged, and sealed the baggies. Sly told the customer to park on the side street and line up behind the other cars. There were always other cars, but none of them belonged on the street, they were other customers waiting for their delivery. Sly put the sacks in her pockets. Her left pocket was for half-gram sacks, the right was for teeners, the back left was for single grams, and the back right was for 8-balls. She had a separate purse for pills, acid, mushrooms, and weed. These orders were less likely to occur during the week, but it being Friday, they would go fast today, kids stocking up for the weekend.

The girls walked outside and make the rounds to each car, Lilly walking ahead to collect money while Sly followed with delivery. They giggled to each other the whole time. As the line of cars grew, so did the caress to their egos. Today was a busy day and Lilly couldn't break away to go smoke with Adam, no matter how much she wanted to. There were too many orders to fill, and Lilly had to help Sly keep up with her demand. More coke sold meant more free coke for Lilly on the backend.

The girls finished the day's orders, ran around, made a few deliveries in town and met Adam back at Lilly's house. Sly greeted Adam with a chuckle as if to say, "I know what you two did last night." Adam laughed back as if to say, "Yeah, yeah, I know you know." Lilly greeted Adam, expecting it to be a romantic encounter, but it wasn't. Adam hugged Lilly the same way he always did, but this time added a look aimed dead in her eye, a reminder of the secret she promised to keep. There wouldn't be any flirting or touching each other while amongst their friends.

The seriousness of it weighed on her shoulders like a sack of rocks, its heaviness pulling the smile right from her face. The giggling stopped.

In the car, they talked about the day, how many drugs they sold, or how much they sniffed in-between sales, normal shop-talk, the events of the night before kept locked up and hidden away in the back of Lilly's mind. When they arrived at JJ's, the rest of the crew was already in attendance. JJ the host, Strange Guy, Bass Man, Freestyle and the brothers from Shade's crew, Stan and James. The brothers became a big part of the party scene and also spent time with the Junglist crew, despite having roots in the Kandi crew. They were both gone for several weeks to work on a pot farm up north and had returned in time to help with Visualize.

"Hey! You guys are back!" Lilly greeted Stan and James.

"Yeah, we wrapped up and wanted to make it back for the party," Stan said.

"Well cool, we can smoke now." Lilly remembered the times before, when Lilly, Adam, Ryan, and Kyle had spent endless hours with Stan and James at their home, smoking pot before or after classes.

As the night wore on, Lilly became preoccupied with Adam and caught herself watching him move about the kitchen as he paced back and forth, rambling and exciting himself with ideas. She could tell that the furthest thing from his mind was her, while he was the closest thing to hers. It was hard to watch once she was high. All she wanted was to be close to him, talk to him, be important to him, but it was as if he was putting an extra space in between them to overcompensate for the secret they were now guarding. It was an act, and she wanted to play along, but it hurt her heart still that, after all this time, she couldn't have him the way she wanted him. He told her it was because he didn't want to disrupt the friend group, but the true reason would soon become clear.

Over the next several weeks, Adam and Lilly spent more and more time together, even taking time for themselves away from Sly. It was easy to do. With the increased pressure of being a more prominent dealer, Sly often needed alone time and would ignore her phone, instead leaving Lilly to take care of customers so she could have the night off.

"Sly left me her box tonight, so it's just us taking care of shit." Lilly told Adam when he arrived at the studio after a long day at the hotel. Her box was a fireproof lockbox that held her inventory, a scale, baggies, and cash. Lilly, being Sly's most trusted companion, held the key.

"Tight! Let's do it."

"No, Adam, we can't just sniff coke all night. This is Sly's and I'm working."

"Oh, come on, she's gonna expect you to do some of it! Open the box."

"No! Adam, she's my best friend, I'm not just gonna betray her like that. She's paying me to do this. She gave me $50, I have to keep everything else straight."

"Perfect, so use the $50 to buy two grams. We'll just hang out here the two of us and I'll help you work."

"Two grams? No way, man, that's not the price."

"Yes! For you it is, you have full access! Come on, open the box, baby…" Adam walked over to her with pouty lips and half-closed eyes. He put his hands around her waist and pulled her into him. Lilly lost herself as her face and chest brightened in rouge.

"Okay, but I'm only getting one gram for $40. And you have to stay and help."

"Okay, yes, of course. I'm here for you. Open the box."

The box opened and their night began. One gram turned into more, but only because Adam had a way of convincing her it would be fine. His sweet nothings in her ear softening her rules of the box. The night wore on.

"Lil," Adam said as he pulled his head up from the glass top of her dresser. "You know you're really special to me."

"Yeah, I know. You're special to me too, Adam."

"No, like, you're really special to me. You don't understand."

"Of course I do, you're my best friend."

"No!" His voice turned stern. "You're more than special. Lilly, we've been doing this dance for a long time. I need you to know how I really feel."

"Okay, then tell me." Lilly remained calm, she could feel it coming, she had waited for this for so long, staying calm was paramount, she didn't want to scare the words back into him.

"Lil, I'm trying to tell you that I love you."

"I love you too, Adam." The release of the words washed over her with a coolness she had been craving like lemonade at a pool party. She had him. Now it was real, and it would be forever. Her entire body tingled as he ran his fingertip across the bottom of her chin and pulled her in for a kiss.

It was these times Lilly longed for, because in these private moments alone, Adam paid attention to her, doted on her, made her feel special. She thirsted for these times because in between, in the view of their friends, he was an almost stranger. Their private relationship was wildly sexual. Adam maintained that they needed to keep it private without ever justifying his reasoning, and Lilly didn't question it. She was lucky to even have him. Alone, Adam told her all the sweet nothings any girl could dream of hearing but made sure she knew they were still just friends, with benefits. These messages were confusing and contradictory but acted as motivation that helped to convince her that keeping the secret was the right thing to do, because if she did, someday he would reward her with real acknowledgement. This he never told her or promised her, but in her mind, she built it into the fantasy.

THE PARTY TO end the summer was among them. Adam in his position of power as regulator, JJ supervising and running gate, Lilly and Sly ran around as dealers, Stan and James worked security, and the rest of the crew DJed. Over 1,000 ravers that showed up to the forest venue. With so many partygoers running around, half of them young girls in lingerie, it was no wonder what happened next. Walking through the night forest alone, from one stage to another, Lilly recognized Adam's voice off in the distance and found his shadow in the darkness. He pressed his body up against what could have only been a sexy young girl. She was playing with him, pretending like she didn't want him to be doing the things he was doing to her, but it was a game of cat and mouse. She giggled for him to stop, only to pull him in closer until the two shadows kissed, groped, and fondled each other. Lilly's mouth fell agape as she watched the shadows disappear into a tent and zip shut the fabric entrance.

It broke her heart, devastated her, obliterated the high from the pills she took hours earlier. She looked for Sly; she was the only one who could help her now. But Sly was nowhere, which wasn't unusual as she had a habit of disappearing when her pills kicked in. Lilly was keener on finding her way to the dance floor while Sly enjoyed finding a nice quiet place to take a nap. Lilly spent the rest of the party wandering alone through the forest, crying to herself because she had no right to confront him outright. To everyone else, they were nothing more than friends.

The dawn came and revealed that the party had shrunk, leaving only the crew, hired DJs, and the few random partygoers who refused to leave. Sly was still tucked away in hiding. Lilly spent time with JJ, but couldn't tell her why her face had dried tears caked in forest dust. Adam emerged from his hiding spot and approached JJ and Lilly with a cheerful demeanor, a grin on his face like he'd just had the best night of his life. Lilly kept her eyes averted and tried not to answer Adam's questions.

"What's wrong? You okay?" he asked like a concerned friend.

Lilly nodded, and turned to walk away, not knowing where she was going. Adam waited until she was a few steps away and not in view of anyone else before going after her. He caught up with her behind a group of trees and yelled at her to stop. "Hey!" he screamed with anger in his voice. "What are you doing, what's your problem?"

"I saw you get in that tent last night with that girl," Lilly said, choking back tears.

"Oh, my god! That's what you're upset about?" Adam laughed at her as if her suggestion that he was doing anything wrong was ridiculous. "Dude! We're just friends, you can't get upset about things like that. Those girls are just for fun, they mean nothing. You're the one I come home with, and you're the one I love. Let me do what I want to do, otherwise we're not gonna be able to be friends anymore, you understand."

"What? So it's okay for you to just go off and hook up with other girls? Fine, I guess I'll just hook up with other guys."

"NO!" Adam scolded. "It doesn't work like that. I do

what I want to do, and you don't. You stay and wait patiently for me and I will always come back to you. And we continue not telling anyone about it because that's the way it has to be, and you can't get upset. You just can't."

"But why?"

"Lilly, you don't question me. I'm smarter and I know what's best for you. Everything I do is for you, even when it doesn't seem like it."

"Adam…"

"NO! That's it." And that was it. He walked off and let her cry alone to herself behind the trees. She took a moment to compose herself before emerging. When she did, Sly was waking up from her nap. She sensed something was wrong and Lilly told her everything that had happened, Adam's reaction, and the new rule he had forced on her.

"Lilly," Sly said in a consoling voice as she held Lilly's shoulders. "You have to leave him. He's an ass. He doesn't deserve you."

"Sly, you don't understand. Look at me!" Lilly cried through her response. "No one will ever want me. It's not as easy for me as it is for you. I can't just go and find any random guy to like me. This is what I get, and this is just how it is."

"No, you're wrong. Plenty of guys like you. You're kidding yourself."

"No, no, no. Listen, this took me three years! Okay? Three years I've been working on this. And I've changed everything. I don't even recognize myself anymore. I mean, look at me! I'm a fucking cokehead junkie, covered in dirt! I'm still fat, no one else wants me."

"Lilly…" Sly's eyes became wet as she listened to Lilly speak.

"No, and you know what? He loves me, he does. He

tells me he does. It doesn't mean anything with these other girls. He's right? He deserves to have some attention from these hot sexy girls 'cause it's something I'll never be able to give him. So, this is just it. It's how it is, and it's my own fault for not being enough for him."

Sly turned her head to the ground, using the palms of her hands to wipe the tears away as they seeped out. The heat in Lilly's voice dissipated. "Come on, let's go back to the party. Happy faces, okay?" Sly nodded, and the girls stepped off to re-join the morning's leftover party crew.

SEVENTEEN

Secret's Out

Months passed. Adam and Lilly fell into a routine that protected their secret bubble, but friends were asking questions.

"Hello?" Adam answered the phone, Stan on the other end.

"Hey man, I just got a big shipment in if you're interested? Come smoke with me."

"Yeah, I will, later. I'm at Lilly's right now."

"At Lilly's? Are you guys fucking?" Stan asked, no tone of sensitivity in his voice.

"No!" Adam exclaimed while laughing away his nervousness. "She's helping me study, these classes I'm in are crazy," was the complete nonsense excuse he used. It was winter break and that meant the end of the last class with new classes to start after the holiday, there were no classes to study for, and Adam was always more interested in smoking weed than getting a leg up on studying for an upcoming class, that hadn't even begun yet. And Lilly, who was no longer enrolled at the college, had no business sticking her head in a book.

"Right, studying is important and over break would be the perfect time to do that. Well, whatever, both you fuckers come smoke then."

Adam's explanation, not by any means a save, was more of a warning call that their friends were onto them. Lilly and Adam couldn't keep their secret much longer if they were to continue on like this. Good news for Lilly, who was wearing thin of keeping her forbidden relationship contained, but bad news for Adam, who wanted to continue eating his cake. The pair stayed in denial, ignoring the vague comments and long glances coming in their direction. Friends, despite growing suspicions, stayed away from the subject, and Lilly and Adam didn't offer any information.

It was February, and Sly announced her plan to throw a Valentine's Day party to mark the occasion. She didn't know the first thing about throwing a party, and also, even though she was a close friend of the DJ crews, was not above them in the hierarchy of rave family culture and couldn't ask them to throw a party for her. Sly needed the help of Lilly to convince the DJ's to spin. With the promise of free cocaine, this was an easy feat for Lilly to complete. They planned the party as a house party and invited everyone they knew. Because the theme was Valentine's Day, Sly encouraged girls to wear lingerie. There was a stripper pole installed in the living room, and the bedroom floors were covered in sheetless mattresses and fake rose petals. There wouldn't be much else in the way of decorations, but there would be copious amounts of drugs and live music. To them, that was what made a party, a party.

Lilly and Adam arrived at the posted address together. Lilly was not in lingerie and Sly scolded her at the door, herself dressed in a black lace bodysuit with no underwear. *God damn it, Sly.* Was this going to be another moment where Adam would find an opportunity to hook up with her friend and Lilly would have to sit in the other room pretending she didn't care? Whatever, she would worry about that later, or she wouldn't, not like there was anything she could do about it, anyway. For the moment, she hoped Sly was a better friend to her and wouldn't fall for Adam's advances, which she was sure would come.

"Hey! You're here! Yay!" Sly greeted them at the door.

"Hi! We made it! You look hot, girl!" Lilly said.

"Thanks!" Sly said in a provocative giggle. "Why aren't you wearing sexy lingerie? There's a dress code!"

"Oh, you're so funny… Now let me in." Lilly was not in the mood to play games. She knew Sly knew that would never happen and was only giving her shit.

Lilly pushed past Sly and walked in to find several friends already in attendance. Freestyle and Stan were in the corner of the living room smoking a blunt while a hired girl worked the pole. Bass Man and Strange Guy were sniffing lines on the kitchen island, and huddled around them were several of Sly's customers, all of whom Lilly knew by name and considered friendly. Lilly went up to make conversation with the crowd around the coke table. Adam and Lilly showed up together, but they wouldn't likely see each other much during the party as several close friends were in attendance and that meant they would spend the party away from one another, trying not to raise further suspicion. The two separated and might find each other later to sneak a kiss in a dark corner when their highs were peaking and the moment motivated them.

As the night wore on, the party grew. Some guests showed up only interested in drugs as this became the pickup spot for the night, others showed up for drugs but stayed to enjoy the party. During the night, a fight broke out at the front door. Sly rolled her eyes at the commotion.

"Ugh, why do guys always fight over stupid shit when they're fucked up?" she said to Lilly as the men fought.

Lilly didn't respond and kept her distance. The fight began when Jermaine, a customer of Sly's and owner of the home they were in, who had become very close to Sly in Lilly's more recent absence, got angry at another male customer who had tried flirting with Sly. Sly ate it up, but Jermaine didn't like it.

Jermaine—or Maine, they called him—was the type that was always looking for attention and not afraid to create a scene to get it. He was a tall and handsome black man with a retro Afro who wore bright, fitted suits—he liked to stand out, and was notorious for showing up to a party wearing a fire engine red tuxedo with baby blue suede shoes, munching on a full-sized box of Lucky Charms for the sake of watching people ask why, or at least guarantee everyone noticed his arrival.

At the front door, a man tried to kiss Sly on the cheek as he was walking out. Jermaine was high and took that as a sign of disrespect in his home. He and Sly had gotten close enough, and she asked him to host a huge, drug bender party for her, to which he complied, despite only being a casual pot smoker before the two had met. He shoved the guy up against the front door, jamming it shut. That was all. He wouldn't likely try to fight the guy any further, and the guy being there alone and on his way out, wasn't about to push a man far bigger than he to continue the fight. In a haste to get away from the situation, he tried opening the door, but it wouldn't budge. In a panic, he hurried to the closest window he could find and hopped through it.

"What the fuck did you do to the door, Maine?" Sly announced to the room but addressed Jermaine.

"What? I don't know, hold on." Jermaine tried to finagle the door; it wouldn't budge. He tried for several seconds, but nothing. A few other males took their turn trying, it stayed stuck.

"Oh my God, are we trapped in here?" Sly asked, half-laughing at the ridiculous situation.

"No, no, we're not. There's a window." Jermaine pointed to the window that, a few moments ago, a scared little man escaped from.

"Back to the party, everyone!" Sly announced to the 50-60 party people all staring at her and Jermaine. "Jermaine, you, come here." She pointed to a bedroom where the two of them would disappear to for the rest of the night.

By the morning, only a select few remained. Dark circles hung heavy under Lilly's eyes and her hair stuck flat to her scalp. This became a common look she carried after partying all night, and everyone still there appeared the same. Adam and Lilly had seen little of each other or spoken the entire time. That was fine though, she was used to this already, and she had plenty of drugs to occupy her, anyway. Before Sly disappeared to the bedroom, she gave Lilly her stash and asked that she supply the party and take care of any orders, that she had to talk to Jermaine about what happened. Also, not unusual, was Sly disappearing and handing over all responsibility to Lilly. It was something that happened often.

Lilly holding the supply not only meant she would be busy filling orders, but that she was free to help herself to whatever she wanted. She had taken ecstasy and cocaine, smoked plenty of weed, and made lots of new friends. The morning party mellowed, and the music turned down, but didn't stop.

When Sly emerged from behind the closed door, she brought with her a NOS tank. The party continued. It was here that Lilly learned the reality behind Shade's warning brought to her attention all that time ago, after her very first party. She had forgotten all about it until it happened to her, when she fished out.

A leftover party of only eight people sat on the floor around the stripper pole, huddled close to the tank. The sun shone itself through the naked windows. A full night of various substances that became the drug salad she indulged in that evening left her with sticky skin and an occasional stench of body odor that emanated from her stinky parts. But that didn't matter now, Sly handed her a full balloon. Lilly leaned her back against the wall and took several long hits of the gas, playing a little game with herself where the aim was to see how many breaths she could take of just nitrous before being forced to take in oxygen.

The next moment, her body detached itself from reality. The left side of her body, from the top of her head down through her left foot, was being pulled into what she could only describe as a static blackness. She could see, out of her left eye, nothing but darkness that went on forever, and from her left ear, that sound that comes out of the TV when you've hit a broken channel or come to the end of a home video. It was loud and all-consuming. From the right side, out of her right eye, were bright neon trees and landscapes. She was inside a Mario Brothers game on the Super Nintendo she loved as a kid, complete with video game theme music! The melody she recognized from the game. She wanted to walk into the video game side, but that left side was holding her down where she was. It was pulling her down and out of her very life and she had to fight against it to stay outside the darkness. She understood that life didn't exist in there.

"Lilly! LILLY!" Adam screamed.

The blackness disappeared, and she was no longer inside a video game, but back in the living room she had left. She wasn't leaning against the wall anymore; she was lying on the floor, on her left side. Adam's hand was on her shoulder, shaking her entire body. She rose, confused, and didn't understand what happened to her, but was relieved to be back.

"What happened?" she said.

"You fished out. Are you okay? Sit up!" Adam said, still concerned. People were all looking at him now. His tone changed and he let out a nervous laugh. What Lilly didn't know was that fishing out was a term used to describe nitrous poisoning, coined for the way a person looks while it's happening to them, like a fish-out-of-water, flopping around on the ground, gasping for air. The experience for the user though, as Lilly learned here, was more real than any power of hallucinogen she had already experienced. Pretty colors and dancing paisleys altered her reality until she left it, and she liked it. It was dangerous, and she understood the risks as explained to her. Fishing out was something that people tried to avoid, but Lilly didn't know if she was going to be one of those people.

The morning had gone, but the party continued. They needed to leave for more supplies. Freestyle and Lilly took an order of beer, more balloons, condoms, cigarettes, and food. Getting in and out was difficult because of the jammed front door, and a back door that Jermaine long before boarded up. Jermaine was paranoid on drugs. In his short time experimenting with them, the last strong trip he'd endured, he boarded up his back door to protect himself from whatever bogeyman he was fighting that time. Climbing in and out of the front window became the only way in and out of the house. Lilly was never hungry on drugs, but she reasoned that if she didn't eat, at some point she wouldn't feel well enough to keep partying, so she forced a sandwich every once in a while.

By the third day, Lilly's legs and knees had bruises on them from climbing in and out of the window, like a kid who enjoyed roughhousing outdoors a little too much. Hygiene became a luxury none of them would give up the party for. They were too busy partying and couldn't figure out how to keep a plate of cocaine dry in a steamy bathroom. That sticky skin was more pronounced, and her hair had strung off in clumpy bits. Lilly smelled odors coming from everywhere now, whiffs that she didn't recognize as her own.

Sly said they were going to keep the party going with more ecstasy. The seven remaining partiers, Jermaine, Bass Man, Freestyle, Adam, Lilly, a random girl named Kourtney and her boyfriend Nate, all opened their palms as Sly dropped free pills into each, and the party continued. For fun, she dared Lilly to take her top off, that if she did, she would give her as many pills as she wanted and forgive her of some debts she liked to hold over Lilly's head as a reminder of her generosity. Sly would never collect the debts. She owed Lilly more than money. But being put on-the-spot, Lilly had to comply. She didn't want to risk Sly not letting her have any more pills, an energy she needed to continue on.

Lilly, now running around topless, provoked the rest of the girls to do the same and the party moved into a side bedroom with a mattress filled floor. In the room, Adam laid next to Lilly on a mattress off in the corner. Sly laid on the bed with Bass Man. Jermaine, seeing this, exploded in rage and left the room, Freestyle followed him out, not wanting anything to do with what was about to happen. Kourtney and Nate took another mattress on the opposite end. Within minutes, all couples were making out, paying no attention to the couples surrounding them.

Lilly and Adam were the first to have sex. The room knew when it happened because neither of them were quiet about it. There was an elation in Lilly's expressions as what was happening held a strong significance. He was acknowledging their relationship that had been progressing over the months and years they had known each other. This prompted the other couples to take their actions to the next level. Within a few minutes, sex fumes filled the air. By the time Adam and Lilly finished, Sly and Kourtney had switched partners with each other. Adam laughed, while motioning to Lilly that no, they would not be taking part. After a few more minutes of watching the rest of them have fun, Adam, not having completed his refractory period, told Lilly they should leave the room and go out to smoke with Freestyle and Jermaine.

The weed was enough to relax Lilly. For the first time in three days, her body weighted down with exhaustion. Her feet planted into the ground and pulled her down, taking all her strength to fight against the urge to collapse into it. The circles under her eyes drooped further, pulling her upper eyelids down with them. Her face told the story that her brain couldn't put together words for. She was tired. An elevated couch propped up on top of a table sat in the living room. She had avoided that couch until now because it reminded her of her bed, but by this point everything she could have wanted to happen at the party had happened. The couch was more than welcoming, and she was ready for it.

When she woke, it was dark out. She had slept through the rest of the day. Would they try partying more, now that night was here again? But she found the room empty and dark, except for Adam who was asleep on the living room floor, near her elevated couch. Sly walked into the living room from the master bedroom where she had stayed cuddled up with Jermaine. Lilly hopped down from the couch when Sly entered and walked towards the kitchen.

"Shit, man, how long was I out?" Lilly asked with a smile, refreshed and rejuvenated.

"Like a long time, you needed it."

"Yeah, I guess. What are you doing? Are you tired? Did you sleep?" Lilly asked, fishing for an opportunity to get the party going again.

"Hey, so, you were asleep for a really long time, and I tried to wake you up when it was happening, but you just wouldn't."

"What? What happened? What do you mean?" Lilly said concerned.

"Um, while you were asleep, Adam had sex with that Kourtney chick." Sly winced, expecting an outrage to follow.

"What!" was all Lilly could say as her heart sank back down into her shoes, all the pieces shattering and slicing through her insides as they fell. "But we had sex in front of everybody. He finally made us public!" Confused and broken, a welt grew in her throat as she choked back tears.

"I know, I'm sorry. I tried to wake you," Sly said, understanding Lilly's pain, but looking at her like a disappointed mother.

Nothing had changed. Lilly looked back towards the living room where he laid resting. Everything she was working for with him was nothing more than a figment of her imagination, a hallucination of her girlish mind wanting it to be more than what it was.

"I don't know what to do," Lilly cried.

"Why do you keep letting him do this to you? It's infuriating!" Sly said in a harsh voice and shaking her shoulders.

"You know why, Sly." Lilly looked down towards the ground, unable to face her reality or her best friend.

"You're just fucking stupid! You know he's gonna do shit like this, it's your own fault for letting him."

"What else am I supposed to do, Sly? Just break up with him? We're not even together! If I tried to do that, he would laugh in my face! This is what I agreed to. I just have to hold on for a little while longer…"

"Longer for what? What are you waiting for?" Sly asked, almost in a rage.

"He's gonna get better. I know he is. He loves me."

"Okay, you know what?" Sly put her hands up in submission. "Whatever, you're delusional. I can't listen to this anymore… Stop crying. Come on, let's go sniff some lines."

"Okay," Lilly said as she sniffed up her sniffles and wiped her eyes. She followed Sly into the bedroom, trying her best not to look at Adam as she passed.

EIGHTEEN

Xany Bar Meltdown

"Can I talk to you about something?" Lilly asked. She and Adam were back at the garage studio now, tired and beaten from the three-day party marathon they had come from, but Lilly was more energetic as she pulled her nose up from a plate of cocaine when Adam came storming in the bath-room to collect her. They escaped out the front window with only a subtle goodbye to Sly and Jermaine.

"What?!" Adam snapped back. He was not in the mood to talk. "Look, if this is just gonna be another one of your stupid drama fests, I don't wanna hear it. We had a fun time, you had all the drugs you could have wanted. I took care of everything for you, didn't I?" He barked at her. "Didn't I?!" He screamed when she didn't answer right away.

"Yes, okay, yes." But he hadn't. It was Sly's drugs they consumed throughout, but that didn't stop him from forcing her to agree with his lie. "Never mind, I mean, I was just gonna ask, that, um… well, we had sex in front of them, and Bass is like your best homie, so what does that mean?"

"It doesn't mean shit! It means everything stays the same, and nobody knows anything they didn't already know. They all knew, Lil, they just weren't talking about it out loud. But nothing changes, you understand?"

She nodded in agreement and changed the subject. Once Stan had asked, it was likely that the friend group had been talking about it for some time. It was only a matter of when it was going to become public knowledge, not if, and the longer Adam and Lilly didn't talk about it, the more the friends would talk about it behind their back. Publicly sex was a way of saying it without words, confirming any suspicions without having to talk about it. This way Adam stayed in control and he didn't have to answer any sappy follow-up questions. He was telling his friends that yes, they fuck, nothing else, leave it alone.

But things changed, and Lilly liked it. The secret was out now. Conversation at the following Fri-Yays now circled around the close group of friends all laughing and talking, opening up about how Adam and Lilly had them all fooled, for at least a little while. As a couple, she and Adam had more influence amongst the group. Lilly had the connection to Sly and her party favors, Adam had influence over the parties as the crew looked up to him now. Whether it was real or a make-believe notion of power, one she convinced herself wasn't the drugs causing her to hallucinate, it was there. In this power, Lilly pulled herself closer to Adam. Her personal identity melted away as she became an extension of him, like a meaningless extra limb. No longer having to hide it, her connection to him became so strong that she couldn't breathe without him, like her heartbeat inside his chest and even the thought of him separating himself from her meant ripping apart the veins and capillaries that supplied oxygen rich blood to her organs and brain.

Adam reveled in this power, too. He wanted more of it, and with Lilly clung to his side, he no longer had to consider Sly and her place in the scene. He was going to take it from her, for no other reason than because he could. Adam revealed to Lilly his plans, hidden behind the guise that it would make more sense for them to sell, without Sly in the picture. They would have more money to support their friends and the party and Lilly wouldn't have to worry about going off to parties with Sly, she could be with Adam and the Junglist crew all the time and they wouldn't have to be apart, ever. This was alluring to Lilly, who knew that if she wanted to be with Adam, this was going to be the next step, always following his lead.

All she had to do was keep him happy and follow orders. Sure, selling drugs wouldn't be a bad idea, Sly would understand and wouldn't take it personally, she told herself. Lilly agreed that this would be best for them and asked Adam how they should go ahead. How would they tell Sly? How would they even get money to buy product? Where would their customers come from? Adam laughed at her cute eagerness, but told her not to worry, he would handle all the details. She only needed to worry about talking to Sly, by inviting her over and telling her in person. Telling Sly that she would no longer be a protected dealer at the biggest parties of the summer, and that Adam would instead take that role, was going to be hard to hear, but Sly appreciated their friendship too and it would be okay. Or at least that's what she had to convince herself of to go through with the plan to break Sly's heart for a boy that was almost hers.

"Hey girl! What you doing?" Lilly exclaimed when Sly's voice picked up the line.

"Oh nothing, just hanging out at home, slanging sacks, bored. What're you up to?"

"Oh yeah, hanging out with Adam at my place. Hey! You wanna come chill with us over here? We got some xany-bars, your favorite!"

"Sweet! Yeah, I'll come, can you come pick me up?"

"Yup! On our way now."

Sly was a sucker for a xany, and bar form was her Achilles. xany was slang for Xanax, a barbiturate prescription pill used for immediate relief of major anxiety and full-blown panic attacks. A 2.0 milligram xany bar was almost never available, you had to know someone super connected to get those, and the 4.0 milligram bar was more or less an urban legend. Lilly had only ever heard of them, but never had the chance to try or even see one. Sly, although she enjoyed a good party drug, she was more partial to the downers vs uppers. Xany's were of the downer category and thus her favorite pastime, when she could get ahold of them.

Adam and Lilly arrived to pick up Sly. As she walked towards the car, there was a glow on her face, a smile stretched across it, and an almost a glitter in her eye. She was excited for the evening, knowing it would culminate in the finishing touch of the ever-elusive xany bar. Many a cokehead enjoyed a good Xanax dose at the end of a long night of sniffing lines, that's why Adam and Lilly liked them. They had an almost magical quality that no other depressant had, that was that enough of a dose could knock out even the most spun up and high-strung junkie. There wasn't enough beer or weed in the world to accomplish the same task after a night of harsh lines. Xanax was different, it was instant relaxation. It helped to calm the mind and quiet the inner monologue that kept the mind reeling. Within moments of wanting to be, anyone could be fast asleep.

Sly, she liked Xanax for a different reason. She wasn't interested in falling asleep on them or using them as a facilitator to come down off of too much cocaine. No, she was ready to swallow them and walk out into the world, fight the urge to lie down and instead let herself drown in the overwhelming feeling of pure and total release of every inhibition, complete peace, absolute joy, and silly forgetfulness. Lilly didn't get that from Xanax. She enjoyed them for the pure sake of what they helped to accomplish after a cocaine bender. It was the serene release she needed to take her away from the anxious and throbbing pain of the comedown. She needed escape from the red watering eyes, clogged throat unable to take in air, inner thoughts that raced inside and wouldn't leave her be, and the paralyzing fear brought on by their intensity.

Back at Lilly's, Adam called attention to the girls. "Girls, I have something special for you."

"Give me my xany!" shouted Sly, excited and ready to drift away.

Lilly and Adam laughed at her excitableness.

"Alright, alright, chill out," Adam said through his laughs. "Okay, look, I had to pull some serious strings to get this shit, so you bitches better be grateful! I want you to repay me with a double blow job!" He was half joking, but testing the waters.

"Oh my god, shut up and give us drugs!" Lilly said, pushing on his shoulder.

"Okay, alright, fine." Adam pulled a small, clear jewelry bag out of his pocket. "These are…"

"Oh my, God! You got fours!" Sly shouted and screamed. Four green, bar shaped pills looked back at her through the plastic. Lilly had never seen green before, she knew white, blue, and yellow. But never green. *These must be them.*

"Relax!" Adam shouted back at her, even louder than her first scream, but excited that the girls were excited.

"Oh my god, dude, are those really fours? I didn't think they were an actual thing?" said Lilly.

"Yes, they're a thing! Oh, my god! Gimme! Gimme! Gimme!" Sly responded as she danced around on her tippy-toes, palms and fingers stretched out in front of her, eyes fixated on the baggie.

"Alright, look, one each now, and then we party, and if we need to later, we can split up the last one, but fours are super strong so we might not even need it." Adam held the bag in front of him and fiddled with the tiny ziplock. He handed one green bar to Sly, one to Lilly, and one he took out for himself. Lilly tossed the bar into the back of her throat, knowing how quickly they dissolve. She didn't want to risk letting it disintegrate on the tip of her tongue as she had plenty of experience with the chemical taste. Lilly's body became heavy but floaty at the same time. A euphoric wave of calm rushed over her. After the pills, it was time to rack out lines. The night moved quickly, as things always do with xanys. The phrase time flies when you're having fun was more than true in this experience. Not because it was moving fast, they were all moving slow without realizing it, but Xanax has a funny way of blurring moments into minutes and further into hours and evenings and sometimes entire 24-hour periods.

At one point, Lilly couldn't have told you when it happened, but the three of them were all so relaxed by the Xanax, they couldn't feel the cocaine they were sniffing, so they switched to smoking it off small bits of foil. Had Lilly ever done this before? No, but logic told her it was the most appropriate thing to do considering it might get her a stronger high. This carried on throughout the night until the breaking point came and Sly and Adam could no longer fight the bars. Sleep was imminent. With reluctance, Lilly agreed. The foil was burning her throat anyway, and sleep might do her good.

Within the next few minutes, Sly and Lilly were laying on the bed. Sly rolled over and was out. Adam was sitting on the desk chair. He tilted his head back and put himself to sleep quick. Lilly tossed and turned for a moment, but sleep was nowhere near her. The bar had worn, and the cocaine had taken hold. She knew it would be a long morning of laying in silence while the sun rose. But there was a fix! Adam had one more bar there in his pocket. She slunk out of bed and creeped over towards his limp body on the chair. His snores were loud enough to mask her rustling through his clothing. She found the baggie, removed the bar, and swallowed it whole. *That should do the trick.* She didn't remember getting back into bed before waking up fourteen hours later, the following evening.

It was the sound of Adam screaming at her that got her up. It was about six o'clock. She woke, confused and disorientated. Sly was next to her, yelling at Adam to stop. She had placed herself in a protective stance over Lilly, worried that Adam might strike her. Sly urged him to let her sleep, go home and come back later. Adam did not appreciate that.

"Lil! You gonna let this bitch talk to me like that? What the FUCK! Get the fuck up! What are you doing? You've been asleep all fucking day! It's nighttime! Get the fuck up!"

"Adam, chill, she's fucking tired! Let her sleep, it's fine, I'll stay here with her," Sly said, hovering over Lilly's waking body, a fear in her eyes that considered Adam might assault her.

"Okay, I'm sorry, I'm up. What time is it?" Lilly said in a voice that could barely rummage through the commotion.

"Fuck! Lilly! We've been trying to get you up forever!" Adam yelled again, his overreaction fueled by the saturation of drugs in his system.

"It's okay, you're just tired. We had a long night," Sly said in a calm and sweet voice, smiling in reassurance.

"No, it's not okay, because Lilly and I have something to tell you, Sly. Get the fuck up and tell her, Lilly." Adam pulled Lilly up by the arm and out of her own bed.

"Fuck, Adam, ok!" Lilly shook the last bit of sleep out of her head and readied herself to deliver the news. His anger, she remained unreactive to. He had changed over the months as their habits took deeper hold, and she accepted the consequences of that.

"Tell her!"

"Tell me what? What's going on?" Sly said to Lilly, her brow furrowed in a show of confused at how the tables had turned.

"Oh, well, uh, you know season's coming up and we're planning a bunch of parties and Adam thinks…"

"We think…" Adam inserted himself as he interrupted her.

"Okay, we think it would just be easier if Adam did the dealing now and that way you can just enjoy yourself and you don't have to worry about always hanging around with me all the time, 'cause Adam and I are like together now, so it just makes more sense." Lilly finished her sentence without taking a breath. The faster she spoke, the easier it was to remain convinced that Sly would understand and agree with them easily as Adam had influenced her first. It was as if she could see the light leave Sly's eyes and fill instead with water, her best friend having crushed her heart. But she couldn't stay sad, this was business, and she was being cut out.

"Are you fucking dumping me for this asshole?!" Sly's eyes turned to fire. "Are you fucking kidding me? After everything I've done for you? I gave you so much free drugs, and paid for everything, and you play me like this, like you think you can just cut me?"

"No, it's not like that, I just meant…"

"Shut up, bitch!" Adam interjected. "You don't own the game, I do. These are my parties and you're lucky we let you in. If it weren't for Lilly, you wouldn't be in, so you should be thanking her!" Adam shouted, his aggression piercing through the encounter.

"Wait, Stop! I just…" Lilly tried to calm the two.

"No, fuck you, Adam! You're a fucking liar and you treat her like shit and she's too stupid to see that you're taking advantage of how she feels about you!" Sly screamed back at him.

The interaction pushed Adam to action as the energy boiled over. Adam positioned himself inches behind Lilly, and with force shoved her towards Sly, inciting the two best friends to engage in physical battle. Their screams alerted the neighbors and Lilly's father inside the front house, not fifty feet away. The altercation moved outside as Lilly tried to run away, but Sly went after her. It ended only when onlooking neighbors announced they had called the police. It was no longer safe for any of them to be there, Adam had to leave, Sly walked off into the dark back alley, and Lilly stayed, now having to face her father and answer for the events that had transpired.

Standing outside with neighbors watching and her father standing a few feet away with his arms crossed, Lilly fell to her knees and sobbed. The weight of her experiences up to that point was too much for her to continue carrying. *What is happening? Oh my God, is this my real life?* Her thoughts jumbled themselves up in knots as she tried to make sense of her reality and how she had gotten there. It was a moment of clarity that lasted only that long.

"Come inside, now," Lilly's father said in a stern voice. Still charged, Lilly pulled her body off the ground and dragged herself inside with her head sunk down as far as it could go. "You gonna tell us just what the hell is going on out there?"

Lilly let out a deep sigh and announced to her father and the child-bride that she was a drug addict, something they had known but hadn't known how else to confront after the first failed attempt so long ago. Lilly rambled off explicit details as to the lengths she had gone to get high and what kinds of drugs she used, ending with a desperate plea for help. It was a breakthrough. It was the first step, and an opportunity for them all to heal as a family and put all this behind them.

"Okay," her dad said to her as his daughter purged the guilt that had been eating at her insides for so long. "We'll get you help, thank you for coming to us. Go get some sleep and we'll deal with this first thing in the morning."

Lilly soaked in a sense of relief. Part of her wanted this nightmare to end. She wanted to be well. She wanted to be in school and productive and working towards her goals; she remembered having goals once. It was a moment of clarity and she left it in the ever-capable hands of her father to guide her through the second part of this. She went to bed hoping the morning would bring a a fresh mind and she would begin the walk to leave all of this behind her.

NINETEEN

In The Game

L illy woke up the next morning to the sound of her phone ringing. It was Adam. It was always Adam. "Hello," she answered in a groggy voice.

"That stupid bitch tried to kill herself! Haha! Dumb bitch." These were the first trite and unconcerned words Adam spoke to her, the morning after the biggest fight she had ever gotten into in her life, with her best friend, no less.

"What? What are you talking about?" The concern coming now from her, being absent elsewhere.

"Sly! After she left your place yesterday, she walked to the grocery store and got arrested after she went through the pharmacy aisle and swallowed an entire bottle of Tylenol PM. Fell to the ground screaming or some shit. I just got off the phone with Maine, I guess she called him from jail. They're transferring her to some facility. Serves her right for fucking with me. Dumb bitch." This was all funny to him.

"What? Oh, my god! Is she okay? Can I talk to her?"

"No! Fuck her! We're done with her. Forget about Sly,

she's done. We're busy. I'm on my way over to pick you up. We have a meeting with Jose." He hung up.

The click of the end call button triggered Lilly into a rage. She screamed, so loud and for so long, it ended in her coughing and gasping for air. Tears streamed down her face as she grabbed at loose objects in her reach and smashed them against the walls. She didn't stop when the broken glass of an ashtray cut through her feet as they continued to walk through strewn ash and cigarette butts on the floor. The next closest object to her was her computer. She picked up the monitor that sat on her desk and smashed it back down. To her advantage, her strength was no stronger than that of a small child and she caused only minor damage to any of it, although she tried inflicting more.

When the shade of red washed itself from her teary eyes, she understood that this would not do. Adam could not see this reaction, the aftermath of a destroyed woman's grief. She held her face in her hands for a moment, let out a single and quick whimper as she remembered the friendship that was over. She took a deep breath and let it out as she shook her head and hands clean of any residual emotion. Adam would be here soon. There was no time to sit or cry. Lilly picked up a broom and cleaned up the mess, then herself.

But wait! She gathered herself and remembered the words her father spoke to her. That he would get her help. In her mind, she played with the decision. *Go with Adam today, or go with my dad?* All it would take is a few steps towards the front house where he would welcome her in and ship her off to some type of rehab or facility where she could hide away from Adam long enough for him to forget about her. She could start over, erase the last several years of her life, hit reset. She sat at her computer desk for a long minute, staring past the blank computer monitor. "I can't do this anymore," she said to herself out loud and got up and grabbed her purse to begin the march out her door and up to the front house where her father would be waiting for her.

Her heart raced as she approached. She heard her breath in her ear. She reached out her hand to grab the doorknob and pushed and turned it while shifting her body weight inside the doorframe. But the door stopped her as she banged up against it. Her eyebrows squinted as she tried to understand what was happening. She jiggled the knob. *Locked? Why is it locked?* She searched her purse for house keys, but when she found them and tried to match them to the lock, she met with resistance. *The lock's broken? Wait... did they change the locks?* A sinking feeling in her chest took her by surprise and almost knocked her over. "Hello! Dad? I'm here! Hello?" She shouted through the heavy wood barrier, the words emphasized by her fists pounding along on the door. "Dad!" She shouted again, this time accompanied by tears that streamed down her face.

Well, I guess that's that, then. She nodded and wiped away her tears. Another short walk back to her quarters where she again sat at her computer desk, letting the silence wash away her feelings and numb her body. "Time to get ready," she said to no one, except maybe herself, with no other options left. In the process, she made sure she shaved her legs, brushed her hair, and held a bright smile. *I guess it's easier this way. Why fight it?* She heard the anxious honk of his car blow through her walls. The muffled thudding of loud Drum'n'Bass music rattling against metal pulled in with the roar of tires coming down the alleyway outside. *Time to go.*

In the car, they didn't speak a word. He didn't even bother turning down the music when she got in, he never did. If he spoke to her at all, it was to tell her what CD to put in next, and if she didn't pull it from its sleeve fast enough, he would let her know it. When they arrived at Jose's, they received the same warm and friendly greeting. Lilly knew them by name now and no longer felt uncomfortable in their presence—tear drop tattoos, bullet wounds, and all. There was a plate of coke sitting out for them on the kitchen table, several tiny lines racked and ready. Jose announced that he had waited for their arrival before indulging himself. It was only ten in the morning, but Lilly grinned towards the plate and followed her nose like a bloodhound on the hunt. She needed it after the night she'd had.

"Please, help yourself, we waited for you guys," Jose said as he handed Lilly a rolled up one-hundred-dollar bill and bowed his head in grace to her. These people respected her, why was not clear, but Jose and his homies were always kind to her. She took the bill in her hand and said nothing about how small they were, not wanting to be rude. She leaned over the table and embraced the rush as it flew up her nose, down her throat, into the back of her eyes and found its way through her veins, electrifying itself into a pulse as it coursed. It surprised her at how such a small amount could have such an impact. It was like the first time again. She rose in ecstasy to find Jose, Adam, and the homies watching her with intent. Taken aback, something felt wrong.

"Well? How was it?" Adam asked.

"Pretty fucking good, like way better than usual. Why? Why is everyone looking at me?"

"Alright, that's what I like to hear!" Jose said. The rest of the homies laughed and clapped in celebration. "This is primo stuff right here, girl. We wanted you to be the first! 99% pure!"

Had she sniffed pure cocaine as a guinea pig? Why hadn't they told her? Warned her? Should she be mad? Because the elation that followed was making it hard for her to feel anything but pure and utter adoration for being so honored. She reasoned they were trying to surprise her with a beautiful gift, and she was beyond thankful for the opportunity.

"Alright, boys…" Jose said as he took the bill out of Lilly's fingers and took a quick sniff off the plate, raising back up to finish his sentence, "you guys keep Chica company, Adam and I are gonna go talk." He finished as he handed the bill over to Adam, whose face lit up in antic-ipation, a fleeting one as it was not a second later that he took his line and was back up again, an extra pep in his step, as the two men walked out of the room behind closed doors. Another happening Lilly was used to. They left her alone with the gangsters, but also the cocaine—she was in good company.

Adam emerged from the meeting room with a package in his hand and a fierce look of dominion on his face. He and Jose shook hands and Adam motioned to Lilly that it was time to go. Lilly said her goodbyes, like she was saying goodbye to her best group of girlfriends. Each of them waved and smiled at her as she left and nodded in acknowledgement to Adam.

"Everyone is always so nice at Jose's house," Lilly said to Adam as they got in the car.

"Yeah, yeah, they're cool," Adam responded in a straight and uninterested tone. It wasn't the social interac-tion he wanted to talk about. He changed the subject as his grin widened and his eyes sparkled. "Listen. Shit is real for us now. We're slanging. Jose just fronted me an ounce and we're going to move it for him. Once we move this one, we get another one up from there. You have to help me keep the money straight. This can't go up our noses, you hear me! This is serious, Lilly! We're in the game and we can't fuck up!"

"Whoa! Okay, cool. You want me to call some people?" Lilly said, now as excited about their new situation as Adam was.

"Yes, call all of Sly's old customers and tell them she's gone away, that we can take care of them now."

"Okay!"

They spent the rest of the day making phone calls and deliveries. It took only a few hours for their new business to be up and running. By the end of the fourth day, they had sold out the entire ounce, twenty-eight grams of pure cocaine, a street value of $25,000, and were on their way back to Jose's to pickup again. With each pickup, the time frame became smaller and the amounts larger. Their customer base grew, and more people became enamored with the new, pure product only they could offer. It was expensive at $90 a gram, but well worth the money.

THE SUMMER PARTY season had come, and with it a new set of challenges as Adam now took on the role of official supplier and regulator. Lilly's dreams of spending moments with Adam at the party disappeared because he was now busier than ever, and she was too, as the two of them became the most sought-after people at the party. Well, it was the car rather. The car was the symbol, like an ice cream truck in a neighborhood full of kids struck by the scorching summer sun. Find the car amongst the desert landscape, was the word at the rave. The car was where party kids could place their order. Adam's new, bright green Honda Element, a small SUV of sorts, that he had purchased for the season. They called it The Nug because it resembled a nugget of their favorite bright green chronic, the drug they used in between all the others when there was a free moment.

This was nothing new to Lilly, who had been down this rabbit hole the season before with Sly, only this time Adam would not allow her to take part so closely, even though she had more experience than he did. Adam hid behind the guise of her safety and instead ordered her to go enjoy the party. He would find her on the dance floor and bring her what she needed or come say hi when he had the chance. But even on the dance floor, Lilly found herself in a much more popular position than she had been in seasons past.

People came up to her to talk about moments they remembered having with her at parties she had long since forgotten, these moments forgotten too. Others asked her for drugs, she pointed them to The Nug; others still wanted to be in her company, hoping for a glimpse or chance into the inner-circle that she herself had fallen into that fateful first season years earlier. They all knew who she was and wanted to radiate off of her. These things were challenges not because they were scary or dangerous, but because they were annoying to Lilly, who only had eyes for Adam, and wanted nothing more than to spend those moments with him, instead of a million friendly strangers. She kept herself interested and engaged with copious amounts of ecstasy pills, acid, mushrooms, whatever she had available to her, and she tried her best to finish her pocket stash as fast as she could as that meant she would have an excuse to leave the floor and go looking for Adam to give her more, who could never tell her no, even when it was already her fourth pill, the sun had barely set, and they still had the entire night to go.

The challenges for Adam were different. He didn't argue with Lilly about how many pills she was taking.

Instead, he gave her what she asked for and brushed her off for the rest of the night, telling her he didn't have time for her, that there was an entire party to regulate, sell to, and police the shadows in. Lilly knew that this business he claimed didn't stress him like he pretended it did. She saw the glow in his face when people looked up to him and heeded his regulator warnings. He often spoke in an accent that mimicked Scarface, his favorite character that he told her he pretended to be sometimes in the privacy of his dreams. The moments when things got scary for Lilly, Adam rose to the challenge, getting them both out of it okay.

One of these times, a drug deal gone bad, involved a friend of his, a stranger friend, that he had only met that evening at the party (this was frequent). The friend got stabbed by an angry customer who was aiming for Adam, but he aimed too high and his blade stabbed into the wrong person's body. Chaos broke out amongst the group of men huddled around Adam, making sure he was okay, he was, while the stranger friend bled-out on the forest floor.

Another time, at another party, a fight broke out over who had first fill rights over the early morning NOS tank. Mornings at the rave were filled with the sound of freshly cracked tanks, and the ravers were desperate for a come-down fix. The tank offered that momentary relief and was worth fighting over. The fight turned into a swarm of left-over ravers all swinging and pulling at each other to get to the tank. Dust filled the air like a cartoon rumble between a starved coyote and an escaped roadrunner. Adam jumped in and used his voice to silence the fight and pull rank. The moment the fighting stopped it was he, standing above every other man in the brawl, at the neck of the tank, who halted the entire situation. It was like watching

Scarface himself as he stood over his domain and claimed it in front of his rivals. Adam celebrated his victory by connecting his balloon to the neck of that tank and taking his right to first fill.

BY THE END of the first month of the summer season, Adam and Lilly brought the new business up to complete operational capacity. They spent the week selling coke to raise money for the weekend. Sales during the week were a little more nerve-wrecking for both of them because they had to happen in open air, exposed to prying eyes of passersby and possible police officers. Adam resorted to using the parking garage of his parent's hotel for most of the meetings, under the perceived protection of security. Adam knew the area and considered it a safe spot.

"Get a sack ready for Phil, he's gonna meet us at the garage," Adam said as he entered Lilly's studio after work one day.

"How much?"

"Teener."

Lilly readied the order, knowing that a teener meant he wanted 1.6 grams of cocaine, and hopped in Adam's car with him for the short ride to the hotel.

"Yo, yo, yo!" Adam said as he parked at the top level of the garage, the customer, Phil, already waiting.

"Finally! Damn, I've been waiting, dog!"

"Aight, sorry, sorry, I know. We're here."

"Hi, Phil!" Lilly said from the front seat, leaning her head over to greet Phil, who had walked up to Adam's window.

"Hey, how you doin, girl?" The three of them laughed together and stepped out of the car to complete the deal.

"Aight, dog, look, we hooked you up, like always.

Here." Adam handed the sack over to Phil, who took it and held it up, sizing it up with his eyes.

"Cool, cool. It's all good, dog. I know what's up." Phil handed three twenties back to Adam, completing the exchange. "Hey, you gonna be around later? I might…"

"Adam!" Phil was cut off mid-sentence by a shouting voice that came from behind them. The three of them together, attention captured, looked toward where the voice had come from.

"Adam! What are you doing? Is that drugs? At my hotel?" A tall, dark man in a business suit ran towards them.

"Oh, fuck!" Adam said silently while Phil ran away and Lilly stood and held her breath, the sight of Adam's father acted as a Medusa character that turned her into a statute.

"Adam! What is this? I saw you on my security cameras! Who is this girl? Did she put you up to this?"

"No, no, Dad, chill. We're just meeting a friend to go get dinner. But look, you scared him away. Calm down, it's not what you think," Adam said. He laughed at his father's overzealous behavior, as if trying to prove his reaction wasn't warranted for the situation of meeting a friend for dinner.

"Who are you? What are you doing with my son? Are you high?" The questions came flying towards Lilly with a finger pointed in her face.

She stayed in her cast of stone.

"Dad, Dad." Adam laughed again. "Stop it. It's not what you think."

"I saw the drugs, Adam! I have you on camera. It's her, isn't it? She's the one!"

"No, Dad. That wasn't drugs, the camera must have been playing tricks on you. Go back inside, we're leaving. Thanks for ruining our dinner plans." It was his attitude that must have sold it, because his father silenced himself and after one last glare in Lilly's direction, threw up his hands and walked away.

"How the fuck did you get away with that one?" Lilly asked when he was finally out of view.

Adam sucked his teeth. "I'll deal with him later."

TWENTY

Cocaine Aggression

The weekend party lasted four days, from Thursday to Sunday, and the two of them bankrolled all of it for them and the party crew. Adam was generous to his friends. None of them had to worry about where the party favors would come from, because they were all supplied by Adam. All they had to do was keep the music going. Adam was giving, but he used it as another form of control to keep his place in his seat in the hierarchy. The crew were his brothers and sisters, his followers, who looked to him for guidance and validation. He answered them by bestowing upon them gifts of chemical elation.

Because she was at his side, Lilly shared in this hallucination with him. She felt revered with adoration, and without having to work for the privilege. Adam made sure of that, for as demanding as he was of her, he made true to his word that she would never have to work for anything. He took care of her. She partied without consequence, all she had to do was stay close to Adam's side and follow his lead. But following his lead wasn't easy and required a lot of Lilly.

As the weeks and months passed on, the demand for Adam's services increased, along with his frequency of re-up and amount he received each time. The more demand on Adam, the more he sniffed the stress away, the more Lilly sniffed alongside him, as was her place. When it got to where neither of their phones stopped ringing, they never found an opportunity to sleep. They used cocaine to keep them awake and meet the demand. One more line meant enough energy to get them through one more delivery, and one more delivery meant one step closer to world domination. It soon became normal for them to make deliveries in the middle of the night to nice, suburban and unsuspecting neighborhoods, where they would stop under a streetlight and sniff a line off of an empty CD jewel case before heading to their next stop.

The habit of sniffing cocaine became serious and toxic, along with the relationship between them, which evolved into a set of rules that Adam expected Lilly to follow. She was not allowed to speak louder than him or stand in front of him. She got used to slouching because she learned that her hunched shoulders brought an unconscious smile to his face. Ironically enough, that posed another problem for her because Adam didn't like her acting unladylike. He wanted her to present herself in a feminine way; shaved legs, nice hair, makeup, cute clothes (another impossibility considering her size). He wanted her to speak with a soft voice, stand with good posture, possess a sweet and happy persona, jump when he said jump, suck his dick when he pointed to it, etcetera.

He expected her to be submissive and excitable, and impartial when he hooked up with other women. Rejecting him was not an option, ever. Lilly never questioned him about any of these rules. Doing so would only cause a fight, one which she could not take part in, because she wasn't allowed to talk back to him or criticize him or have an opinion about anything that didn't mirror his own. Arguing with Adam was pointless because he was smarter, stronger, more experienced; he was better than her, and he made sure she felt it.

"Lilly, what the fuck is the matter with you? Why'd you tell Strange Guy I hadn't picked up for the party yet?" Adam asked Lilly as he hung up the phone as she entered her studio, in full confrontation mode, having just heard from Strange Guy that they needed him to have a full supply ready for that evening's party.

"What? He asked if you were on deck and I said you only had a little bit and didn't get a chance to re-up yet."

"You don't fucking speak for me! Do you understand? I make the rules, I answer the questions. You keep your mouth shut and do what I say."

"Ok, but what am I supposed to do when they ask me?"

"Don't ask me any questions, either!" Adam screamed at her and paced around the room a few times before banging his head into the wall several times.

"Adam! Stop! Please! I'm sorry!" Lilly pleaded with him. She approached, wanting to calm him, but he swung his arms around in a helicopter fashion, forcing her backwards into an adjacent wall.

"You make me fucking crazy!" Adam's rage was full and overflowed out of him. He cornered her and punched his hand into the wall an inch away from her face. Lilly shut her eyes and let out a quick yelp as tears fell down her face.

"I'm sorry, I'm sorry! I didn't mean anything. I didn't know. I won't do it again, I promise." Lilly blubbered the words and Adam's face softened. He grabbed her shoulders passionately but without hate. She winced at first, but released her breath when his mouth latched onto her neck. What happened next, she submitted to. The act left Adam calmed and her with only a few bruises on her arms, a consequence she relinquished for upsetting him. It was her fault.

After a time, this became normal too. The sexual episodes became so intense that in secret she attended a women's health clinic for an exam, sure she had contracted an STD when she discovered a constant and penetrating sting in her vagina that refused to go away. At the clinic the nurse told her she had some inflammation and soreness, but that there were no signs of infection, no open sores or pus. They let her go with simple advice to stop having such hard sex, no matter how fun it might be. *Fun?*

No, the nurse didn't ask if she was in a situation where she felt unsafe. She told her she was some crazy kid who would benefit from taking a break from the rough sex for a little while. As if she had a choice. The nurse didn't question her about the bruises on her arms or thighs or neck, probably assumed it was another part of the role play. Lilly didn't offer this information either. The *rough sex* was a casualty, a price her lifestyle made her responsible for.

Soon enough this grew into a stress in her body that manifested itself in open sores and ulcers in her mouth and throat, accompanied with spasms of her neck muscles anytime she tried to eat or swallow. Was this herpes? Another doctor at another clinic took one look into her larynx and couldn't understand. It wasn't herpes; it was something else. When he got to her nose with the scope, he jumped back in horror at what Lilly could only assume must have looked like the raw, bleeding, abused inner membranes of her nostrils from the constant cocaine abuse.

The doctor backed himself into the corner of the room closest to the door, waiting for the moment he could escape from her, the lowly junkie not deserving of treatment or kindness. The roughness of the inside of her nose had scared him from speaking to her further. He offered no advice other than to take it easy, relax, no mention of drug counseling or even a question to her about any possibility of a drug problem. The doctor wanted out of the room and away from her.

After the doctor's quick retreat, a nurse came in to give her some literature on stress and told her to stay hydrated. He didn't know what the sores and ulcers were, but they were most likely related to stress and would go away if she took it easy. Lilly went home and, not being able to eat, quieted her rumbling stomach with a few lines before she and Adam began their evening route. On the plus side, Lilly began losing weight because of her inability to swallow. Adam complimented her new, slimmer figure. He knew she wasn't eating; she picked at her food when they stopped at local fast-food restaurants, a behavior he encouraged. He never questioned her or asked her if she was okay. She never alluded to the fact that she was in pain or suffering, afraid that if he knew about the blisters, she would disgust him, and he wouldn't want to touch her anymore. None of their friends recognized her recent weight loss as anything more than an accomplishment and praised her for her efforts.

THE TIDE SHIFTED for both of them as addiction took a stronger hold. Adam, who once promised Lilly that he would take care of her, that she would never want for anything and that he would always provide for her, was falling behind in paying back Jose and now looked to Lilly for help.

Now that a debt was looming over them, Adam asked her to gather anything she could find of value so they could pawn it. They came across DVD titles, CD's, an old keyboard, and some of her father's tools he kept stashed away in the garage. But these items didn't fetch more than a few meals for the two of them and didn't dent the ever-growing debt they were racking up beside their lines of cocaine.

It wasn't enough, but Lilly would sell whatever she possessed that Adam perceived to have value. She would always do what he asked. After leaving the pawnshop with a measly twenty dollars, Adam received a phone call from a prominent customer. He was a man of means and didn't have a problem spending hundreds of dollars at a time on a single pickup. Adam enjoyed receiving these calls from him and wanted to keep this customer happy.

"Hey, man, you on deck?"

"Yo, yo, yo! Yes I am! What you need, man?" Adam responded, expecting for a big order to come through.

"Sup, let me get two 8-balls, and can you drop off over here at The Inn, the boys and I got a room for the weekend."

"On my way!" Adam said as he hung up the phone and rushed Lilly to ready the order so they could head over. When they arrived, the customer greeted them and introduced them to his two friends, the boys. When they completed the deal, the men invited them to stay for a line and a beer. Lilly sat herself down at the desk and poured out the sack, racking out one for each of them.

"You know, your girl is sexy with that coke, man, she knows how to rack it," the customer said to Adam.

"Haha," Adam laughed in agreement. "She's had a lot of practice."

"Hey, would you sell her too? I'll give you $200 right now, for just a quick one," the customer said, a joke to test the waters.

"Oh, shut the fuck up, you dick!" Lilly responded, also laughing but making sure they knew she was not for sale.

"Hey, you heard the lady." Adam laughed along with the tone of the room.

"Alright, well, how 'bout I just take her from you then!" the customer responded without hesitation, pulled a gun from his back, and pointed it right at Adam. The other men in the room stood at attention as the mood changed from light to dark.

"What! No! No, no, no!" Lilly screamed as she stood and froze in place.

"It's ok, Lilly." Adam said as he held a hand up in her direction, gesturing her to stay calm. "Look man, it's cool, we're cool. It doesn't have to be like this. Not over a bitch."

"Oh, I know it's cool. But come on, you can't be the only guy to taste a piece of that fat ass!" The man, holding the gun steady, took a few steps over towards Lilly and looked her up and down while he sucked on his lips. "I thought we were homies? You don't wanna share?" Standing an inch away from her, he reached out his arm and with his hand grasped onto her crotch. Lilly shivered and let out a light scream with a few tears.

"Get your fucking hands off of her!" Adam yelled. But, staring down the black barrel of a gun, stood still. The other men stepped closer to him, only an arms-length away, tense in their posture. "It's cool, it's cool. Just let her go, man, you can have whatever you want. Just let her go. Please." Adam's tone softened as he dropped his head and whimpered with Lilly.

"Oh, it's cool. Now? Yeah, it is cool. You know what?" The man let go of Lilly and again faced Adam. "It is cool, man. You don't wanna give me your bitch, maybe I'll just take your coke."

"Fucking take it! Go!" The man dropped his gun and held it at his side. Adam rushed to grab Lilly's arm and pull her from her state of fear. The two of them left the room without their coke or the money owed to them.

Lilly broke down once inside the safety of the car. She hadn't cried that hard since her favorite childhood dog died when she was nine.

"Oh my, God! Oh my, God! He could have killed you!"

"Shut the fuck up, Lilly! You don't think I know that? I'm the one who had the gun pointed in my face!" Adam let his aggression out onto her, having missed an opportunity to do so at the true source of his rage.

Lilly continued crying, holding her face in her hands and wiping at snot that fell from her nose.

"Fuck!" Adam banged his fists on the steering wheel. "You know what this means, Lilly! We're even more in debt than before, and we just lost one of our biggest customers! God, fucking damn it!"

"What are we gonna do?"

"I don't know, I don't fucking know!"

TWENTY-ONE

Bar Fight

T he summer was over, another successful season wrapped up. By the end, Lilly and Adam had taken over their local market and were always on call. They spent their days and nights in ten and twenty-minute increments, ten minutes at this person's house for this delivery, twenty minutes at another where they might stay to smoke a bowl. Their customer base had grown, and they never had over twenty minutes to spare at any single drop off. The newest group of customers included a a few people introduced to them by Jermaine, Sly's old friend. There was no loyalty in this game. As soon as word got out that Sly was "gone" and Adam was the fresh face, all calls went to him. There was no talk of mutiny or hostile takeover, only a simple switch to the new supplier. Jermaine was now Adam's newest best friend and tried to show his newfound allegiance by introducing him to a fresh set of consumers.

This new group comprised Amanda, Jermaine's new blonde-haired, blue-eyed girlfriend; her roommate Claire and boyfriend Bret; and Jermaine's close friend Ronny, a skinny blonde guy who smoked way too much weed for his stature and listened to just as much Reggae music. Also in the club was Ronny's innocent girlfriend Kristin, who knew about his drug habits, but didn't take part in the festivities herself. You wouldn't have known, though. She hung out with everyone and had energy equal to the rest of them, despite not having the elemental motivation. Lilly and Adam gravitated towards this new crew when Lilly discovered that Jermaine was friend's with Sly's old boyfriend Tom; the one she broke up with all those years ago, and who was also Lilly's old acquaintance from high school.

Because of this connection, and no upcoming parties to plan for, Adam and Lilly spent lots of time with this group in-between drop offs. Fri-Yay at JJ's house turned into The Yayzel at Jermain's house, a term Jermaine coined one coke-filled evening when they were all laughing and having fun. The Yayzel happened every Thursday night at Jermaine's, Thursdays because Friday had become the busiest night of the week for Adam and Lilly. They still stopped by JJ's for FriYay, but only to supply it, always too busy with other customers to stay longer than twenty minutes. However, they found more time on Thursdays and ended up spending many endless nights at Jermaine's. By now, Jermaine had fixed the front door, making it accessible, an inside joke Adam and Lilly liked to remind him of every once in a while.

Over the weeks and months, Lilly and Adam spent more and more time with Jermaine and his friends, and a familiar tingle of muted jealousy crept up inside her. It was the same feeling she got during the summer party season as she competed against the random girls Adam was still hooking up with under the desert moon, or in the dark shadows of the forest trees. Despite the two of them being together, that never stopped or waned. She looked forward to the off season, the brief weeks before and after the party season, when she would have his full attention. This was that time, yet his attention was still being pulled away. He had been sitting close to and talking with Claire, Amanda's roommate, who was always part of The Yayzel and also was always around anytime they were hanging out with the group.

There wasn't anything she could do about it though, at least not in the public space of her friends. She would, however, bring it up the next time she and Adam were alone. If one good thing came out of her official status with Adam, it was that she now had authority to bring up her discontents with him during the privacy of a personal conversation. She told herself he owed her at least that much after the symptoms of stress she'd allowed to happen to her body, for the sake of this relationship. Within reason, as he was still the boss and still the leader of the relationship and wasn't afraid to threaten her with its devastating end when her displeasures became too much.

At this Yayzel, Lilly overheard the conversation between Adam and Claire, her silent envy kept her listening. Her interest piqued when Claire giggled, followed by Adam telling her he liked the way her eyes sparkled when she laughed.

"What the fuck, Adam? Her eyes sparkle? Really?!" Lilly criticized him and for the first time in public.

His glare towards her intensified and burned through her. The rest of the group, thinking it was some kind of joke, oohed and awed and laughed at the ridiculousness of it all.

"I was joking, Lilly, calm down," Adam said to save the fight for a more private encounter.

"Yeah, whatever. I'm sitting right here, dude; you can at least be a little more subtle." Lilly let the words leave her mouth without hesitation, knowing she would pay for them later. She had become tired of the constant fight for his affection. Even now, amongst friends, there was no guarantee he belonged to her. Her compliance and silence against his transgressions had gotten her nowhere except to the throne at the head of a two-bit drug empire she never wanted. She accepted the seat because it was the only one right next to his. But there was nothing she could do about the endless line of women scheming to steal it from her. Another look from him in her direction and she silenced herself. She had already gone too far.

"What the fuck is your problem, Lilly?!" he screamed at her as they left the house and walked towards the street to their parked car. The Yayzel had become tense, and they had deliveries to make, anyway.

"Why the fuck are you disrespecting me like that in front of everybody?! You can't play me like that around our friends."

"I can do whatever the fuck I want!" he yelled and checked her, lunging forward without making contact but coming less than an inch away from her face.

Startled, she stepped backwards and slipped, falling sideways towards the passenger door of the car. The impact of her face cracked the window, and she fell completely into the wet and molded gutter, her body sandwiched in between the car and the raised curb. Silent tears and her complete submission followed as she slunk down further into the ground. She put a hand up to her cheek and pressed down on the swelling that had already begun.

"Listen," he breathed, "why do you act like this? You see what happens? I hate you for making me this crazy! Just chill! You know the rules. If you would just follow them, you wouldn't be sitting in a gutter, right now. But you don't listen, you bring this upon yourself." Lilly nodded in agreement, keeping her eyes averted towards the concrete. "Alright, now apologize to me, so we can move on and enjoy the rest of the night."

"I'm sorry." Her voice cracked as she spoke the words.

"Good girl... Now get in the car and rack me a line real quick, we gotta go meet Phil and Sarah." He walked to the driver side of the car without helping her up. There was no time, they had to meet Phil and Sarah, more customers they would see for a few minutes that evening, and again later in the evening or early in the morning when their sack ran out and they found another $20 to spend for a second pickup.

Exhausted, Lilly wanted to go home to sleep, for once. Adam allowed her to forgo the rest of the evenings deliveries and dropped her off at home. She woke up the next morning to no calls or texts from Adam, which usually happened every twenty minutes when they weren't together. He hadn't given her the night to herself. His obsession with her would not have allowed for that. A sinking sensation in her chest told her he had gone back to Jermaine's house after dropping her off. Claire's boyfriend Bret was not in attendance for the Yayzel. She called Jermaine, no answer, then Amanda, no answer. The last person she called was Claire, no answer. Knowing they were all in the same house, someone would have answered, because with the amount of cocaine still out on the table by the time she left the night before... they were still awake. She and Jermaine had a special connection because of their friendship during the Sly days. She called him again, and again, until he answered, wide awake and happy to talk.

"Where is he, Maine? I know he's there with Claire."

"I don't know. I don't know. I don't know if he's with her or not. Her bedroom is closed. I'm not going in there. I don't know what happened last night. I don't know anything."

"So, you admit he's there! I knew it! Just tell him to answer the phone right now! I'm not stupid, Maine! Put him on the phone!"

"Look, I don't know what's happening, I'm high—it's The Yayzel! Try calling him again, he'll probably answer, but I don't know where he is or what's going on."

"What the fuck! You know he's there! Stop playing! Put him on the phone!" she screamed into the phone, having had enough of the bullshit.

"Uhhh, fuck, uh, my dog is pissing on the rug, I gotta go, bye," Jermaine blurted before hanging up. He didn't have a dog.

"Fuck!" Lilly cried to herself, with no one listening. She turned in bed and screamed into the pillow, tears exploded from her eyes and bloody snot dripped from her nose. He was there; Jermaine confirmed it, in not so many words. But she could do nothing. This was her punishment for testing him, for pushing him, for daring him to chase after her and ignore the batting eyes of another pretty girl who was being nothing but sweet to him and welcoming of his attention. All she could do now was wait. He would be back when he finished with his plaything. She needed him to be. Even if Adam didn't want to admit it, Lilly helped him control the money and made sure they were selling more than they were sniffing. Which, if she was being honest with herself, wasn't happening anymore, but that didn't matter right now. They were a team, and one did not work without the other. Adam would never admit that, but Lilly knew it. Exhaustion got the best of her and she dried her eyes, showered, and waited by her phone for a call from him. In the meantime, her phone rang plenty. Customers asking for sacks, asking why Adam's phone was off, when they could deliver, etc. *Adam's phone is off because he was out partying last night, and I wasn't there to remind him to charge it, duh!* See, he needed her.

By mid-morning, the party would have been winding down and Adam would either go home to sleep it off, or head straight to her to charge his phone and answer the many missed calls from the night and morning. Yes, people still wanted cocaine at 7, 8, 9, 10 am, and they were always awake and ready to deliver. She was right. It was 10:30 am, the roar of the tires ripping down the alleyway, and the thud of Drum'n'Bass from his speakers announced his arrival. She rolled her eyes and crossed her arms as she posed, waiting for his entrance.

"Dude! Check me! Nothing happened! I swear!" he announced as he let himself in. He was in high spirits, while Lilly was close to tears.

"Check you?" Her face puzzled.

"Check my dick! I swear nothing happened, I just went back over there and passed out."

"I'm not gonna smell your dick, dude. That's gross! Plus, hello, you probably just took a shower," Lilly reasoned.

Adam laughed at her, maybe trying to lighten the mood. It worked.

"You're so crazy, you know nothing happened, I just wanted you to relax and rest and have a night off." He said this as if to convince her, or himself, that he was too good of a man to wrong her in such a way. How could she even fathom he would do that to her? But that wasn't the truth. There was an unspoken understanding between the two of them. Adam was to go off and play his games with other girls, because it was fun, and boys are allowed to have fun. In return, he would pretend that Lilly was the only girl, or that she was the most important one, and that none of his other toys meant as much.

In not so many words, he promised her he would always lie to her, because he loved her. And he did that. Lilly always had money for shopping sprees. He kept her appetite for the party satisfied, and she held the seat steady right next to him at the top of his game. It was all eyes on him, as the dealer, the supplier, the homie, and the hookup. And because all eyes were on him, she was in the peripheral, and the second most important role in the scene they had built.

Maybe she was crazy? What right did she have to ask more from him? It was no more different today that it was when they began this arrangement. The only difference was that Adam had become a prominent drug dealer and Lilly was lucky to be right there with him.

He embraced her and cuddled her on the bed. Locked in his loving gaze, she nuzzled her face in his shoulder, careful not to disturb the right side, tender from the car window that got in the way. Her anxiety melted away as he held her. A tender moment that became passionate as they made up for the lost time that harsh evening had taken from them.

IT WAS NOVEMBER, Lilly's 22nd birthday. Adam wanted to do something special for her, so he invited their friends, Jermaine's group, out to a bar. In attendance were Jermaine and Amanda, Claire and Bret, Ronny and Kristin, Tom and his new girlfriend Samantha. Lilly had been on edge that day, her throat had been hurting more than usual, and she was nervous about seeing Claire. She hadn't seen the group since that Yayzel two weeks earlier when she made the mistake of calling out Adam for flirt-

ing. They had long made up, but this would be the first
time she would reconnect with them all.

They arrived at the bar in two cars, and the night
began. The group celebrated the occasion like nothing had
ever happened. Drinks were free for Lilly and by the
middle of the night, she was rather sloshed, the bumps of
cocaine they were sniffing out of recessed cigarette filters
not enough to sober her up. At about midnight, she
wanted more. Sneaking bathroom bumps was more of a
tease than anything. She leaned over to Adam and asked
him to take her out to the car so they could blow a few
lines.

"Okay," he responded, "let me see if Claire wants to
come too." That was enough to set her off.

"Why? Why Claire? Why do you give a fuck about
her?" Lilly said loudly enough to grab the attention of the
entire bar. The crowd now focused on her, even over the
music and commotion of a packed house.

"Nothing! Chill!" Adam yelled to calm the situation
down, but not realizing he was only adding to it. They
were all drunk, control was not something any of them
could have possessed at the moment.

"No! Fuck this! I knew this would happen! You're
fucking her, aren't you?! Why do you care about Claire?!"
Lilly screamed, even the bartenders now stopping to see
what was going to happen next.

Adam, without saying a word, grabbed Lilly by her
arm and pulled her out of the bar. The rest of them
followed, knowing this wasn't a calm-down-and-get-back-
to-drinking situation.

Outside, the screaming match continued. Lilly accused
Adam of cheating, Adam called her names and told her to
shut the fuck up. It was enough for Lilly. After four years of
quiet subordination, she could no longer keep up the

charade. She approached Adam, and in front of all their friends, slapped him across the face three times. Jermaine, acting quick, grabbed Adam and stopped him from pummeling Lilly to the ground. His force wasn't enough, as both Ronny and Tom had to also offered resistance against his rage. Bret stood back, confused at why his girl-friend's name had caused such an altercation.

"Fuck you! You fucking asshole! I fucking hate you!" Lilly scream-cried towards the pile of male bodies all enveloping Adam's.

"Amanda, get her the fuck out of here!" Jermaine yelled to his girlfriend.

"Come on, Lilly, let's go." Amanda grabbed Lilly and pulled her away towards Bret's car. Bret followed and gave Amanda the keys before returning to his girlfriend, who stood there frozen with a hand held over her gaping mouth.

The bar was only a mile from Lilly's and the two girls arrived within minutes of leaving. Lilly was a weepy mess and needed help inside. She cried while Amanda tried to comfort her.

"He's gonna leave me, he's gonna leave me!" Lilly wailed.

"No, he's not, he loves you. This was just a fucked-up situation, it's gonna be fine. Don't worry. Just try to get some sleep, okay?" Amanda's reassuring voice calmed her, although she didn't believe it.

She fell asleep and slept deeper and harder than she had in a long time, considering she never had time to blow those rails...

TWENTY-TWO

Aftermath

I t was the morning after. Lilly woke up in a cold sweat with anxious breaths as she reflected on the events that transpired the night before. A heavy chest came back to her when she looked at her phone. There were no missed calls or texts from Adam. It would be hard to fix this one, but she was going to try. She called, but there was no answer. Texted, no response. She spent the entire morning calling and calling, each ring only adding to her anguish.

There was a party that following weekend. *He has to call by then.* They never showed up at parties without each other. *I still have his coke. He wouldn't not come back for that, at least.* He couldn't re-up without paying back the front for the last one, and Adam was already short this time, he wouldn't risk not trying to sell every gram to make as much back as he could, and he would bargain with Jose for the rest of it.

The day wore on and Adam didn't call. He didn't call for the entire week as Lilly spent those days alone in her studio, crying, starving, and listening to Alanis Morissette's Jagged Little Pill album to get through the daylight hours. She spoke to old friends, they all offered her support, but none of them could offer her any relief from her broken heart. With nothing else to keep her going, she kept hoping Adam would remember all the sacrifices she had made for him and come back to her. She reasoned it was the stress of everything that was keeping him away for this long. No one else knew any different, until she got a phone call from someone who did. It was Tom who called. Her old friend Tom, always reliable and sensitive.

"Tom? Hey, what's up? Have you heard from Adam?" Lilly asked as she answered the phone, wasting no time cutting to the chase.

"Actually, that's why I was calling. I wanted to let you know because the party is this weekend, and I didn't think it was fair to have something like this surprise you." He had a tone of sadness in his voice, like he was already feeling sorry for her.

"What do you mean? What is it?"

"Well, I haven't even told Jermaine yet because honestly, I thought you should know first..."

"Tell me, please!" Lilly cut him off. She couldn't help her anxiety at this point.

"Um, Amanda broke up with Jermaine yesterday, but didn't tell him why, I called Adam today for a sack and he pulled up with Amanda riding shotgun. So, I guess he's with Amanda now, and that's why she broke up with Maine."

"WHAT?! Are you fucking kidding me?!"

"I'm sorry, Lilly, I really am."

"Oh, that bitch thinks she's gonna steal my seat?" Lilly said, half-yelling, half-crying.

"Huh? Look, I just thought you should know because

he's probably going to bring her to the party this weekend."

"Oh, we'll see about that!" Lilly, too upset to continue, hung up. Tom was only trying to help, but her emotions got the best of her. She called Jermaine before she gave herself a chance to process the information on her own.

"Hello?" Jermaine answered, ignorant of what had happened to his relationship and the real reason Amanda left him.

"So, I just got off the phone with Tom. Amanda's fucking Adam!" Lilly said, no longer crying, but screaming.

"Oh? Wow! Okay, that's fine. Fuck her and fuck him, fuck both of them! She can go get hit by a fucking bus!" Jermaine's response was excitable and peppy, it still upset him, but he disguised it well behind a facade of toughness.

"Yup, that's what I thought too! Fuck them! That asshole still hasn't even had the balls to call me and tell me what the hell is up, he just goes and fucking steals your girl and he thinks he's gonna bring her to the party this weekend and disrespect me like that in front of all our friends!"

"Nope, nope, fuck them, I'm not letting that happen. You and me will go to the party this weekend then. You down?" Jermaine had come up with the perfect plan for redemption.

"Yes! Fuck 'em," Lilly responded. Determined not to let Amanda get away with this, Lilly fumed. No tears left. She was full of only rage.

The evening came, and it was time to go to the party. Lilly had to find another ride because Jermaine called at the last minute and said that he couldn't go through with the confrontation. No biggie, Lilly had a million friends and all of them were going to the party. One of them would have an extra seat for her, the Royal Highness of the subculture. Another friend from another crew came to get her, Kitten. Someone she knew, and her crew knew, but this person belonged to another party crew all together and was more of an acquaintance than close; but everyone was a friend at the party, so it made no difference. Kitten's was a different kind of party crew, not the kind that organized parties, but more of a group of friends that always attended them, you could count on them to come and for that they coined themselves the Stay High party crew. Kitten from Stay High was a sweet girl, she was always friendly with Lilly and always down to help a raver in need with a ride when she could.

Lilly got picked up, and they were on their way. As per usual for Lilly, they negated the map point, a perk Kitten hadn't experienced before. Straight to the gate, no cover, no ticket price with Lilly in the car. Another fun perk that Kitten and the two other ravers with them appreciated. Regardless of what was happening with her and Adam, she was still family and the crew would not charge her gate entrance. She was a friend to them, and in Adam's absence, this did not change. The crew at the gate was Stuff, Neil, and JJ. The three of them surrounded the passenger side window to say hello but also offer condolences. JJ took a moment to confirm for her what Tom suspected, that Adam was already in attendance and that he had in fact brought another girl with him. She didn't know the girl's name, didn't want to, but she was here, clinging to Adam's side and not saying much. Lilly thanked her friends for the warning and took a deep breath, ready to take on the night.

The party was awkward at first. By now everyone had heard the news, and no one looked down on Adam for bringing a new stand-in to replace Lilly. There she was, across the clearing in the forest floor that would become the dance floor that night. Her eyes stayed pointed down towards the ground as she stood behind Adam for refuge from Lilly's glare. It was a scowl so strong that it cut through the air and slapped her right in the face. But Lilly wasn't there to start drama, only to make her presence known and stand tall, showing everyone that she would not be the sullen, lost little puppy dog sitting home alone on a Saturday night when all her friends were out having yet another amazing night. She found her close group of friends that had been there since the beginning, before she and Adam were ever a thing, her old 1 Earth, 1 Rave buddies. She stuck to them and they welcomed her presence. Once the pills kicked in, it was easy to ignore Amanda, who stayed away from her, anyway.

By the early morning, Lilly was ready to make her point and test the lengths to which she could pressure Adam. He watched her throughout the party. Amanda stayed back and tried to avoid Lilly's eyes, but Adam's followed her as she moved throughout the party, his eyes turning fiery when she spoke to other men that were not him, the reaction lighting her own fire within. One that made her believe she was winning.

Kitten mentioned, in the early dawn, that she was ready to leave, but it was far from the time when the party was over. The crew always stayed late to tear down and party amongst themselves. It was here that Lilly found an opportunity. Lilly approached Adam, half-scared that he would ignore her, but hoping that he wouldn't.

"Look, I know this sucks, but Kitten is leaving, and she's taking home someone else in my seat. I don't have a ride." Tears welled up in her eyes from the sheer nervous energy she had built up inside her.

"Shut up, Lilly! She's not gonna leave you! No one's gonna leave you in the forest!" Adam yelled back at her, annoyed that she would even ask for something so inappropriate.

"I'm not lying! Look, she has someone else in her car and they're getting ready. Please!" Lilly was begging and crying now. She had exhausted herself during the previous full night of partying and felt emotional from the comedown off the pills.

"Fine! Just stop crying. But you're sitting in the back!" Adam couldn't stand to see her cry, still. Lilly walked away from the encounter before he changed his mind and waved goodbye as Kitten and her car drove off. It was a minor battle, but another she had won. A few more hours passed, and she enjoyed her time with her close circle of friends, the family, now that the rest of the random party kids were gone.

By the early afternoon, the crew took down the party and packed the trucks. Shade was pleased with the money he made that night, and they were ready to take the party back to his place for the celebratory afterparty. Only Lilly wouldn't be going to this one. Adam would make sure of that. Still trying to keep her distance, Adam motioned to Amanda that it was time to go. Lilly, from a distance, headed the signal too, and both girls walked towards his car.

"Alright, Amanda, should Lilly sit in the front or back?" he asked, giving Amanda the option, and as if to sign to Lilly that she was above her now. But Amanda wasn't that bold, she would not test her luck and risk an altercation. She kept silent and shrugged her shoulders. Maybe Adam guessed she would, because the next words that came out of his mouth were, "Aight, Lilly in the front, Amanda in the back." Another win and she hadn't even tried.

A half an hour down the road, they made it out of the

forest and stopped at the first fast food spot for a refuel from the long and exhausting night. They all sat together at a table. Lilly and Amanda acted friendly towards each other, as they always did in their times together before. Adam ordered and paid for both of their meals. At the end of the meal, Adam suggested they both use the restroom. It was still another hour and a half before making it home. They followed one another to the bathroom. Lilly sensed nervousness seeping from Amanda, and felt it in her own skin just as much. After the toilet, both girls found themselves at the sink at the same moment. Amanda kept her head down still, knowing she had no right to be there, in the space or situation that she had inserted herself.

"Why did you do it?" Lilly asked.

"Huh?" Amanda responded, stunned, not able to find the words and taken over by fear of the impending wrath.

"You ruined a perfectly good relationship with Maine, for what? You think you can have him? Let me tell you something, Amanda. He's mine. He's been mine, he's always gonna be mine. All you did was take advantage of a situation that you shouldn't have because you're gonna really miss having anything to do with him once I'm done here. Do you understand?"

"Uh, huh," was all Amanda could muster out of herself.

"Good. Because you just lost not only two great friends, but your connect and your own boyfriend. Good fucking job," Lilly said, confident in the submission she evoked in Amanda. She walked out of the bathroom collected, as if nothing happened. She knew now, more than ever, that the events that happened since that morning re-cemented her status again in Adam's eyes and that it would only be a matter of time before she got him back. But she would learn next that it wouldn't be that easy, and her confidence was perhaps premature.

LILLY SPENT days after the rave in the same Alanis Morissette sinkhole that kept her in bed but unable to sleep, hungry but too sad to eat, skinnier still with only a personal sized stash of cocaine left to keep her going. It was a deep depression that she couldn't escape from. She considered her options. Did she have enough cocaine left to sniff quick and hard enough to allow herself to drift off into oblivion? No, not with the tolerance she had developed. Instead, she used what was left to follow that rabbit down into his hole where she succumbed to sniffing cocaine alone, surrounding herself with darkness behind tin-foiled windows and a forever locked door.

Without the option of overdose to ease her suffering, she considered how easy it would be to string herself up in the rafters of her father's garage using his utility rope that hung in the corner, the one the pawn shop owner had no use for and wouldn't accept. Ironic (thanks Alanis), Adam tried to get rid of that rope for her, but now it was there, sitting, waiting, mocking her as the tool she would use to end her suffering. Adam still hadn't called, still wasn't answering her phone calls, but why would he at this point? She crept into the sting that Amanda had taken her seat for good, maybe she would have to live with that, or not, an out was right over there, taunting her as it hung in the corner.

TWENTY-THREE

Wanna Roll?

I t was FriYay again. Lilly received a call from her old friend JJ. The two spoke at the party, but not to the extent that JJ wanted to with all the people and chaos happening around them. JJ revealed she had been wanting to reach out to Lilly, but that she didn't know when the right time was. She understood Lilly must be hurting and wanted to extend herself to whatever she might need, even if that only meant a shoulder to cry on. It was a welcome phone call as Lilly struggled with no real friends left.

Because JJ knew Adam wouldn't be attending FriYay, she took the opportunity to re-invite Lilly, who more than accepted the invitation. Her heart jumped at the invite. Fri-Yay was a refuge and everything that she needed to help pull her out of the depression that engulfed her in Adam's absence. All of her closest Junglist friends were there, Freestyle, Bass Man and Strange Guy, Stan, and JJ.

It took Lilly some practice before she settled into the evening. Within the first 20-minutes of arriving, she found herself confronted with a debilitating panic attack that sent her screaming into the bathroom.

"Lilly? You okay?" JJ's kind voice said from outside the locked bathroom door.

Inside, Lilly shook and trembled as she gasped for a breath she couldn't find. Her vision blurred and her heart thumped in her chest. Lilly did nothing while her helium-filled head floated up to and bounced off the ceiling, and sweat dampened her clothing, keeping her body stuck heavy on the bathroom floor.

"Let me in, it's okay. Let me help you."

Lilly couldn't hear her friend's concerned request; she was focused on trying to keep the walls from swallowing her up. It wasn't until the door broke open that she came back to her senses and distracted herself from the experience. Her friends rushed in and joined her on the cool floor, the sight of her body curled up and shivering too much for any of them to bear witness without offering comfort.

"I'm sorry, I'm sorry..." Lilly mumbled through tears. "I... just... I don't know what's wrong with me..."

"It's okay, don't trip, we're here for you, girl," JJ said.

"Aw, man, we get it. Shit, my last breakup with my ex, pfft. Damn, that shit was hard," Bass Man said, easing her embarrassment. The rest of them nodded along, as if they'd all been there before.

"Hey, you made it a full twenty minutes!" JJ exclaimed. "You guys never used to stay here that long, always so busy slanging. But now you can just chill. Come on, I'll rack a good one for you."

"Thanks," Lilly said with a smirk as her body come back to her. They helped her off the floor and moved on from the moment.

. . .

THE EVENING CENTERED on cocaine and the rumors that had been spreading since the party. Everyone took their turn sharing stories, Adam being the major topic of interest.

"Yo, I saw him last Wednesday at a house party. Amanda was with him. She kinda just sits behind him and doesn't talk to anyone. People were all talking shit, too. Like things just aren't going well for him," said Bass Man, shaking his head like a disappointed father. "I think he's in trouble with his connect, whoever that is." Bass Man didn't know, but Lilly did.

"Yup, I saw him last week too when he came by for weed. Fucker asked me for money and weed! I said, sure homie, hook me up with a sack. But he didn't have none," Stan chimed in.

"Oh yeah, I know. Me too! He hit me up for money and said some shit about how he really needed help. He got aggressive with me, dude! Like he's given me so much free coke and I needed to pay him back or some shit," said Freestyle, corroborating the stories.

Lilly listened to them document his fall from grace as she imagined her king tumbling down off his throne in such a public way, hearing in her mind the loud crashing noise his skull made as it hit the concrete. She knew how deep in debt he was with Jose, and the sack he left with her after her birthday blowout hadn't helped the situation. Amanda wasn't ready for the responsibility; she didn't have a clue what she was walking into. The stupid girl didn't realize that Adam was a sensitive man that needed to be taken care of. She was supposed to protect him from himself, keep him from sniffing too much, make sure he kept the money right. Amanda was to blame for this fall, even though he had been slipping for far longer than the girl had been around. But look where he was now, what a stupid man he was. Letting his ego pull him away from the only woman who understood him and could keep him safe and cared for.

LILLY FOUND herself that next morning still at JJ's house and not ready to go back to the darkness that consumed her little studio garage apartment. The panic followed her, but this time it was not as intense as it was the evening before. She taught herself to breathe through the rising heartbeat and waited for it to calm itself. JJ offered her refuge in a spare guest room; she could stay as long as she wanted. In the guest room, there was little sleeping. The cocaine made sure not much of that happened for any of them. Lilly only rested her eyes in the still darkness of the room as the sun rose outside the blanket covered windows. Days and nights and weeks passed for her in that room, each one the same as the last.

JJ WALKED AROUND in the kitchen, stirring Lilly fully awake. It was already two pm. She must have dozed off for at least a bit since the last time she checked her phone around 9am when she retreated to the darkened room, still up from the night before. Two in the afternoon meant it was time to get up and begin the day. Sitting at JJ's break-fast bar, that familiar sadness crept in. She fell into her longing for Adam. Even though they were done, even though he was never coming back to her, she missed him ferociously. It was 2:10 pm. She remembered looking down at her phone again when JJ stepped outside to smoke a cigarette. Lilly contemplated joining her, but her solemness kept her heavy in her seat. Her throat still charred from the long night of smoking, and the days and nights previous, she instead would wait for the next one. Sitting there, sulking over a glass of water, her phone rang. The caller ID read Adam.

In an instant wave of excitement, her heart skipped and fluttered; her eyelids widened and her pupils dilated; a flush of blood rose to the surface of her skin and she became warm, while a simultaneous chill ran down her spine. "Hello?" she answered with apprehension.

"Hi," said the voice on the other end. It was in fact Adam. The voice she hadn't heard in too long and the sound of which stimulated a happy sting in her chest.

"Hi," was all she could say back.

"You wanna roll?"

"Yeah." Yes, a million times YES! That was what she wanted to say. Her answer to him was always yes, if it meant she could be in his presence, or if it would please him.

"Where are you?" he asked.

"At JJ's."

"Really?" he asked, puzzled.

"Yeah, I've been spending a lot of time here."

"Okay, cool. I'm coming over," he finished without saying goodbye, and hung up the phone. The conversation was short and simple, as they always were. Lilly jumped up from that breakfast bar and rushed outside to inform JJ.

"Wait, he just called you right now? And he's coming over here?" JJ asked for clarification. Lilly only nodded in confirmation. "And you want him to come over? You sure?"

"Yes, yes, I do. Is it okay?" Lilly asked. Her voice almost in fever.

"I mean, yeah, it's cool. As long as you're cool?" JJ asked again, double checking that her friend was making the best decision for herself. But Lilly had never been surer of anything in her life. There wasn't anything in the world Lilly could have asked for that she wanted more than for Adam to be in her presence, willfully. She hurried through a shower and a light sprucing and waited for the sound of his tires screeching down the road, the thumping of his speakers that would announce his arrival.

Adam arrived, and it was as if nothing had ever happened between them. There was no talk about the separation, the fight, Amanda, and she didn't question it. She was happy to be back and wasn't keen to the confrontation, anyway. She didn't have any right to question him or his motives anyway, because she was the lucky one. He smiled at her and hugged her and handed her a deep blue pill embossed with the symbol of an ice cream cone. Blue Ice Cream Cones had been going around and were a popular choice amongst her circle of friends. He offered one to JJ, who also indulged herself. Adam was the last to partake, but followed once the ladies had taken theirs.

The trip was insignificant but memorable. Lilly couldn't tell if it was the previous night's partying, or if perhaps her brain hadn't had enough time to recoup the lost feel-good chemicals? But this roll was less euphoric and more emotional. Could have been the pills, all pills were different, and Lilly was accustomed to the variation. Some pills were "amp-y" and made her want to dance until her legs fell off, others were super "roll-y" and turned her into a puddle on the floor. There were pills that gave her a strong euphoric body high, others that had a mild hallucinogenic feature, and some still that invoked a strong sense of connection. These were the latter. *It must be the pills*. Because Adam becoming emotional with her was something that never happened in the presence of others.

He shared with her what had been happening with him

over the last few weeks in her absence regarding his connection to Jose. That he didn't blame her, but he hinted at the fact that if she had not done *that thing she did*, things might be different, and he wouldn't be in trouble. Both Lilly and JJ listened as he told them he had fallen far behind in his payments to Jose, that he had been so distraught with Lilly estranged from him that he had been sniffing way more than his profit margin could account for. A few days earlier, Jose had gotten fed up with him and come to collect the money that Adam owed to him, but he didn't have it. Instead, Jose took the rest of his sack, only a gram but still significant to him, and cut him off. Adam no longer had access to cocaine. Now, there were other dealers and Adam had many friends, but the cocaine he got from Jose was pure, Adam never had to pay upfront, and he had access to as much of it as he wanted, or used to, anyway. This was a condition that would turn even the most casual user into a certified addict. Adam was now in panic mode. He owed money to Jose and he no longer had a means to repay him or get any more cocaine.

Lilly and JJ listened to this story as if he was recounting the tragedy of war. Their faces showed concern and horror as he spun them through his tale, the theme of which sung woe-unto-him. In a heightened state of emotional outpouring, JJ and Lilly were both pulled towards helping him. There must be something they could do, they couldn't sit back and let their poor friend suffer like this. It was JJ who came up with an idea first. JJ had sold cocaine in high school and only stopped when her habit became too much for her to continue hiding from her parents. But now, older, living in a house her parents gifted to her, and with an appreciation for coke that had grown again since she and Lilly had become close, there was an opportunity. JJ knew Adam had the market cornered on the best cocaine and plenty of customers looking for it all the time. What if *she* became the dealer and Adam worked for her? She would maintain possession of the product while Adam would sell to his customers, and a portion of the profits would go back to Jose to pay off his debt. He would give over the reins and stepping down, but he was desperate for a solution and almost relieved to let go of the responsibility. He would regain his access and the party would continue on as it had, only with more control over him, which he very much needed.

The first step in this new master plan would involve introducing JJ to Jose. Lilly came up with the next idea for JJ to host a Snow Party, inviting all their friends and Jose and the homies. Adam agreed that this was a great idea. A Snow Party, which as the name suggests, is a party centered on the sniffing of cocaine, like any other FriYay but larger and louder, as is a side effect of a larger guest list. This would be the perfect introduction to show Jose that JJ was cool and trustworthy. Without hesitation, and still high on ecstasy, Adam called Jose and passed along the invite, letting him know that the main event of the night would be a mountain of cocaine provided by the host (and purchased in advance from Jose), free to anyone who wanted it, racked out and served by two of her hot stripper friends.

They set the party for that FriYay. JJ invited all of their closest friends, plus a few more, and Jose showed up with the homies. The air was thick between Adam and Jose, but they were still friends and Jose could put aside the tension for the sake of meeting new customers. As promised, JJ had invited two beautiful women, who were in fact strippers and adult film stars, and had them sit at the table behind a mountain of cocaine that rivaled the one Tony Montana sat behind the night he was assassinated in his home, planning a war. The topless girls racked out lines on demand as the men stood around and gawked at the glittery pasties that bounced with the movement of them cutting coke. They gracefully kept the party served through the night.

Several hours into the party, Adam asked Jose if he would come outside for a cigarette. He motioned to JJ and Lilly to join. Once outside, Adam, subdued by the ball of cocaine in his throat, introduced the idea to Jose. "Okay, I know I owe you a lot of money, and I appreciate you being so cool with me, we're homies, and I wanna take care of it, so we came up with an idea." Adam paused the pitch and looked to JJ for validation. "This is JJ, this is her house, she's the homie."

"Hey man, what's up. JJ," she said with a smile and a friendly tone as she held her cigarette with her mouth and reached out a hand to shake his.

"Oh, this is your house? Cool, cool. Thanks for having us over," he said, referencing his band of homies all standing behind him who followed him outside but kept a few feet back to give him privacy.

"Cool, man. Thanks for coming," JJ responded with similar pleasantries.

"Alright, so look. JJ has this house, she also wants to get in the game, and I have the customers," Adam began… "JJ would like to pick up from you, and I will work for her, slanging. She's cool to front, she's good for it, and when we finish the sack and pick up again, she'll give you a little extra towards my debt." Adam laid out his plan and searched Jose's face of stone for an endorsement.

Jose took a long moment to think before responding.

"Hold up…" Jose paused. "Does she know how much money you owe me?" His face was more serious than Lilly had ever seen.

"Dawg… come on. It's chill, we can fix it," Adam assured Jose and himself with a posture that sunk his neck down into his shoulders and hands that held themselves out in front of his body either as a shield or a sign of submission.

"Look, let's start small, like one to two ounces, and then when we finish selling, I can give you like $200 on top of the next pickup, and we'll just keep doing that until it's paid off," JJ answered with confidence.

"$200!" Jose scoffed and laughed. "This fool owes me $5,000! I need at least $500, and I want $500 right now for coming out here." He addressed JJ as if Adam wasn't standing right there. The real gangster was coming out now. For the first time since they met, Lilly was uneasy and scared in his presence.

"Alright, alright, let's calm down. It's all cool," Adam said with a smile, trying to diffuse the tension. "JJ's gonna pickup, right now, two ounces. We can't do the extra $500 right now, but I know I can sell off at least an ounce by the end of the weekend and JJ will give you an extra $1,000 off that, and then $500 for every ounce after. So, once I'm done with these two, that'll be an extra $1,500 in your pocket, that's already a lot, come on dawg, it's cool. We're homies." Adam was rambling now, something he some-times did when he was excited or not feeling confident. He knew Jose didn't want to play this game anymore, he wanted his money.

Jose took a long time to think, showing no emotion on his face. "Alright, we can try that," he said. "Just don't give this fucker any coke, he's cut off!" Jose joked, to lighten the mood and get the group back into the party spirit. Their business handled.

"Aw fuck you, dawg!" Adam said, and the rest of them laughed along.

Back at the party, tensions released, and Lilly was among friends again. She talked with the homies again, as she often did. Jose joined in and shared with Lilly more about the situation that Adam had not filled them in on. "Lilly, you were gone, and I don't know why, but that fool stole four ounces from me. You know how much money that is, like $4,500 and the other $500 is from when he started slipping when you were still there. I can't keep making excuses for him."

"Wait, he stole it?" Lilly said in shock.

"Well, that's how my boss sees it," Jose responded. "You think I'm the boss? I'm not the boss. I'm nobody, but somebody knows me. The boss knows who I do business with and he keeps track. I tried to keep Adam out of it cause he's the homie, but boss know, and he don't fuck around." Lilly's face held tight with wide eyes and a mouth lightly gaping. "Yeah! I'm telling you. And it's not even about the cash, yo. This fucker is crazy. He'll kill you over $500, he don't give a fuck, so $5,000? Fuck, you better watch out! I'm telling you he's watching, he knows where Adam lives, where his sister goes to school, where his mom and dad work. He knows about you too, Chica. He knows everything and he let me know that if he keeps fucking up, it's gonna be a problem. I covered for him again this time, but I can't keep doing it. I don't have that kind of money either. If he fucks up again, it's gonna be me, or him."

Lilly was less sure about their genius plan now. This wasn't a game, and it wasn't about partying anymore. There was money at stake and the threat was real. Did Adam grasp the significance of it all, or was he still only looking for a chance to get high? Maybe he did, and that's why he was so eager to hand it all over to JJ.

"Look, just remember," Jose added, "if it ever goes bad, you just tell me onions."

"Onions?" Lilly questioned.

"Yeah, onions. It's onions. I'll know that's it. We're done. Shit's gone bad."

Lilly nodded to give the appearance that she understood, but she didn't, not yet.

TWENTY-FOUR

A Cab Ride Home

I t was going to be a big weekend. Adam had planned to take JJ's coke out to several parties and come back with cash in hand. It was Thursday and instead of picking up two ounces like they had discussed at the party, Adam convinced both sides that they needed five, five ounces of pure Mexican cocaine, a grand total of $5,600 now owed to Jose by JJ, plus agreeing to paying off Adam's debt of $5,000 that would trail them. If all went according to plan, Adam would sell ALL of it for a total street value of $12,000, leaving plenty of room to pay back the front, a portion of Adam's debt, and leaving a profit for JJ. But all would not go according to plan, Lilly and JJ both expected some of it they would party away. JJ asked Lilly to make sure Adam came back with at least $11,000 or enough left-over cocaine to match the value. She relinquished the brick right over to Adam, who took possession and headed off to the weekend's shenanigans. JJ preferred to stay behind and let Adam do all the hard work that came along with selling drugs. It was grunt work and she would rather be the moneyman who sat safely away from risk. Adam was fine with assuming all the risks if it meant he got to hold and control the drugs. He was on top of his little world and his confidence shown through in the ego that swelled around him.

The first stop on the tour was a house party in the neighboring mid-century modern city of Pasadena. The house sat on top of a hill, a beautiful marvel hidden away from the busy streets in a quiet neighborhood, full of tall windows and backyard palm trees. They wouldn't be here long, they stayed nowhere for very long. This was business. Before the two even entered the home, Adam's customer Paul greeted them on the front lawn. He was another a customer that had first belonged to their old friend Sly. Paul was a lanky dude who would have identified himself as a street kid. He spent his free time tagging buildings hidden behind locked fences and skateboarding on private properties that had banned the act all together. He had a shaved head and a kind voice. It was Paul who had invited Adam and Lilly to the party, knowing full well the cocaine wouldn't be in short supply.

"Yo! You made it! What up!" Paul shouted to Adam as they walked up the driveway.

"Yo, yo dawg! I'm here!" Adam shouted back as the three met and exchanged handshakes and half-hugs.

"Alright, you ready to go in? I got a few people to introduce you to," Paul said, looking at Adam.

"Let's do it!" Adam responded. The pure anticipation of the party caused endorphins to release into their bloodstreams.

The scene inside was an iconic mix of raver kids, the DJs, and their crews. Through the front entrance and into the living room was a wall of speakers stacked to the ceiling, much like the ones she had first seen at Shade's apartment, what felt like a million years ago now. The back wall of the living room held a sliding glass door that led out to the pool area, where she found a bar that was only offering water and orange juice. Laser lights and glow sticks flooded the walls of the house and lit up the palm trees that protected the back yard. There were girls dressed as fairies and princesses splashing in the pool and tangling themselves up in their wings, makeup dripping down their faces. There were guys dressed in full, neon body suits covered in lights, and the DJ's were always the easiest to spot standing next to their record cases or wearing headphones around their necks.

Paul began the introductions, and the sack came out. Someone wanted a twenty, another wanted a gram. Each time the sack came out, Lilly took on a new role as a server as she weighed out the orders and packaged them up. Adam held the money and made time for them to sniff a line in between customers. They hadn't planned on staying as long as they did, but as the party grew, so did the customers. As Lilly soaked in the rave energy of the party and thudded along to the music, she became bored with cocaine and wanted instead to do ecstasy. Adam agreed and ordered her a few pills from the water bar's secret menu, and sent her off to enjoy the party. Lilly took one pill and stuffed the other three in her pocket for later.

By the time her pill kicked in, she had run into her friend, Kitten. They hadn't seen or spoken to each other since the party right after the breakup when Kitten offered her a ride. Kitten was someone who always popped up at parties and clicked with Lilly when the two of them were high. Each time they met, they acted like best friends who hadn't seen each other in far too long, but neither of them attempted to keep the relationship going outside of those party encounters. Regardless, they were fast friends and spent the party close to each other.

Lilly and Kitten had been sharing stories of their lives since they had seen each other at the last party, and the subject of Adam leaving Lilly for that other woman came up again, considering it had only recently resolved itself. "I figured you two were getting back together that next day 'cause you left with him," Kitten said. "I can't believe he still left you hanging way longer than that."

"I know, but you know what, I fucked up. Like bad. I really am just happy that he came back. I kinda wanna show him how much I appreciate him. Do something special, ya know?" Lilly said, looking to Kitten for any kind of suggestion.

"I have a great idea!" Kitten said with a seductive grin on her face. "Ok, hear me out. What if we," she pointed to herself and Lilly as she spoke, "gave him a threesome!" Kitten jumped in the air as she let out the words in pure excitement. That energy poured over into Lilly as a wave of ecstasy hit her.

"Whoa! That is a great idea! He would totally love that! Oh my god, you would do that for me?" Lilly said, shocked that Kitten was such a good friend that she would offer herself like that in an act to save her and Adam's relationship. A few weeks ago, something like this would have been the furthest thing from her mind, but having won him back, she wanted to do something big. A grand gesture like this would be perfect.

"You're my girl, I'd do anything for you!" The two girls embraced and pouty-faced their foreheads together. With a new mission in mind, Lilly and Kitten left the dance floor looking for Adam. Lilly wasn't allowed to bother Adam after he had sent her off to the dance floor with her pills, but for something like this, she was sure he would make an exception. By the time they found Adam, they could see that he was in the middle of another deal, and not interested in being bothered. He waved his hands at Lilly, shooing her away. He didn't have time for her. Lilly wasn't taking that. This was important. She told him so much with eye contact and her unwillingness to walk away. Adam finished up his deal and excused himself from the small swarm of guys surrounding him.

"What, Lilly, I'm busy? Hi Kitten," Adam said, addressing both girls at once.

"Hi, okay," Lilly said, the tone in her voice playful and excitable. "Kitten and I were wondering, if maybe..." She was acting coy now, Adam's face telling her to get on with it... "What if, the three of us, maybe, went and had some fun?"

"Like what? You girls want coke? Fine, you can have whatever you want but I have to get to work, take what you want and leave," Adam said very matter-of-factly, holding out his open baggie of cocaine to the girls, missing the innuendo and needing clarification. Lilly was unimpressed, but the look in Kitten's face was one of adoration and astonishment as she stared into the open baggie.

"No, silly, like, you know... a threesome," Lilly said, whispering into his ear and batting away the open bag.

"Oh! Really?" His whole tone changed as a wide smile found its way to his face. His eyes softened as he pondered the implications of the opportunity.

"Yeah!" Kitten said, inserting herself into the conversation, her eyes following the bag of cocaine he was still holding in his palm.

"Okay, great! Let's get out of here!" Adam said as he looked at his phone. The time was already 3:30am. "This party's over, let's go get a hotel?" The girls nodded and followed him out, without saying goodbye or addressing the still angry swarm of guys he left behind.

The three packed themselves into Adam's car and traveled a few miles down the road to the first motel they came across. There was a room available, a suite with the heart-shaped jacuzzi tub, *how perfect*. Inside the room, Adam helped the girls relax a little by offering them lines of coke. The girls had worn through their pills and wanted to keep the party going. After a few lines, Kitten suggested she and Lilly get into the tub together and Adam could watch. Kitten disrobed and left Lilly dumbfounded by her figure. Her beauty was striking. With pale skin and full breasts, she had not a single curve out of place. Her long dark hair fell down her back and stopped only at the top of her round buttock that complimented her thick but firm thighs. In comparison, Lilly was a child's first attempt at pottery class. Insecurity and anxiety ate at her as she looked over to see Adam grinning so widely he couldn't even speak.

This is happening, Lilly's inner monologue told her, *you might as well pretend to enjoy it*. She shook her head and hands and responded to Kitten beckoning her from the tub. In the tub, Lilly let herself become captivated by Kitten. She was the most beautiful woman Lilly had ever seen, and she almost forgot that her boyfriend was also gawking at her, only a foot away. To Kitten's direction, the girls kissed and touched and rubbed their breasts together as they giggled and flirted. Adam was all too happy to sit back and take it all in. He celebrated by taking several pictures with his phone, although the frames only included Kitten. The girls giggled themselves out of the tub and Kitten asked them both to join her on the bed. It was the first time Lilly had witnessed Adam taking direction from a female, happy to at that. Kitten guided the three of them through a sensual experience that lasted long enough through the foreplay, but once Adam mounted Lilly, the anticipation had gotten the best of him and the grunts of his climax ended the occasion for all of them.

Adam left the warmth of the women on the bed to fill his nose with more cocaine. He pulled out the sack that was much smaller than it had been before they arrived at the house party. This concerned Lilly, but she didn't want to question him in front of their guest. Instead, she sniffed her lines with grace and the three of them continued to flirt and pet and have deep, emotional conversations.

By the time Kitten tired, the sun had long since rose and was well into setting again. She had called a friend who came to pick her up from the motel while Lilly and Adam readied themselves for the next event. It was now Friday night and they would head out to Hollywood to link up with DJ Sunrise at The Avalon, a club he frequented and could get the pair free entrance.

The packed club held a scene that reminded her of the same she had seen the night before, and many other nights before that. Lilly, more tired this time around, wasted no time popping a pill to get her going. It was more of the same, Lilly danced her life-force away while Adam ran around the club, pretending to be king of the party. She kept herself awake with pills from her pocket and water from the bar. When the club closed at 2 am, the party moved to an after-hours club that kept them going for another four hours. By 6 am, the bouncers shut the doors and the forced random clubbers out into the bright morning light that cast on the Hollywood Walk of Fame. The DJ's always stayed, their entourage included, and because Adam and Lilly fell into the group of Sunrise's, they stayed inside with the rest of them, none of whom were ready to stop partying. They didn't have to face the world yet and could stay in the darkness believing that time was standing still.

They spent several more hours in this state. Sunrise invited them back to his house, along with the rest of the remaining party. Here, there would be music, more pills, smoke, darkness, and friends, all they needed to become whole again and stave off the effect of the enormous amounts of drugs they had already taken. The Saturday escaped them, and they never found sleep. It was nighttime again and time to move on to the next stop.

Saturday night found them at an outdoor party. It wasn't one of theirs, as it was out of season, but one of the DJs they had partied with the night before that was playing and so they tagged along with him. All the while they continued the flow of ecstasy pills, coke, and smoke. The party didn't end until the sun rose on it Sunday morning, but the DJs weren't ready to leave, so it continued on well into the morning and early afternoon. It wasn't until Adam offered his cocaine that any of them would be motivated to leave for shelter of a house where they could sniff their drugs in comfort, shielded from the outdoor sun that burned their bloodshot eyes.

Another DJ's house was where they found themselves. They were worn, but not tired, and their noses still had quite an appetite. Among friends, Adam was never stingy. He shared his cocaine among them like a blessing and reveled in his own generosity. It wasn't until the sun set on that Sunday that Adam would allow them time to lie down. Lilly, exhausted herself, followed him into a dark guest room where they found an empty space on the floor, the bed already being taken up by another couple of exhausted friends.

Her rest was over in a blink. Lilly had laid her head down and closed her eyes, only to have them forced open again a moment later to the sound of Adam in agony.

"Fuck! Get up! Get up! Get the fuck up!" he screamed at her.

"What? What's going on?" Lilly asked, confused and more tired than ever.

"It's fucking 2:30 in the morning! I was supposed to be home hours ago! My parents are going to kill me!"

"Okay, okay, let's go," she said as she helped him rummage around in the darkness for their things. They slinked out of the house, being sure not to disturb the several other bodies strewn sleeping on the floor.

They were deep in the valley of Los Angeles and home was at least an hour away, if they drove fast enough down the 405. Adam, more comfortable now that they were in the car and on their way, asked Lilly if she would like to stop at Norms on the way home for a meal. He assured her that if he drove fast, he would still have time to take her out to eat and make it home before sunrise, when his parents would wonder where he was. Lilly smiled as he pressed on the gas and entered the freeway going one hundred and twenty miles per hour.

The dark and empty freeway flashed with bright blue and red lights. The lights surrounded them and swallowed them up. Lilly looked over at Adam as sheer dread and terror melted into her.

"Pull over! Pull over now!" The police intercom demanded their immediate submission. Adam kept cool and slowed down only enough to search his pockets.

"Here, put this in your bra," Adam said as he handed her a single ecstasy pill in a tiny plastic jewelry bag. Lilly, not knowing what to do, took the bag and stuffed it away in her bra. The police intercom became more fervent in its demands.

"Exit the highway, now!" the intercom called out to them. Adam complied and pulled into a dark parking lot of a closed fast-food restaurant and stopped the car. "Turn off the engine, put your hands up, touch the ceiling!"

Lilly sucked in shallow and fast breaths. Hands up on the ceiling meant guns drawn. She was sure of it. They were about to die. *Where was the coke? Had he hidden it? Was she going to jail?* Her mind raced and her heart beat hard and fast in her chest. While still in thought, the officers pulled her body from the car and over to the front of the police cruiser parked right behind them.

"Put your hands on the hood, miss," a police officer directed her as he frisked her and asked questions. Where were they coming from, what had they been doing that night, were they under the influence, what's in the car? The questions continued on and shot at her so fast, she couldn't speak before the next one came. It was a distraction, because while they were only stern to her, they abused Adam. On the opposite side of the squad car, Adam was in a headlock by one officer and punched in the stomach by another. He lost consciousness and fell to the floor, while a third officer kicked him and spit profanities at him.

"Adam!" Lilly screamed as he fell. Her cries alerted the officer handling her. She was witnessing the event and, rather than let her continue looking on, he pulled her further away and asked her more questions. From her viewpoint, she could see two officers now searching the car.

"Look, miss, if you tell me what's in the car, nothing will happen to you, do you understand? I don't want to take both of you to jail, but he's going no matter what. What's in the car?" The officer stared deep into her eyes.

"Nothing. Nothing's in the car," Lilly spoke through her tears.

"Back on the squad car," said the officer, disappointed that she hadn't cracked under the weight of his pressure. The officers continued searching the car and came up with nothing. They ended on the conclusion that Adam had been driving under the influence, even though they found no substance. This meant the police would impound his car and take him to spend the night in jail. The cash Adam was carrying they offered to Lilly as the officers told her she could legally maintain any cash found on his person. The officer handed her four one-hundred-dollar bills.

It was cold while Lilly waited for her cab that the police had called for her. Adam was already in the squad car and the police couldn't leave her unattended. They waited in chaperone for her cab, and in the meantime let her walk into the neighboring 7-11 to keep warm. Back at the car, the officers took a second, long search inside the vehicle. Her heart pounded harder as she waited for the inevitable. It happened. She knew it when one officer exited the car and double-timed it over to the entrance of the 7-11.

"You're going to jail!" he screamed at her as he pulled her by the arm out of the store. "You're going to jail, what's in the car!?"

"What? I don't know," she mustered.

"Don't play dumb! I told you, if you lied to me, you were going to jail too, so now you're going to jail."

In that instant Lilly couldn't respond. Fear had taken over her and she was becoming faint. By the grace of whatever eternal power must have been watching over her, a yellow cab pulled up and stopped right next to the squad car. Another officer, still over by the vehicle, called over to Lilly, still frozen in the confronting officer's glare as he towered over her. "You can go now!" he yelled in her direction. She didn't wait for the officer standing not an inch away from her face to respond or call back. She took her escape and walked toward the refuge of the idling yellow cab. As she did, she passed in front of the squad car and looked Adam in the eyes. They exchanged words through glances as he told her he was happy she got away, but scared for what was to become of him.

That cab ride home was the longest ride of her life. The driver was an older man with long curly hair, a Hawaiian button-up shirt, and coke-bottle glasses. He was kind and understanding as he offered his ear, figuring something strange must have happened to her considering the circumstances he was picking her up in. Lilly was all too happy to divulge her experiences. With an open heart, the man listened to her vent and offered what advice he could, although none of it stuck with her as she wasn't interested in listening as much as she was in the mood for an emotional purging. By the time she arrived home, the sun was rising. She knew what had to happen next. The phone trilled as she waited for Jose to answer. When he did, the only words she had for him were, "It's onions, man."

TWENTY-FIVE

Clap

L illy took the entire day to sleep. Rolling around in her bed, she wasted time until she couldn't anymore. Her phone had been ringing, but she knew it wouldn't be Adam calling, so answering was not important. The sun had set and only out of boredom did she convince herself to grab her phone. JJ had been calling. Thirty-two missed calls and twelve text messages had been waiting hours for her response. As she scrolled the list, her chest became heavy with the gravity of her situation weighing on her. *So much money, so much money.* Her eyes lost focus on the screen and her head dropped into her chest. A deep breath in brought her back, standing tall and ready to face the consequence that JJ would have waiting for her. It was her job to control Adam, her job to make sure the money was right, but she had failed. Adam wasn't here to save her, Jose would not bail her out. There was no one else to face but her fate.

"Finally! I've been calling you all fucking day! What the fuck?!" JJ said on the line.

"I know, I know. I'm sorry. Shit's fucked up, dude."

Lilly's voice quivered as tears released from her eyes and her nose filled up with snot. Blubbering wouldn't help, but the emotional overload of the last 48 hours had caught up to her and it was all she could do.

"Well, you need to get the fuck over here, right now. I don't know what the fuck is going on, but Jose is pissed and won't tell me, so you need to. Where the fuck is Adam? You guys need to get here now." Her tears made no difference to JJ, who held strong in her tone.

"Adam's not here. He's locked up."

"What?!" JJ responded with a fright so pure it surprised Lilly. "Fuck. Okay, I'm coming to get you."

The car ride was all but silent. JJ did most of the talking, a symptom of her state of mind. It was dark now, and Lilly knew JJ had racked her lines hours before that. In little bits and pieces, Lilly got out the important details of the previous night and how it all happened. Because JJ insisted on talking over Lilly, some details she filled in herself, like the major detail of what happened to the $11,000–JJ assumed the police had confiscated it, and Lilly didn't correct her. This didn't stop JJ from being livid about the situation, but it at least redirected the anger away from Lilly and onto a force she had no control over.

"So, while you guys were gone, I had Jose front me another two, because the profit from you guys would have more than paid for it, and I had a few people here that I needed to take care of," JJ said.

"Oh, fuck," Was all Lilly could respond.

"So now you guys owe me for the original five which was $5,600 to Jose plus my profits, plus two more of my price is another $2,250, plus Adam's original $5,000 debt… and we have nothing? Is that what you're telling me?"

"JJ, I'm sorry, we fucked up. I just… wait, what happened to your two?"

"I still have some, but I had people over. Like I said, the profit from you guys was supposed to cover it!" JJ was just as guilty for her crime of being a coke head. "Shut the fuck up, shut the fuck up. Let me think." She paused, but not long enough for any amount of thought to run through her. "Listen, this is what we're gonna do. When we get back to the house, we're gonna sniff some lines, and we're gonna brainstorm. Also, I need your help with the TV, something's off with the colors. I think the bulbs inside are dusty or something I need to clean them. My TV is all fucked up."

The girls arrived back at JJ's house. Money talk or what happened to Adam became unimportant as the girls refocused on the pile of cocaine sitting out on the kitchen table waiting for them. Lilly sniffed a few lines back-to-back as the rush dissipated any negative feelings from moments before. Lilly stopped worrying about anything. Jose would understand. It wasn't their fault; he would have to cut them a break. Nothing was that serious.

"So, look." JJ said to Lilly as she pointed at the large, flatscreen box TV that stood in its alcove. "See how the bottom of the screen here looks kind of grainy? Like something's wrong with the bulbs inside. I might have to replace them, but I wanna look inside and see if I can fix it first." The TV was old and not worth saving, but JJ would not give up on it.

"Okay, yeah, I see what you mean. Here, let's pull it out so we can get behind it." The girls heaved and hoed the large box out of place. Dust balls and debris wafted into the air and stuck to their fingers, clothing, and the soft tissues inside their lungs.

"Grab me the screwdriver in the junk drawer." JJ

pointed to a drawer in the kitchen. Lilly made her way towards it but stopped at the coke table for a sniff on her way. As Lilly dug through the drawer and found the tool, JJ made a trip to the table herself.

"Here," Lilly said as she handed over the tool.

"Thanks. See, we open it here and then we can see what's going on in there," JJ said as Lilly stood over her, ready to lend a hand when necessary. They removed the back and peered inside, not knowing what they were looking for, but playing the role of some type of television mechanic who did.

"Oh shit, it's fucking dusty in there."

"Oh fuck! Grab me that rag." At JJ's request, Lilly fetched a damp kitchen rag and JJ got to work wiping down the bulbs that had dust caked to them so thick, it created a film that wouldn't wipe clean. Still she persisted, and Lilly stood back as her assistant pointed out missed spots and what still needed cleaning. The particles thickened the air even further now as they choked through the task, although the cocaine may have been equally to blame.

It must have been hours that passed, considering how significantly the coke pile had shrunk before them, when the doorbell rang. They looked at each other and with their eyes asked if either of them were expecting someone.

"Who the fuck is that?" JJ asked aloud.

"Uhhh…" Lilly shrugged her shoulders. JJ made her way over to the door and opened the screen. Once the barrier broke, five men draped in black clothing and black bandanas across their face pushed their way in, knocking JJ down. Lilly wanted to scream from the living room, but the sound of a clap silenced her. A bullet whizzed past her and shattered through the back window. The men rushed inside and overtook the space. They held JJ by the hair as they pulled her to her feet and back inside the kitchen area where Lilly was already on her knees, the cold barrel of a gun sliding around on the sweaty skin of her forehead.

"Where the fuck is the money?" The mechanically altered voice demanded an answer.

Lilly tried to scream again but the ball of coke caught in her throat muffled her voice.

"I have some, I have some, here, it's in the drawer over there." JJ panicked and pointed with a shaky hand towards a kitchen drawer.

One man walked over to the drawer and found two twenty-dollar bills and one rolled up one-hundred-dollar bill. He held the articles up for the rest to see. Not a second later, another clap, the sound she now recognized as a bullet leaving its silencer. Only instead of being followed by the sound of shattered glass, JJ let out a grunt as this one penetrated her skull. Not able to scream, Lilly's eyes widened as she collapsed in time with JJ, who was finishing her fall to the floor.

Lilly regained consciousness at the impact of her body banging against hard metal, her hands now tied behind her back and her ankles bound. She was lying on the floor of a vehicle that had taken a hard corner and sent her flying to the side. Her eyes were free. Three of the men huddled around her. Two were sitting in front, one driving, one riding shotgun. The men's faces no longer covered, she recognized two of them as being guys she had seen before at Jose's house. She had partied with these guys, sniffed lines with these guys. Why the hell were they doing this to her? Out of instinct, she tried to plead her case to them and beg them to take pity on her. But the words couldn't escape her lips. A tightness around her mouth and the back of her neck sealed them shut. From the pulling sensation in the hair follicles around the back of her head, and the stickiness on her cheeks. It must have been tape, wrapped all the way around her mouth and head.

"Shut the fuck up, bitch!" one man shouted at her as she struggled to yell and gnaw through the binding.

She made a guttural scream in frustration. One man met her response with a swift smack to the temple by the handle of a pistol.

"Haha!"

"Pistol whip that bitch!" The others chanted and cheered as she lay dazed on the floor.

Blood trickled down from the wound and into her eye. Her vision blurred and a wave of nausea sat itself in her belly. Unable to wipe the blood from her eye, she closed it, and the pure stress of her condition put her to sleep.

SHE AWOKE AGAIN to her body being pulled out of the vehicle. Wherever they were going, they had arrived. With the cool air on her skin, she attempted to glimpse her surroundings and gather any data that might tell her where she was, but she couldn't. One man grabbed her by the neck and pushed her head down so she could see nothing but the ground beneath her feet as they dragged her inside. The deep and angry bark of pit bulls jumping on chain-link fences echoed around her. She could only assume they were coming from fenced-in front lawns, a relic of a neighborhood she had in fact been too many times before. This must be Jose's house. It was dark inside, but there was a dark outline of a couch, a lamp, in what must have been a living room area, and a kitchen island on the opposite side. But none of it looked familiar. She didn't know what to believe anymore.

There were tall dark figures standing and sitting in total silence. Dark outlines of men stood through the space. She couldn't get away. They took her down a long hallway and unlocked a door fastened with three separate deadbolts, keeping whatever was inside from getting out. The door opened. Inside were the dark outlines of three trembling figures. They held together like a pack of hikers caught in a storm without shelter. A dim light flicked on and Lilly recognized the people standing in front of her.

The first one who recognized her, almost relieved to see her, was Adam's younger sister, Sasha. Lilly smiled at her fondly as she flashed back to the first time she met Sasha, back when life was far less complicated than the situation she found herself in now. In that dimly lit room, it meant she wasn't alone.

The next two people huddled next to Sasha she wasn't so excited to be standing in front of. It was Adam's mother and father. These two people hated Lilly more than any of the men in black holding them there now. In denial of their perfect son's true involvement in the drug trade, they blamed Lilly for the state of being that their son had fallen into over the years. The authentic run-in with Adam's father in his hotel parking garage, enough evidence against her to fuel their rage. Lilly felt their disapproval, she had been so accustomed to feeling it from her own parents, in her own home, her whole life.

"We'll leave you all to get acquainted," said one man in black as she shoved Lilly into the room and onto her knees in front of the family.

"You!" Adam's father shouted as he stood over her, dominating the space of the tiny room they were being held, the door now shut and the dangerous men locked out on the opposite side, for now.

"Daddy, no, it's okay." Sasha said to her father, holding her hands up in a wave of surrender. The father's lock on Lilly weaned as he softened at the sound of his daughter's voice. "She's scared too, just like us." Sasha knelt down to help Lilly.

"Get away from her!" Adam's mother screamed as she grabbed at her daughter's arm. The family rallied around this girl to show any bit of kindness would not be tolerated.

"Mommy. It's okay. It's okay." Sasha pulled herself away from her mother and finished her task of ripping off the tape that bound Lilly's hands, feet, and mouth. Lilly waited in silence for her bindings to be removed.

"Thank you," Lilly said.

A look of disappointment rained down on her. Adam's parents wanted more.

"Well? What do you have to say for yourself?" Adam's mother demanded.

"Look, all I know is that these guys want money, and they have all of us, because Adam's in jail."

"Money?! Oh for Christ's sake, this is about money? What kind of scheme did you get my family into, you scum whore!" Adam's mother shouted again, unable to control her rage.

"What did I get you into?" Lilly's voice raised as she began fuming. "This has nothing to do with me, this is all your son's doing! He stole from them! I tried to help him so this wouldn't happen, but he fucked up again, and…" In the drama Lilly flailed her arms and head around in enormous gestures of frustration. A vessel in her nose burst and blood spewed out of it and onto the mother's blouse before falling in a stream down Lilly's face. "You know what, fuck you! My fucking friend is dead!" Lilly screamed as she held her arm up to her nose in a meager attempt to stop or even slow the bleeding. Emotions were running high, Lilly was coming down and feeling sick, and the situation she was in was no closer to being a bad dream than pigs were close to learning how to fly.

"Look at you, you disgusting addict. Your shame is bleeding all over the place and you think this is my son's fault? How dare you try to pin this on my Adam! He's an angel, you are the one who has corrupted him and turned him against our family!"

"No, no… No! That's not what's happening here. Why don't you pull your head out of your ass and open your fucking eyes!" Lilly, still holding her nose, felt far less powerful now than when she had begun.

"Enough! I will not tolerate you speaking to my wife in that tone!"

"Mommy! Daddy! Stop!" Sasha stepped in to diffuse the tension that was only escalating. "Listen. She's right. Adam has been doing this for a long time, he was doing it before on his own."

"What? How do you know? What do you know, Sasha?" With a wilted voice, her father turned to her. The mother began weeping, not needing anymore information for the reality to sink in.

"Well, Adam sold me weed once before. That's when I met Lilly."

"See! I knew it! You were there, so you must have been the one to give it to him!" Adam's mother said as she pointed a scolding finger towards Lilly.

"No! No, mommy. It wasn't like that. Lilly was there, but she wasn't involved, she wasn't even friends with Adam, Adam got it with another guy and then Lilly made fun of Adam for selling drugs to his little sister."

Adam's mother collapsed into her husband's arms and sobbed.

"Okay, look, I'm sure you guys all have a lot of questions. I can answer all of them, but right now I'm feeling ill and I need to lie down, please. None of us are getting out of here soon. They're gonna come in here asking for money, but until then I think we should all just try to chill out a bit." Lilly crawled over to a stack of old cots and dirty blankets in the corner of the room.

"How could you even think about rest in a time like this?" Adam's father scowled at her.

"Look, there are at least 10 guys out there, and three deadbolts on the outside of that door. And look around, no windows, phone, nothing. We're not getting out of here, and if it's money they want, they're not going to expect a respectable guy like you can get it until business hours, so…" Lilly shrugged her shoulders and collapsed on the cots. Sleep was the only coping mechanism she had power over, and she took advantage of it.

TWENTY-SIX

Help Us!

Sasha shook Lilly awake, her face and gestures panicking at the sound of the deadbolts coming undone. The four of them remained alert, eyes on the door as it opened. The hallway behind the door was no longer dark, a slight natural light crept through. It must have been daytime. Three men in black stood in the doorway, one of whom was looking down and standing behind the others, almost like he was hiding. But no amount of hiding could save him from identification. Lilly knew who he was, she would have known even if she could see only the tips of the curls on top of his head.

"Ryan?!" Lilly shouted, pushing her way towards him, ignoring the imminent danger the other two men might have posed. "Ryan, help us! Please! Oh my God, Ryan, please!" It was none other than her old flame, Ryan. Her first boyfriend, the one she spent happy moments with all those years ago, when raves were still about having fun, and ecstasy was still a novelty. But what was he doing here? Where was Jose? How did he even know Jose? A million questions ran through her head as she tried to piece the puzzle together, but nothing made sense.

"Shut the fuck up," he said to her as he batted her off his leg. The other two men finished pulling her back and tossed her back towards the family.

Lilly was more confused than ever about what was going on. The family looked around and at each other, trying to understand, but their faces revealed them as mystified. Thoughts twirled around inside Lilly's head as she tried to make sense of Ryan's presence. How could he toss her aside? Why was she here? Was this some sort of jealous ex-boyfriend bullshit that her parents would watch on the next *60 Minutes* special?

"Well, well, well…" A voice came from behind the three men standing in the doorway. They moved aside to reveal another man that Lilly recognized, but not as fondly. Milo. "Looks like we're finally going to get this ungrateful bitch back for how she treated you, huh, homie?" Milo nudged Ryan's elbow while he chuckled. The men in black grinned and snickered along.

"Milo? What the fuck? What is this? What do you want?" Lilly demanded in a shaky voice, peering back at Ryan every few moments, searching for a signal of her salvation that never came.

"I want my money, bitch! And you know I don't take too kindly to bitches trying to take me for money!" Lilly flashed back and remembered the story of Cuddles, the poor girl who was murdered over $500 and how Milo had given up his friends and rave family connections over the dispute. She remembered the first time she met Milo and how Ryan had sworn her to secrecy. The pieces were coming together. After Lilly and Ryan broke up, Ryan, being outcast by the family, must have joined forces with Milo and ended up the coke game? But what about Jose?

"Your money? It's Jose's money." Lilly said, fishing for connections.

"Jose!" Milo screamed behind him into the belly of the house.

"Boss!" It was Jose's voice who answered. He came running down the hall. In front of her now were Ryan, Jose, and Milo. The cocaine hierarchy of Lilly's world, and she had never even known it.

"Fuck." Tears streamed down Lilly's face as she fell apart in front of them, their safety now more in jeopardy. The personal ties all these people had together made the situation about more than money.

"If this is about money, we can pay," Adam's father chimed in.

"Shut the fuck up, old man." Milo pointed in his direction, but never took his gaze off of Lilly, a silent command that caused one of the other men in black to approach the father and pistol whip him to his knees. The women screamed and fell with him. "I wanna hear from Lilly. How the fuck are you gonna fix this, Lilly?"

"He can get you money! He has it, he'll pay it!" Lilly shouted through tears. Milo motioned towards the father again. The two other men in black grabbed the father and dragged him to the center of the room. One held his arms behind his back while the other began wrapping packing tape tightly around his face and neck. The women screamed. Jose held them steady at gun point. "No! Stop, please! I can do it, I can get it!" Another head nod from the Milo and the taping stopped, but it made little difference as the constriction around the father's neck was so tight that his face turned red as he struggled to breathe.

"Well?"

"I, I... I know someone. Another dealer, like JJ. They have money. We can take it from them." Lilly was panicked, her voice trembled with her body. She didn't know anyone else like that. Not anyone that had the money Milo wanted. But being a hardened criminal, the idea of a robbery might entice Milo more than a simple trip to the ATM by Adam's father.

"I'm listening…" Milo responded.

"Um, I… I just…" Lilly was panicking still. "I have to call and set up a pickup. We can set it up like a sale. They bring the cash, you provide the coke, but, uh, not…"

"And how the fuck are you gonna convince some person I've never heard of to purchase $20k of cocaine, at cost?"

"$20k? But we only owed you like…"

"It's $20k now, bitch!" Milo shouted at her as he interrupted. "You think it's cheap having to kidnap and murder people? I gotta pay these guys to get you, I gotta pay someone to come clean up the mess… This is your fault! You fuckers with your greedy nostrils caused all this!" As Milo screamed, he got close enough to her face, she could taste his breath.

"Okay, okay. $20k." Lilly cowered before him. "Um, I need a phone… a phone to call, and some privacy, please."

"Privacy?! Bitch! What kind of game you think you're playing here? Fucking zip him up, I'm tired of this bitch." Another command followed that led to Adam's father's tape covered face now being held still while one man pulled an extra-large zip tie from his pocket, fastened it around his neck, and pulled tight. The poor man struggled, the women screamed behind the face of the gun, but there was nothing they could do to stop it.

"No! Please! Ryan! Help! Please!" Lilly begged and pleaded to the memory of their relationship, hoping something in him might act to save her, to save the poor man now choking on the floor. His red face turning darker shades of purple as his eyes strained themselves to pop out of their sockets. The entire room was in chaos—three women screaming and begging on the floor, one man dying, and Milo laughing like an evil villain. Ryan kept his gaze averted down. He flinched at the sound of his name being called, but stayed at attention.

Only a few minutes later the spectacle was over, but in the perspective of the three screaming women, those few minutes had lasted a lifetime. A moment later, the man stopped struggling, his bloodshot eyes glazed over with death. The wailing women stopped their exhibition to sit in shock and disbelief, waiting for the pinch to wake them from this nightmare.

"Alright, boys, let's let these bitches have their periods over this asshole in private," Milo said with an evil laugh still in his voice. The men, including Ryan and Jose, followed Milo out of the room. Ryan was the last to leave and trailed behind for a moment. His eyes were heavy as he looked at Lilly. He waited, gauging if the other men were far enough ahead. When they were, he tossed something to the back of the room. It landed silently on the stack of cots. He slammed the door and fastened each deadbolt.

"What was that?" Jose's muffled voice came from behind the door.

"Huh? Nothing, just locking the door."

Lilly stayed silent for a moment to ensure no one would come back in the room before rushing back over to the cots to reveal what Ryan had given her.

Lilly left the grieving women to tend to the body of their dead loved one while she rushed over to the cots to find the article. It was a cell phone. A not-so-silent shriek jolted itself from her throat. The women looked over to see what she was holding in her hand and shrieked in kind.

"Shhhh!" Lilly urged them to quiet their excitement as she tried to contain her own. "Keep crying over him," she whispered and pointed to the body beneath them, the one they had forgotten about for a moment. With salvation in her hand, she flipped it open and dialed 9-1-1.

"9-1-1, what's your emergency?" They were the most beautiful words she had ever heard in her life. Another sigh relieved itself from her and more tears streamed down her face.

"Please." She whispered into the phone while cupping her hand over her mouth to let as little sound escape as possible. The walls were thin. "Please help. Someone has kidnapped us. One man is dead. Please hurry!" Lilly's voice screamed with urgency while remaining silent.

"Do you know what your location is?"

"Yes… I mean, I think. We're in South LA. 422 121st Street. Is that familiar?"

"Residence of Jose Gutierrez?"

"Yes!"

"Okay, ma'am, sit tight we're sending units over now. Are there firearms in the home? Are you in immediate danger? Do you know how many people are in the home with you?"

"Yes, yes! Several men in black, all armed. They killed one of us already. They're coming back any second. I can't stay. Are you coming?"

"Ma'am, I need you to put the phone down, try to hide it if you can, but don't hang up. I'm going to stay on the line until help arrives. They're almost there." With last instructions, Lilly hid the phone under a thin blanket and went to join the women huddled around the body.

"They're coming for us, it's okay, they're coming." The news of rescue sent the women into an uproarious celebration, the tone of which no longer matched that of lament

and sorrow. Thin walls did not help their case. Fast footsteps soon came down the hallway, followed by the familiar
sound of deadbolts becoming unfastened.

"What the fuck is going on in here?" It was Ryan,
yelling, creating a scene for the rest of the men outside the
door.

"Nothing, nothing." Lilly responded, trying to divert
attention away from the stack of cots where her active call
to the police was hiding. "These women, they're just… he's
dead! They don't know how to deal!" She was screaming
now, trying her damnedest to act natural, but there was
nothing natural about the setting they were in. No movie
or TV show could ever prepare her for the real-life
scenario of this plot.

"Keep it the fuck down! Milo's trying to figure out
what the fuck to do with you bitches." Ryan finished his
statement with a fake lunge towards their huddle that
made them each flinch and scream. He laughed at his
accomplishment. The men standing behind him laughed;
they were still in charge. The door slammed, and they
refastened deadbolts.

Each of the women breathed out a silent sigh of relief,
and anxious smiles snuck back into their faces.

Silence fell upon the room as the three of them listened
for any sign of their rescue. When it didn't come, Lilly
worried she had given them the wrong address, that maybe
they weren't at Jose's after-all and they were seconds away
from being killed instead. Then they heard it. A megaphone coming from outside announced the coming end of
this trauma.

"This is the LA County police. We know you have
hostages inside. Come out with your hands up or we will
break entry." The warning was clear and confident. This
would all be over soon. Lilly grabbed onto Sasha and her

mother. The three of them huddled together in the corner and waited for a police officer to come bursting through the door. But the muffled panic on the other side ensured that this would not be a peaceful end.

"Get the bitches! Get the bitches!" One voice screamed, Milo's, the only voice sadistic enough to worry about grabbing a helpless female amid an unavoidable bullet spew from the police force. More footsteps came and approached the door.

"No!" Ryan's voice. A struggle ensued. The sound of two men grappling outside the door, their bodies banging up against it, vibrating the wall and cracking the frame. The next sound was the crack of a gun. From right outside the door, the single bullet came and shot itself through. The women flinched, gasped, and held each other tight.

"Shots fired! Shots fired! Go! Go! Go!" The megaphone called to action by the act of a gun fired. Everything was happening. Inside the house, grown men panicked and turned into screaming children. They fired shots through windows that shattered in response. The police burst through the front door and the women knew when the police had taken over the space because a confident calm rushed over them as they heard the officers clear out each room and handcuff whoever they had spared a bullet wound.

"There's a body blocking this bolted door. They might be in here," an officer called out to his team.

"Yes! We're here! We're in here!" Lilly screamed louder than she had ever screamed before. Sasha and her mother screamed along but did not, or could not, make those screams into coherent words. For the last time the deadbolts were unfastened and on the other side of the door, rescuers appeared as three uniformed police officers in full riot gear.

TWENTY-SEVEN

Confession

The officers led the women out of the room in thin blankets and couldn't stop them from witnessing the carnage that had ensued in pursuit of them. Milo lay dead on the living room floor; a bullet hole disintegrated his left eye. Jose lay in the hallway. A couple other bodies were strewn along the floor as officers took pictures and pointed to various things, talking over them like they were nothing more unusual than the staple water cooler in a common office.

They brought the women outside. The sun was bright that day, despite the winter chill that rouged their noses. Still, there were other men in black, alive and in handcuffs. Ryan was one of them. He was wearing cuffs, but instead of being put in the back of a police car, he was waiting for an ambulance to treat him for the bullets he held inside his leg and ribcage. Lilly asked the officers if it would be appropriate to speak to him, justifying her need with the information that it was him who provided the cell phone and protected them as much as he could while they were inside. The officer rolled his eyes at her but allowed it.

"Thanks for saving us," Lilly said. He couldn't respond anymore than with a grunt and nod of his head.

"Alright, come on," the officer said as he led her away again. "We have an ambulance over here waiting to transport you three to the hospital. An officer will accompany you and get some more information."

The ambulance arrived and loaded the three women inside. The women all sank into the release and cried together. Sasha and mother held each other tight while Lilly held onto herself. The mother pulled Lilly into her and hugged her. "It's okay, dear. We're all okay."

In that moment, Lilly experienced the warmth of a mother she had only ever known to exist in storybooks and make-believe games. The three of them held onto each other the entire trip. Instead of asking questions, the deputy onboard held off, letting the moment complete itself before he interrupted.

At the hospital, the nurses and doctors separated and examined the women. Lilly was alone in her room when an officer entered.

"Lilly, you've been through quite an ordeal, haven't you?" She nodded in agreement. "Listen, I need to ask you some questions, and I need you to be truthful with me. I need you to tell me from start to finish what happened here today. We also know about Adam and his recent arrest. Is he involved in any of this?"

"Um, okay, but, what's gonna happen to me? If I tell you… everything?" She was fishing for some sort of assurance of protection. She knew she wasn't innocent in this. Because of her, her friend was dead, Adam's father too, and she was a hopeless drug addict. No police officer would take pity on her.

"There are some things we already know, I need you to fill in the gaps. If you do that well enough, and you give

me the full story, no matter what you say to implicate yourself, you will have immunity, do you understand?"

Lilly nodded, but the look on her face said she didn't
believe him.

"What I'm telling you, Lilly, is if you give me the full
story, every single detail that you did, Adam did, this Milo
character did, all of it, you walk out of here today a free
woman and you never hear from us again. Okay?"

"Okay. Um, I want to cooperate. I do. But there's so
much that happened, and I need more time." Tears welled
up in Lilly's eyes.

"Alright, this is what I'll do for you, Lilly. I'm gonna
give you some time to rest and catch your breath. You're
being held overnight for observation. Looks like you're
dehydrated, couple scrapes and bruises..." the officer
said, pointing to her medical treatment chart. "I'll be
back tomorrow before they release you, and I'll escort
you down to the station to have a brief chat. Sound
good?"

"Okay, thank you, sir." She was polite, one thing her
mother had gotten right before forfeiting her over to
adolescence.

"See you then." The officer stood and began walking
out of the room before turning back to say one last thing.
"By the way, they released Adam early this morning before
we received your call. Out on bail for now."

Lilly's heart leapt in her chest. Adam was out!

As soon as the officer's feet left her room, she searched
for a phone. There was one by her bedside. An alarm went
off in the room and within seconds, nurses surrounded her.
She rolled her eyes, annoyed at the fuss. They checked her
vitals and determined that her heart rate monitor must be
malfunctioning. The jump in beats per minutes had set off
the alarm. But all else being fine, they told her to rest and

lay back. She waited impatiently for them to leave so she could make her call.

The dial tone was excruciating. She called once, no answer, twice, nothing, three times, four, five. By the sixth time it went straight to voice mail and left her with the "Yo, message, after the beep," of Adam's recorded voice. Frustrated, she kept calling. She would have continued endlessly, but her parents walked into the room at that moment. Her concerned father, the child-bride hanging on his arm, and a mother who was more disappointed in her spawn than she had ever been before. More than the time Lilly threw a house party that disrupted the entire neighborhood. More than the several times she had run away as a high school student. This was beyond and into the realm of resentment.

"Hi sweetheart, how are you?" Her father spoke first. His face told a story of worry, but he held his arms crossed against his chest.

"Hi, Dad." Lilly looked down towards her legs, not able to face them.

"Oh my God, Lilith. Look at the mess you've gotten yourself in now! I cannot believe this. I hope they take you to jail to rot! You deserve nothing less. Maybe a little time in there will finally teach you a lesson." Lilly's mother spoke to her with a hot scowl in her voice. Her father might have said this was a little too harsh, but even all these years after the divorce, he hadn't the balls to stand up to the woman.

"I know, Mom…" Lilly trailed off.

The child-bride remained silent and kept her distance in the background, perhaps intimidated by Lilly's mother's intense presence.

"What the hell happened, anyway?"

Lilly regaled her parents with the story. Beginning with

the breakup, on through how Adam had racked up a debt and her master plan to get him out of it had failed, and culminating in the murder of her friend, JJ, her subsequent abduction, and everything that followed.

"Well, you really shit the bed this time, didn't you?" Lilly's mother shook her head and turned towards her ex-husband, "and this happened under your watch!"

Her father had no response other than to hang his head.

"Mom, I'm an adult! I fucked up! I'm sorry!" The moment was emotional, but Lilly was all out of tears. Dehydration and sheer exhaustion had pulled them all out of her body.

"So, what now? Are they taking you to jail?" Another stern and demanding question from her mother.

"There was a detective here. He told me that if I told them everything, nothing would happen to me and I could walk away."

"Well, I guess that's what you're doing then! Problem solved!"

"Yeah, but what they really want is to condemn Adam. They want to pin this all on him just so they can lock someone up, because they already killed the real bad guys."

"I don't give a damn about that little shit! He's ruined your life, Lilith. Don't you see that?" Lilly's mother began shouting again.

Her father stepped in as he held his hand out to calm the woman and add his own thoughts. "Lilith, what you've told us is some really serious stuff. Do you understand what might happen to you if you don't cooperate with them?"

"Go to jail?" Lilly shrugged. "But what if I got a lawyer?"

"Honey, it will not be that easy. This isn't the movies.

Your mother and I can't afford a lawyer, so you'd be on your own with a public defender. You will take all responsibility for everything that happened; they may even pin the deaths on you. You will spend the rest of your life in prison and Adam will go on, not looking back once. Has he tried to contact you yet?"

"No."

"No? Because he doesn't care, sweetheart. We care. We are here for you. We have your best interests at heart, and you're being given a second chance."

"Oh, really? And where the hell have you guys been? I've already asked you for help! I came to you! You said you'd help me and then you just didn't! You fucking changed the locks on me! You pretend you care, but you don't!" Lilly took her own defense. They were asking her to give up the only person who had acted like he cared about her in years. Logic told her it was the correct thing to do, but this we-love-you bullshit she was getting from her parents was less than believable.

"I know we've made some mistakes. I wish I could go back and do everything differently. Your mother and I dealt with it in our own way. Maybe it was the wrong way, but you were an adult. We couldn't force you to stop, even though we knew how badly you might hurt yourself. As far as what happened that evening you asked me for help, I wanted to. And I changed the locks because you weren't our daughter anymore, you were someone else and hanging out with dangerous people. We didn't know what you were capable of. I'm sorry that came off as us not wanting to help you. But foremost, we needed to protect our home. We had every intention of helping you, but the next day, by the time I got home from work, you were gone, and I didn't see you again for weeks. I knew you had to want help, and you weren't ready for it." The emotional monologue from her father sent the room into sniffles and wet tears, all except Lilly, whose eyes were dry. Even Lilly's hardened mother couldn't stop herself from feeling all of it.

"I just don't know if it's right," Lilly mumbled through a clenched throat.

"This is the right thing. Save yourself. Give yourself a chance," Lilly's father finished.

"When do you have to decide by?" Lilly's mother asked in a calm and collected tone.

"He's coming back tomorrow when they discharge me to take me to the police station."

"Do you need us to be here when that happens?" her father asked.

"I guess, I won't have a ride home afterwards."

"You guys can handle that. I have meetings tomorrow. I wasn't planning on having to be in LA to bail my junkie daughter out of jail." The harsh tone in her mother's voice was back, which did not surprise Lilly.

"Okay, we'll be here," her father said, ignoring the comment and making sure his daughter understood he would be there for her. "Until then, get some rest. I know you've had a rough couple of days. We'll see you tomorrow, Lilith."

"Bye, Lilly," the child-bride said, halfhearted, the first words she had offered that entire time.

"Yeah, bye," her mother said as she was already walking out of the room.

TWENTY-EIGHT

Bounty

E ven after the heartfelt message from her father, Lilly's heart still ached at the thought of having to betray Adam. The connection was still so strong, and without being able to contact him, her thoughts refocused on his remaining family. She had a bond with the mother and sister that she missed in her own mother. Sitting alone in her hospital bed, she called the nurses' station and asked to be connected to Adam's mother and sister's room. She hoped some sort of clarity would come from the conversation. She got exactly that.

What Lilly imagined would be a warm and comforting conversation was a vile and threatening one. The poor mother, distraught over the loss of her husband and still unable to reach her son, spoke hatred to Lilly and blamed her for the misfortune her family had suffered. She assured Lilly that she would make the rest of her life a living hell, that she would place the entire blame on her, and charge her with the murder of her husband as well. Lilly found her tears again and let them flow out of her. Her pain soaked her skin and hospital gown, and filled her room with the sound of her broken heart. This last conversation would cement the decision that she would move forward with the detective to condemn the boy she still loved.

By the time Lilly re-settled her nerves from the events of the day, she relaxed enough to sleep and drifted off. The night was full of nightmares, and though devastating, were deep enough to keep her there in sleep. She woke mid-morning to the sound of the detective entering her room.

"You ready to get this over with?" the detective said light-heartedly.

Lilly took a moment to look around her room and remember where she was. Sleepy eyes did not deceive her, her father was there, standing in the corner with still crossed arms.

"Yeah," she said.

"My wife and I will meet you there. Thank you, sir." Her father addressed the detective and shook his hand.

"Do you mind if I make a phone call really quick?" Lilly said to the detective in one last and final attempt of desperation. The detective nodded and stepped out of the room, following her father who had already left. She picked up the receiver and dialed the number with a shaky hand and a quickened breath. The line trilled.

"Yo, message, after the beep." It was her love's voice, but it wasn't him.

With no other option and no more time, she left a message. "Hey... it's me." Her words welled up in the base of her throat. "Um, please call your mother. I have to go talk to the police... about everything. I'm sorry. I love you." She clicked the receiver back to the base and held her hand over her mouth to silence more tears.

"You ready?" The detective poked his head back in to gather her.

"Yeah, coming." Lilly gathered her things and took a

quick few minutes in the bathroom to change from her hospital attire, brush her teeth, and wash the dried tears from her cheeks.

THE DETECTIVE ESCORTED Lilly into the station and took her to a back room. Her father, already in the waiting room, offered her an assuring smile as she passed. Once in the room, she granted permission for two officers to record her. They confirmed that her cooperation today will grant her exoneration, and they expect full details about the events leading up to the incident. Lilly agreed, and the interview began. In the hour they were in the room, Lilly left nothing to the imagination. She divulged every piece of relevant information, going back to the first time she saw Adam in English class, up and through the murder of her friend JJ and Adam's father, and her 9-1-1 call.

As she spoke, she reminisced about Ryan and their fast-burning love, about how she first met Jose that day she sped down the highway in Adam's Rav4, listening to happy trance music and joking with her friends at the gas station. She told them about Milo and the rumors he had murdered a girl named Cuddles over a $500 dispute, and how she was sure he would do the same to them once she connected all the dots inside that small, dark room. Recounting the scenes was cathartic to her. She followed the expressions on the faces of the officers who pitied her, but not so much that it made her unique, just another unfortunate girl who fell into a trap set perfectly to catch her.

By the time it was over, the officers had all the information they needed, and she was free to go. They walked her out to her father and repeated for her a script of information that reminded her Adam had not checked in with his bail bondsman and was now considered having skipped bail. Additional charges would now be placed against him because of the information Lilly had provided them, and a new warrant placed for his arrest. Should he try to contact her, she was to call them. They told her he would go under bounty, in which case her phone would be tapped and she would be monitored for at least the next six-months, but assured her that this did not mean she was in any trouble, but that she was a police cooperative and this was part of the protocol. Lilly understood, her father thanked them for the information, and they were on their way.

The drive home was long and silent. Lilly sat alone with her thoughts and a nose clogged up with the last several years of a bad coke habit. Her body ached, her heart hurt, and she doubted her decision to save herself. She told herself she wasn't worth saving, that she was the reckless one who deserved to rot for the crimes that led to the death of her friend, the demise of her social circle. Lilly clutched her phone in hand, praying for a phone call that would never come.

They arrived home, and she walked into her studio garage apartment. It had never felt so small. Suffocated, she wanted to run, but she was too weak. By now, word had gotten out among her friends. They knew JJ had been killed, and that Lilly was involved. None of them wanted anything to do with her. She didn't have drugs to offer anyway, so her calls went unanswered. Her connection was dead, and with no access to drugs, she had no choice but to sit in the comedown and let it wash through her.

The first eleven days were the hardest. Her nose leaked blood and her sinuses swelled shut; her eyes burned like they had bathed in chlorine. Each muscle in her body contained a deep ache that no bodybuilder on steroids could match with a thousand hours in the gym. With each movement, it felt like razor blades cutting through the cartilage and connective tissue inside her joints. No amount of Tylenol or accessible pain killer would lessen the edge. Sleep was impossible, the nightmares were rampant, and insomnia claimed most of the nighttime hours. She tried to pass the time by watching her favorite movies, classic gangster films like Blow, Casino, Goodfellas, but even that caused issue. The second the image of cocaine passed into her sight, an urge came upon her so strong, it sent her into a rage she couldn't control by any other means except screaming into the small space that surrounded her.

Loneliness fill the next several weeks. She missed Adam; she missed her friends, and her old life. When the weekends came, those nights were hardest as she imagined her old friends all getting together to party and enjoy life, as she sat alone and isolated in her personal pity party. It wasn't until the third month that some amount of energy returned to her, her muscle pain only a dull ache in the background, and with that came back her drive. She contemplated leaving the studio. Was she ready to go back to school? Once the idea came into her head, it motivated her to action. A visit to the school showed her what she needed to do to get back in good standing and when she could register for the next semester. Her parents were pleased with this progress and supported her decision.

The months passed by and life was mundane. She was enrolled in classes and making new friends. Thoughts of her old life came to her every so often, either on Tuesdays, or on the days an undercover police car follow her to school. The officers inside didn't bother her with her new friends and didn't make themselves a problem in her new life. She tried her best to ignore the presence and be happy in the positive direction she was taking and stay excited about finishing the degree she had started so many years ago. It was a freedom she didn't even know she was missing, from the constant pull to find and consume drugs, and from the pressure to please her boyfriend that was destroying her.

Lilly had stopped keeping track of the time until one day the undercover car was no longer following her on her walk to school or waiting for her when she walked home again. *Had it already been six months?* That same day, she received a phone call from the detective.

"Hello Lilly, this is Detective Richards."

"Oh, hi. I haven't seen you guys around today. Everything okay?"

"Everything is fine. I wanted to call and let you know that the six-month statute on the bounty is up and we will no longer be following you or monitoring your phone. I also wanted to tell you, on a personal note, that I'm happy to see you've made good choices and I hope you stick to it."

"Oh, uh, thanks," Lilly responded. "I guess I hope I never have to talk to you again, then?"

"That's right, Lilly," the detective said while laughing along to her humor. "But, listen, if you do ever hear from Adam or see him again, don't hesitate to call, please. There's still a warrant and we still want him to pay for what he did, to you, to everyone involved."

"Okay, I will."

"Thanks Lilly, and good luck." With that, the call ended and Lilly considered it a symbol of the end of her life before and the beginning of something new. A new life full of aspirations and dreams and accomplishments. This time around, she was free from the prisons of her past, both metaphorically and physically, and she would savor every day outside of them.

. . .

IT WAS THE FOLLOWING TUESDAY. Despite working so hard to let go, Lilly still had an affinity towards the day. On campus, Lilly walked past the smoking section, full of unfamiliar people, but couldn't help but soak in the rosy nostalgia. That same moment her phone rang with an unknown number. Her brow furrowed at the same time as her curiosity peaked. Who could be calling her from an unknown number?

She answered. "Hello? Who is this?"

"Wanna roll?" The voice revealed itself with two simple words.

In an instant, Lilly was paralyzed. Her heart jumped into her throat as its beat became hard and fast, sweat gathered in tiny beads on her forehead and upper lip. She snapped back into reality when all she could hear was the sound of her own hard breaths.

"Uh... Um, Adam?" she responded with a trembling voice.

His next two words evoked an identical response that scared her. "Miss me?"

Her stomach twisted over on itself. She panicked as questions swirled around inside her head. Overwhelmed, she fell into an instinct that told her to cry and let her body fall into a wall nearby that saved her from collapsing in a puddle on the concrete ground. Through the tears and an all too familiar ball in her throat, she choked out the words that demanded answers.

"Where have you been? Do you have... any idea... You don't know what I had to do... I... wait, why did you... where are you?" Unable to speak a complete thought, her words came out chopped and jumbled.

"I've been away, hiding. Yes, I know everything that's

happened, and I don't blame you, I waited because I knew they'd be looking for me, through you, and I couldn't risk it. I'm close, and I want to see you. Meet me at our favorite spot, on time, today." The couple understood each other perfectly, he her emotionally charged and frantic questions, and she the where and when he would expect to see her. "I'll see you soon, okay?" Silence from her end. "Okay?" he asked again, louder this time, as if she hadn't heard him the first time.

"Okay, okay, I don't know… maybe… probably not, but yeah. Okay. No." Her responses insecure and questionable, but she was in shock. Adam and she both knew where she would be when the time came for her to be there.

The chemicals that released themselves from hidden spaces in her brain collided with each other in a wave of anger, euphoria, and anxiety. It was a rush that would have knocked her all the way down if not for that wall holding her up. She waited a moment for the feeling to run through her and burn itself out, but that didn't happen, not before her vision blurred and she was on the verge of passing out. A wave of emotional out pour followed the physical sensation as memories came flooding back. Times she had never remembered before, moments the two of them had shared that were so precious she had buried them away as a defense mechanism against missing him too much. All it took was four words from him and she was putty in his grasp once again.

Over the next several hours, Lilly tried her damnedest to focus on anything but Adam, to no avail. Her mind reeled with the possibilities of what he could have to say, and what he wanted with her now. Until the last possible minute, she contemplated her options. Call the police right away and tell them about where he would be and what time, or go alone, or not go at all.

She played with each scenario and imagined the outcome. Calling the police would have been the most logical, adult, new-Lilly thing to do. Not going at all would be second best. In the end, she followed her heart and went alone, told no one where she was going or who she would be with, and she met Adam at 4:20, that afternoon, at The Tree.

Along the trek towards the secluded area, she remembered fondly all the times she had made that walk with the friends who became her family. She imagined them laughing along with her as the dusk settled into the mountain backdrop. As she crossed over the last hill that separated the rest of the world from the bubble that held The Tree and its landscape, in the distance stood a figure, waiting for her arrival. To say her heart skipped would be inaccurate, as it was more like a complete stop that a moment later erupted into a violent fit of excitement. She kept walking and used the time remaining on the walk to breathe deep and calm her nerves.

When she was close enough, she saw his face covered in the sweet smile that had captivated her the first day in English class—the same one that had activated her desire to pursue him, to follow him after class, to smoke his cigarettes, to sniff her first line of coke, to offer herself to him as a clay he was free to mold into whatever was to suit him best. Without even saying a word, he had a hold on her again, and this time she knew it.

"Hi!" he said as he approached and came in for a hug so bearish, she melted into him, like their bodies fused to become one.

"Hi…" she said back as she breathed in a giant breath of his hair. The two held each other for a long time. Longer than any appropriate time, neither wanting to let go of the other nor suggesting the separation. When they finally untangled their bodies, Adam held her at arm's length and took a long gaze at all of her.

"You look great!"

She blushed and lowered her gaze to the ground to hide her smile.

"You look... different?" she said, posed as a question. And he did; he had changed everything about him. His clothing was different, a style she never would have guessed belonged to him in his flannel button-up shirt and tight jeans. He had grown a beard and hair long enough to tie back in a messy bun, an anomaly he explained away as helping him to stay out of sight and under the radar, blending in with the surrounding crowd.

The old lovers talked like nothing but time had passed between them. Lilly let herself fall into the fantasy of him again and didn't bother trying to catch herself. The evening fell into dark and the conversation waned away from light-hearted and jokey when she told him about getting back into school and being excited about the new direction life was taking her in. She talked about how hard it was rebuilding the broken relationship with her parents and asked him the hard questions that had been plaguing her, like where he'd been and why he abandoned her. Adam answered every question she had. He told her that once he was released, he skipped town and headed up north. The first few weeks he spent working on a pot farm, trimming branches and making spare change. It was an easy place to hide out because the farmers were very private and protective who never allowed cell phones on the property, and no one there had access to a television or radio. Once he wore his welcome out there, he moved into the city of Bend, Oregon, where he worked in the back of a local coffee shop, baking pastries, making sandwiches, and washing dishes. He lived a simple life there, he said, but he spent most days counting down until he could return to find her.

Lilly asked if he knew about what had happened to JJ and his father, if he had spoken to his mother, and what his plan was now. He told her that yes, after he left the farm, he contacted his family and his mother told him all the gory details about what had happened with the kidnapping. It saddened him, but he still could not come home, it was too soon. His mother also told him about his bounty and that thanks to Lilly, the police were looking for him in connection with the murder of JJ and his involvement with the drug gang, Jose, Ryan, and Milo.

"Once my mom told me everything, I knew it wasn't safe to contact any of our old friends, and that I would have to stay away for a while. My mom begged me to come back, but I'm not stupid. I knew it would be safe to contact you, though. I knew I could still trust you. Actually, I haven't even called my mom since that last time, just in case. You're the only one who knows I'm here, and I'm here for you." His words, a hopeless romantic plea to come back to him, she leaned into without reservation.

"Adam, I just…"

"Wait, listen. I know I fucked your life up. I know that if it weren't for me, none of this shit would have happened, and I'm sorry. I'm sorry for bringing you into this life and I wish JJ hadn't died, but we have fun, right? Don't I always take care of you?" A heartfelt apology turned into a manipulation. He had spoken those words so many times before, when he wanted something from her.

"Well, it's getting dark…" Lilly said.

"Exactly! That's why I brought you a present." He presented a small, clear baggie, with six bright, colorful pills inside. She knew without having to ask that they were ecstasy pills as he waved them back and forth in front of her face.

In a swift POP, her bubble burst. He was no king over her, no big shot boss of anything. Just a sad, manipulative little boy who only cared about himself and feeding his id. He didn't care that she had spent the last six months rebuilding her life from the rubble he had left her in, that her parents were only beginning to trust her again, that she was happy to get up early every morning for school. She had said all of that minutes ago, and it was like he wasn't even listening.

"Adam, you know what…" She spoke with a direct and powerful confidence. "I can't let my life go down that path again. I'm committed to being sober and finishing school. I like being sober, and I wanna stay on the right track. I'm sorry, but I can't do this."

Adam's face first looked confused, but a moment later he laughed at her, as if he was trying to soften her up. "Oh, come on, it'll be fun! Let's go back to your place and party like we used to." He grabbed her thigh and sucked his lips in a flirtatious style.

"I can't."

"Lilly, stop. I came all the way here for you. I just want our lives back. Nothing bad that happened has to matter as long as we have each other. Come on!" His voice changed as he absorbed her rejection. "Please, Lilly. I love you. We can have everything back."

"Adam." Tears crept out of her eyes as she continued. "I know you think you love me, but you don't. I know you don't because I didn't love myself, and I let you treat me like I wasn't worthy, like I wasn't good enough. But I know now that I'm worth more, and that means you can't be a part of my life anymore."

"What the fuck!" He was shouting now. "You can't do

this to me! I did this for you, for us! What are you even saying right now?" His gestures and movements intensified as he boiled up in anger. Lilly did not say another word. She took his fit as her opportunity to leave, and she did. She got up and began the long walk back, away from her youth, and into the rest of her life. "You're gonna fucking regret this, Lilly! You'll never get over me! Do you hear me! Lilly!" She heard his angry yells but did not turn around, their power becoming less and less with each step she took until he became a faint noise in the background.

By the time she crossed back over that hill, the noise of the city, now in view, drowned out any remaining whisper. The freedom that she had so come to cherish over the last few months belonged only to her, and with it she went on into the rest of her life.